A heart betrayed… A soul crushed… Plotting revenge never felt so sickly sweet…

Ignoring her mother's warnings, Tabeka forms a relationship with Lord Cidus Milhella, the man chosen for her by the gods as shown her by the goddess Rania. However, her vision does not prepare her for the terrible price she must pay.

Betrayed by Cidus, disowned by her father and abandoned, Tabeka forges a life alone in the forests of Wildevein.

Years later, Cidus seeks Tabeka's healing assistance to help his mate birth him a healthy heir. His request plants the seed for a plan of vengeance in Tabeka's heart—one that will destroy Cidus and his goal for Wildevein.

Tabeka's Revenge
Copyright © 2019 Taryn Jameson and Gabriella Bradley
ISBN: 978-1-4874-2465-7
Cover art by Angela Waters

Published by eXtasy Books Inc or
Devine Destinies, an imprint of eXtasy Books Inc
Look for us online at:
www.eXtasybooks.com or www.devinedestinies.com

TABEKA'S REVENGE

CRIMSON REALM CHRONICLES BOOK 8

BY

TARYN JAMESON
AND
GABRIELLA BRADLEY

To our readers…

PROLOGUE

Shivering, Tabeka moved closer to the fireplace and gazed at the flickering flames. She held her hands toward the fire to warm them. Winter had come with a vengeance. The wind howled around her shack, and she wondered if the walls and roof would hold. She had built it herself after her family had cast her out because she had brought shame upon them.

Her father was the ruler of the Hakania Realm on Ierilia. Many of the Hakanians were travelers that traded their goods and crafts throughout the many realms, moving from village to village, only going home during the winter.

People were afraid of the Hakanians, of their gifts and all-seeing powers. More than often, the group was blamed for a catastrophe in a village, or for thievery. Their music and traditional dances were frowned upon, and their young women labeled whores because of their different style of clothing and their ability to perform as dancers. Yet many a villager had braved their camp, seeking healing, or to know their future.

Tabeka's thoughts wandered back to the time she had first arrived in Wildevein. The valley below the Dreaded Peaks had been picturesque then, abundant in wildlife, flourishing orchards, and farms, and the people had wanted for nothing. From the rumors her father had heard during their travels, the Sirona Realm was ruled by a kind young lord, Cidus Milhella. Her father had gone to see him, and Cidus had graciously allowed them to set up camp in the forest on his property, not far from Wildevein Manor.

She had seen the young lord riding through the forest, and sometimes in the village. From the moment she had laid eyes on him, she was enamored. She dreamed of him at night and spent her waking hours fantasizing about a celebration of their joining. It was her deepest secret, and when the goddess had shown her he was her lifemate, she had waited impatiently for the day when they would meet in person.

Her father had invited Cidus to attend their Festival of Light. When Tabeka performed her dance, Cidus had approached her afterward, and she had fallen in love with him. Tabeka sighed. Her heart still stirred as she pictured his handsome face, framed by shoulder-length, curly blond hair, his chiseled dimpled chin, his deep blue eyes, his straight nose. For her he was perfection, and he was so tall and strong.

Every day, she relived that evening over and over. Occasionally, that brief time of happiness overshadowed the hate she bore in her heart for him now. She had loved *that* Cidus so much, but then he had changed… From one day to the next. Closing her eyes, she sighed, her mind filling with visions and memories of the evening he had asked her to go riding with him.

It was a festival in worship of the goddess of light that was celebrated widely on Ierilia. All evening they had heard the celebrations in the village and at the manor from afar, at times overshadowing their own festivities.

Tabeka finished the closing act of her solo dance. With a

final twirl, she swayed her hips causing the little bells hanging from the chain around her hips to jingle, then she swooped down gracefully to the ground and leaned forward, her arms outstretched.

The spectators, mainly her own people and just a few daring young people from the village, clapped and shouted loudly. She jumped up and bowed in acknowledgment of the applause and studied the crowd. Her heart skipped a beat. There he was, casually leaning against a tree, chewing on a piece of grass. She could hardly believe that he had actually left the celebrations at the manor to come to their camp. She felt the blood rise to her cheeks when their gazes caught and held. He smiled and sauntered toward her.

"Hello. My name is Cidus. What is yours?"

"Tabeka."

He bowed elegantly, as if she were royalty, causing her already flushed face to heat even more. "How nice to meet you. Your dancing is mesmerizing."

"Thank you." She felt shy and stupidly tongue-tied.

"Would you like to go riding with me tomorrow?"

"Yes, Lord Cidus, I love to ride. I will ask for permission." Her heart beat so fast, it thundered in her ears. Her visions had shown her she would meet her lifemate here, in this realm, but she never believed he would be Lord Cidus Milhella of Wildevein Manor, no matter how she dreamed of him and adored him or what the goddess had shown her. It just did not seem possible. "I will be back in a moment." Her heart sang as she hurried to ask her father's consent.

She approached her father whose mind was already fogged from the cosmic mead he had consumed that evening. "Father, can I go riding tomorrow?"

"By yourself?"

"No. The lord of the manor asked me to go with him."

"Is that so. He is a kind young man. I suppose you will be

safe with him. Yes. You may."

"Thank you, Father."

She ran back to Cidus, barely containing her excitement. "Father said yes."

His broad smile flashed perfect white teeth. "I will meet you at the manor gates just after sunup."

When he took her hand, bowed, and kissed her fingers, she almost swooned.

Just before she bedded down for the night, Jacina, her mother, came to speak to her. "Tabeka, your father told me you are going riding with the young lord tomorrow. You must not go. I had a vision that sorrow will befall you."

"Mother, he is my lifemate. The goddess showed me."

"Yes. I know. I had the same vision. But you must remember, you are promised to Koko from birth. We may have lifemates destined for us, but it does not always mean we meet them, or if we do, that it will be good. Taking this man as your lifemate will bring you nothing but pain and heartache, and you will anger your father. Your all-seeing powers have not yet fully developed, or you would know."

"Would I go against the goddess? The goddess Rania spoke to me. She said it was destined to be. It was written in the book of knowledge."

"Child, you have barely seen eighteen summers. Learn patience. I will say no more. Be careful tomorrow. Our hunters saw black dragons yesterday."

She hardly slept that night and was up before sunup. After dressing in her prettiest skirt and blouse, she brushed her long, flaming red hair until it shone and left it hanging loose. Softly she tiptoed to the door and left the wagon, then ran barefooted into the forest in the direction of the manor.

Holding the reins of a black stallion and a white horse, Cidus stood waiting just outside the tall wall near the gates.

4

She ran toward him, and he helped her onto the white mare, though she did not really need his help. The touch of his fingers as he held her hand sent prickles up and down her spine.

"Her name is Tatine. I chose her for you because she is quite tame. I do not know how well you ride."

"Lord, I can outride you. I have been an accomplished horsewoman for many years."

He chuckled. "Next you will tell me you are an accomplished swordswoman, too."

"I am." She only felt mildly insulted. After all, he did not know her yet. "I am an only child. Father taught me archery and swordsmanship as he would have had I been a boy. Mother warned me that our hunters saw black dragons above the forest. Have you seen them?"

The horses trotted leisurely. "Yes, I see them often. The dragons are friendly. They were once jewel dragons. The sorcerer Cewrick turned them into black dragons, and he owns them now. Before he traveled to the realm of dreams, my father told me we do not have to fear them."

"How did your father know?" She glanced sideways at him. Oh, he looked so stately on his horse, and he was even more handsome than last night. Her stomach fluttered, and her skin tingled.

His lips curved into a crooked smile. "He just knew. I do not know how. My father fell off his horse not long ago and is now in the realm of dreams. But he spoke the truth. The dragons have never harmed me."

She gave him a sidelong glance. "Yet they have snatched villagers and travelers and carried them off. How is it that you are safe from them?"

He shrugged. "My father never told me, and I cannot ask him now."

"So… Where are we going?"

"I am taking you to my secret place. I have never shared it with anyone."

"You have a special place? Where?"

If she had not been so enchanted by him, she would probably have thought twice about going. Young women did not accompany men to secret places. It never boded well for the woman. But she trusted him. The goddess would have warned her if she should not go with him.

"My secret place is through the forest beyond your camp, at the base of the Dreaded Peaks."

Even though it was a warm day, she could not suppress the shiver that overtook her body. "The men told me they have seen monsters in that forest. Father forbade me to go there, and the Dreaded Peaks are fearsome."

"I go there all the time. I have never seen a monster." He pulled his sword halfway out of its scabbard, indicating he was ready for anything dangerous that crossed their path. "You will be safe with me."

Tabeka did feel safe with him. Rania had shown him to be her lifemate. No matter the warnings her mother had given her, she knew deep within that this man would cause her no harm. She felt the connection forming within her soul, and she knew he must sense it as well.

She spurred her horse into a gallop to settle her heart and the flutters he caused within her. When they reached the edge of the forest, she pulled the reins to stop her horse.

"Are you sure about this, Lord Cidus?"

"Yes, I am sure. I ride through the forest all the time. And please, call me Cidus?"

She felt her cheeks burn. She had been taught to show respect. Call him by his first name?

Following him into the forest, she rode behind him, glancing from right to left and looking up at the branches. From the tales she had heard, the forest scared her a little, but she could rely on him. If he rode through it almost every day, he would know better than her people if there was danger or not.

The ride through the woods did not take long. When they exited, she continued to follow him toward the craggy mountains beyond the forest. He rode into a crevice that seemed to appear from nowhere. It was narrow, but her horse managed the path well. When they came to the end of it, she gasped.

She was facing a glorious waterfall cascading into a pristine clear pool. Flowers and greenery surrounded the small lake. Small birds twittered and darted back and forth over the surface of the water. Shimmering white sand flanked the banks of the crystalline water, and an intricately carved statue of a woman stood nestled within a burst of colorful flowers.

Tabeka had no idea who the woman could be, but just the sight of the statue filled her heart with joy and love. It had to be the likeness of a goddess. Which one, she did not know. She had never seen an image of her before, not in any of the images of the gods and goddesses on her tablet.

She sighed and gazed at Cidus. The oasis was magickal, a place of such beauty, it took her breath away. Yet it looked oddly out of place within the hideous, craggy peaks surrounding it. How could such an entrancing sanctuary exist here?

Cidus dismounted and held his hand out. She placed her hand in his and got off the horse. "This is magnificent. How did you find this place?"

"One day when I was riding I decided to explore." He took a basket and wineskin off the side of his saddle, and taking her hand, led her to the silvery sand. She sat and buried her feet in its warmth, letting the fine grains run between her toes.

Cidus sat beside her. "How much longer will your people

be trading in this area?"

"I do not know. Trading is very good, so we will probably stay a while."

"How old are you, Tabeka?"

"I have seen eighteen summers. And you?"

"I have seen twenty-four summers."

Cidus opened the basket and took out bread, cheese, fruit, and meat, along with two small goblets. He filled the cups with wine and handed her one, then cut some bread and cheese for her. Tabeka could hardly believe it was all real — she was sitting beside the man of her dreams next to a magickal pool.

After that first day together, they had met every day and sometimes in the evening if her father allowed it. Her father quite liked the young lord, and even her mother had softened toward him, though she still warned Tabeka constantly. But she chose to ignore the warnings. The goddess had not cautioned *her*. Her mother's visions had to be wrong, perhaps conjured up by the fear of losing her daughter to Cidus.

After several weeks had passed, they sat by the pool late in the evening talking about the stars. Polarium's golden glow shimmered across the surface of the water, filling the air with magick. Cidus shifted closer and suddenly took her into his arms. Oh, it felt so good. So right. When he tilted her chin and tenderly kissed her, she thought her heart would jump out of her chest. He slipped the blouse off her shoulders exposing her breasts. His hand moved down, his fingers playing with her nipple, then he gently kneaded her breast.

"Cidus, we should…maybe…we are not joined…we should wait…"

He caressed her lips with his own and whispered softly, "Tabeka, you are the woman of my dreams, my lifemate. That is why I brought you here. No one before me has set foot in this magickal place. When I first laid eyes on you in the village and in the forest, I knew then that you were the one. It was written in the book of knowledge that you and I would meet."

"Yes, I know. I had a vision that told me we were to be lifemates."

"You have the gift of all-seeing?"

"I do, and the gift of healing and the goddess Rania sometimes speaks to me, but I am only eighteen. My gifts have yet to develop. I cannot see farther than that we will love deeply. How is it you know what was written in the book of knowledge? Do you have the gift?"

"No. If I have any special gifts, they have never surfaced. My mother did. Before she traveled to the realm of dreams, she told me of her vision. She described you in every detail, your beautiful hair, your dark eyes, and that you would be a traveler."

"You have lost both your parents. I feel sadness for you," Tabeka said.

He did not answer her. Instead, he claimed her lips again, this time his tongue exploring every crevice of her mouth. She molded her body to his, then pressed her breasts against his hard chest. He teased the blouse down further, then slipped her skirt down to her ankles, making her squirm in his embrace. He quickly undid the laces of his tunic and pulling it off, threw it onto the sand. His boots and pants followed. Taking her into his arms again, he pressed his hard body against hers and lowered her to the sand.

Deep down she knew this was too soon, too fast, but she could not stop herself. Thrusting her hips against his erection, she felt it caress her moist folds. He kissed her again, then pushed into her. She was ready, oh so ready. He was so big he had trouble inching in. In one push he broke the shield and was completely inside her. She gasped, then felt fulfilled. He began to thrust, slowly at first, then faster. A surge of electrical impulses shot through her, from between her legs, to her stomach, her toes, throughout her whole body. He leaned on his hands, his torso raised, his blue eyes darker than the night sky, as he gazed down at her.

A shudder shook her. Waves of passion flooded through her body as he reached his orgasm, and she felt her own release seep its juices.

They made love many times that day. They made plans — talked of their joining, their future, and when he would ask her father for his permission to legally make her his mate.

Two joyous months had gone by when Tabeka's parents finally spoke of leaving for the next realm before winter set in. That evening, while they lay on the sand beside the pool, she told him, "Cidus, Father and Mother are talking about moving to the next realm for a short while and then going home. Winter is coming soon. But there is something I need to tell you. I am with child."

He placed his hands on either side of her face and gazed into her eyes. "I love you so much, my dancing queen. I was waiting for the right moment to speak to your father. But now, I will speak to him in the morning and ask his permission for us to join. If he agrees, we will hold the ceremony next week."

"How could he not agree? I am carrying our child. He will be angry, but I am sure he will be impressed that you will do right by me."

He brushed his fingers through her hair. "I have already begun the arrangements, but I will speed them up. We will have the ceremony and celebration at the manor. I had already decided it was time we officially join and intended to ask you tonight to become Lady Milhella, so I brought you a betrothal gift. Surely your father will delay their departure to attend our joining?"

Tabeka thought her heart would burst with joy when he

placed a gold chain with an oval pendant around her neck. It had the manor's crest engraved on it and precious gems around the edges.

"It was my mother's. She told me it was a gift from the gods," he whispered against her lips. "My sweet dancing queen, I love you with all my heart and soul, and I will be so happy when you are forever by my side." He leaned forward and rested his face against her belly. "And now you are carrying my heir. We will soon be a family."

She giggled. "It could be a girl."

"Whatever, boy or girl, we will have more than one and fill Wildevein Manor with the joy and laughter of children."

He took her back to the camp late that night, but her parents were already asleep. He promised he would come early in the morning to speak to her father.

But he did not come. Several days went by without a word from him, and her people were ready to leave.

Her mother had a vision and knew she was expecting a child. When she questioned Tabeka, she admitted it was true. Her mother told her father, and he was furious.

"You have brought shame to your family. Cidus is done with you now. We are leaving this day, but you are no longer a member of this family."

She had cried, begged, told him that Cidus was coming to speak to him, to ask for her hand, but it was of no use. Cidus had not come, and she realized now, would never come as he had promised. Her mother's pleas for her father to change his mind did not help. The caravan departed, and she was left alone with nowhere to sleep, nowhere to go. She gathered her clothing her father had thrown out of the wagon, the blanket her mother left for her, her sword, bow, and arrows, and her dagger, then she found a hollow tree and spent the night in it.

The next morning, she decided to go to the manor and

demand to see Cidus. Something had to have happened to him. She was sure of it.

The guard refused to let her through the gates. She had crouched beside the gates and waited until he finally rode through them.

"Cidus! Wait!" she called out.

He reined in. The stallion reared, whinnied, then stood snorting. Tabeka noticed the horse was unusually restless.

Cidus looked down at her, disdain clouding his face. "What do you want, wench?"

Was this the man she had fallen in love with? The man who was so tender, so sweet? The man she had allowed to take her? His face was chisel hard, his eyes like steel.

"Cidus, you did not come to speak to my father. He was outraged that I am carrying your child. My father has disowned and abandoned me."

She would never forget his amusement. He had broken out in laughter and belittled her.

"Child?" He glared at her, disgust blazing in his eyes. "I do not blame your father for casting you out. You are nothing but a whore. It is not mine. Next week, I am to join with the Lady Ivia, daughter of Lord Schollen from the Getaga Realm. Get away from here, wench. Do not ever let me see you near my home again!"

He might as well have pierced her with his sword. He spurred the horse and galloped away. Tabeka was crushed, her heart torn to shreds. She ran as fast as she could, across the fields, through the forest, then tripped over a protruding root and fell, hitting her head hard against a rock.

She woke after sundown, her skirt wet and stained with blood. She knew she had lost the infant. After finding a hollow tree, she crept into it and curled up. She had no more tears. All she felt now was the pain of losing him and the infant in her womb, and hatred began to fester in her heart.

The next day she gathered the bundle of clothing into the blanket her mother had left for her and she went to the dark forest. She would have to learn to fend for herself now.

Five years later…

She had become known as the sorceress in the forest, someone with the gift of healing and the ability to foretell the future. Once the villagers got to know her, Tabeka often went to Wildevein and helped to birth a child. People paid her. Sometimes in coin, sometimes in food or wares, and as winter approached, she had been able to trade with the locals for materials and tools to build a little shack.

It was her anger and hatred that drove her. One day Cidus would pay for what he had done.

The village women that dared to brave the forest came to her for herbs or healing and loved to gossip, especially about the lord and lady. They told her that Lady Ivia could not bring a child to term and had lost one infant after another. This knowledge brought Tabeka some satisfaction. Cidus would not have the heir he longed for. Yet a vision she had, showed Ivia giving birth to an infant, a girl.

Banging on her door startled her out of her musings. Who could that be this late at night? None of the women from the village were ready to begin birthing. She opened the door and stepped back, shocked. It was Cidus. *How dare he show up after so long? Why?*

Her heart betrayed her. The love still festered there, alongside her hatred for him. When he asked to come in, she hesitated at first, then nodded and stepped back.

"What brings you here?" she demanded to know as she lit a candle on the table and sat.

"You live on my property. I have a right to go where I please. I am the ruler of this realm. You forget yourself, woman."

"I will find a place in the village if you want me gone."

"The reason I am here is for Lady Ivia. I will reward you with gold if you will use your magick to heal her, so she is able to carry my heir."

Oh, what it must have cost him to lower his pride and approach her. Tabeka sat at her table, never taking her gaze away from his face. He still had that steely look, his eyes reminding her of a frozen pond. How could this man have duped her father? Fooled her, with his pleasant ways, his smile, his promises. "The lady is with child again?"

"Yes. Are you able to use your magick to help her keep this one? And to make sure it is a male child?"

Why does the idiot think I have magick? I am a healer, not a sorceress. Oh well, let him believe it. "Maybe I can, maybe I cannot."

"Woman, do not play words with me."

"Was that not *your* game, Cidus?"

"What do you mean?"

"Did you not toy with me? Play games? Only to discard me after your betrothal to Ivia?"

He frowned. "Woman, you are delusional. You and I never lay together, but what happened to the child you claimed you were carrying?"

Oh, he had the gall to deny their love and to ask her that? But he had never loved her. He had toyed with her, got from her what he desired, then dumped her like garbage when she had told him about the infant. "I lost the babe. How far along is Ivia?"

"Four months or so." He took a pouch from his pocket and emptied the contents on the table.

Tabeka gazed at the pile of gold coins. She already knew she could help Ivia bring the child to term. She had seen in her vision it was a girl forming in Ivia's womb.

"I cannot change the sex of the child. What if it is a girl?"

"You are to deliver the infant. If it is a girl, kill it, then enable her to carry another until she gives me a male heir."

She gazed at his ruthless face, his icy eyes, a shiver running down her spine.

"She appears to conceive easily. As long as you can bring her to term for one boy child, I will be satisfied. Come and live in the manor so you can care for Ivia and guide her through this."

Kill it? Surely he was jesting. A brief vision came to her. It was fleeting, but it showed if she did not agree, Cidus would find someone else, a healer from another village, and the infant Ivia gave life to would die at that healer's hand. Looking at his face, she knew he was serious. A plan formed in her mind, one that would save the infant and in years to come, she would get her revenge.

"I need more than this meager pile," she fingered the gold coins.

He took another pouch from his belt and threw it next to the coins. "I have heard of your magick. Make sure I have a son, and I will give you more gold than you know what to do with."

Her wounded heart threatened to burst its poison, but she controlled herself and made up her mind. "I will come to the manor tomorrow, but I will not sleep there. I will leave when the lady is sleeping, and each night, I will go home after sundown. Be sure to warn your guards to allow me entry whenever I please."

"If you can guarantee me an heir, I will be in your debt. Come to the manor tomorrow. The guards will not trouble you. I will tell Ivia that you will be taking care of her from now on."

Before going to the manor early the next morning she went to the village and sought out Vilore. The woman had just lost her mate and was left to raise five young ones on her own and expecting another.

"Tabeka, I was not expecting you today."

"Can you send the children outside to play? I need to talk to you in private."

Vilore sent her children out, then poured Tabeka a cup of tea. "What is it you want to talk to me about?"

"You are about four months now. Correct?"

"Yes. Why do you ask?"

"I have seen it is going to be another boy. You already have three sons. I will give you gold if you will sell him to me."

Vilore dropped her cup and broke it. "Sell the infant? Are you crazy?"

"Vilore, you have no mate, and you have enough trouble raising the five you have by yourself with no income. How can you manage another? I can give you enough gold to keep you in food and clothing for years. The infant will be well cared for. I can promise you that."

Vilore frowned. "I will think on it."

Tabeka already knew the woman would agree. She left a few gold coins on the table with the promise of a bag of gold if Vilore's answer was yes, to be paid to her when the infant was delivered.

It was almost dawn when Tabeka hurried home carrying her precious bundle in a cloth bag. Ivia had delivered that night, but nothing Tabeka did, or the herbs and potions she had fed the woman, had stopped the bleeding. Tabeka had called out to Rania, but all the goddess said was that all would be as it was written. Ivia had passed on to the realm of dreams shortly after the birth of the feeble girl child. The infant had cried. Not a lusty wail as it should have been, but a soft mewling sound. Nevertheless, Tabeka had given her a few drops of sleep elixir. She could not chance Cidus hearing the child.

Earlier that night, she had brought the boy that Vilore had delivered a few days before to the manor the same way — wrapped up well and hidden in the cloth bag, sleeping soundly from the elixir. He was a beautiful infant, healthy, and had a lusty cry.

Vilore had come to Tabeka's shack three days before to deliver him there to avoid questions from her older children and others and had left, happy with her bag of gold. She had told Tabeka she would tell neighbors and friends the infant had died at birth, and that she was taking her children the next day and moving to another realm to start a new life.

For three days Tabeka had cared for the boy, in between visits to the manor, until a servant came banging on her door in the middle of the night to tell her that Ivia's time to deliver had come.

Cidus had not seemed to care that his mate was gone. He was only interested in the boy child and charged a servant to find a wet-nurse in the village. "I will call him Evior," he had told Tabeka. "I am in your debt, and if you continue to weave your magick to make sure the boy reaches maturity, you will receive a bag of gold every year from this day forth until he has seen twenty-five summers." He had handed her a large bag of gold.

Once inside her shack, Tabeka threw the bag of gold on the table and took the tiny girl out of the bag. She still slept but breathed normally.

"Your name will be Iridia," she whispered as she held the infant against her heart that already overflowed with love and tenderness. "I will give you a good life, little one."

Unwrapping the old blanket, she carefully washed the baby, then dressed her in the clothing she had bought over the last months and swaddled her in a new, soft blanket. She was so tiny, it worried Tabeka. Now that she had a daughter to care for, she would use Cidus' gold to buy land and have the local carpenter build a cottage not too far from the village, and she would raise her properly. No one would ask questions. The type of clothing she wore could have hidden a swelling belly easily. And the villagers liked her services so would not question her.

She sang softly and rocked the infant, gazing into her now open eyes and stroking her downy black hair. She promised to be a pretty little girl. Then again, Ivia was a beautiful woman with her long black hair, brown eyes, and a heart-shaped face.

"You are *my* daughter." Tabeka rested her cheek against the tuft of hair.

Her vengeance was almost complete, but it would take quite a few years for her revenge to come to its final conclusion.

CHAPTER ONE

Twenty years later...

As Tabeka walked into her small cottage with Evior by her side, she saw the curious expression on her daughter's face.

Iridia flung her arms around Evior's neck. "Where have you both been?"

Evior took Iridia by the waist and set her on a chair. "I am sorry. I needed your mother's help."

"With what?"

"You will never guess. I met the king!" Tabeka responded.

"King Biryn?"

Evior chuckled. "Who else? We only have one king."

"Where? And why did you need my mother's help?"

"Iridia, you know of my father's alliance with the evil god, Zohmes. You and I have talked about it. Zohmes is set on destroying the royals and taking possession of the crown and throne."

"Yes, and?"

"It appears Zohmes has once again attacked someone close to the king. At least, that is as much as I know. When the king contacted me, he asked me to talk to my father to find out about Zohmes' temples. He requested I meet with him and his team at the base of Dreaded Peaks. I talked to my father, but he is becoming suspicious of my questions. I confided everything to your mother because she knows a lot more than I do. I took her with me, and she was able to tell the king of another of Zohmes' temples."

"Truly, Mother? You never speak to me that you know of these things. I hate it that you have so many secrets from me, yet you talk to Evior about it all." Iridia frowned and wrinkled her nose.

"Child, I do not want to trouble your mind with such dark matters, and I am glad you do not have the gift. Sometimes the visions are too much to handle."

"In a way, I am glad I did not inherit any of it, though it does seem to come in handy sometimes. Maybe it skips a generation," Iridia said.

"Maybe it does."

It was all Tabeka could think of saying. Yet sometimes she could see an aura around Iridia. She had asked Rania about it, but all the goddess told her was that she would know in due time what the aura meant.

Iridia looked at Evior. "Why do you not leave the manor and Wildevein if you are so against your father and his alliance with evil? Mother and I would go with you."

Tabeka grunted. "Iridia, he is afraid. Not of his father, but of what that nefarious god could do to him. Cidus would call on Zohmes to assist him in finding his son. He is a powerful god and is aided by the most wicked of all sorcerers, Odoxon."

"And now *you* have become involved. All the more reason to leave Wildevein and go elsewhere. Evior, you would go with us?"

He shook his head. "Zohmes will find us wherever we flee. It is not a good plan."

Tabeka suddenly clutched her head.

Evior stepped toward her. "Iridia, your mother, what is

wrong? Help her."

"It is all right, Evior. She is having one of her visions. Mother... Mother, what is it? What do you see?" Iridia called out anxiously.

A realm filled with evil.

Iridia and Evior with blood dripping from their bodies, their faces.

A man with wild hair, redder than her own, laughing evilly, pointing at Cidus, then at Evior and shaking his head.

More terrible laughter.

Eyes that spit fire.

Two men fighting, their faces covered in blood.

Tabeka snapped out of her trance and took a deep breath to calm the fear that pooled in her belly.

Zohmes knows my secret. The children. Iridia and Evior are not safe.

Iridia cast her mother a worried glance. "Honestly, Mother, you scare me when your eyes roll back, and you become so still."

Tabeka saw the concern in her daughter's eyes. She raised her trembling hand and caressed Iridia's cheek. "Child, you have witnessed it many times. I am fine." The image of Iridia and Evior covered in blood flashed before her eyes. A wave of nausea wracked her body. Wildevein was no longer safe. "The vision I just had showed me we *must* leave here. When I spoke with the king, he invited us to move to Cront. That is our destination."

Evior handed Tabeka a cup of tea. "Here. Drink this." He shook his head. "I cannot leave, Tabeka. You know why."

"But you must. Zohmes knows of our allegiance with the king. He will tell your father. We must go. Now. This day."

"My father would not let him harm me. I am his only heir." Evior paced back and forth.

Tabeka sipped from her tea, then sighed. How could she tell them what she had just seen? The vision had terrified her.

Zohmes somehow knew Evior was not of Cidus' blood. If he told Cidus, not only would her life be in terrible danger, but also Evior and Iridia's. Her vision had shown that. And not only would they be in danger from Zohmes, but Cidus' fury would know no bounds.

"Your father is in league with that abominable god. Do not assume you will be safe from their wrath." She placed her cup on the table beside her and gave Evior a pleading stare. "Iridia and I will need your assistance to reach Cront. It is not safe for us to travel alone. We will not make it without your help."

Tabeka knew that playing on Evior's chivalry and the growing love he had for Iridia would be enough to convince him.

He stopped pacing, let out a deep breath, then nodded. "Of course. I will accompany you on your journey, then I must return to Wildevein Manor."

Tabeka sighed in relief. Evior would keep his word, but before they could leave, she would have to cover their tracks.

Cidus had no idea where she currently lived. With the gold he had given her after the birthing, she had bought a small piece of land far outside the village and had paid the local carpenter to build the small cottage on it. The location had served her well. She had managed to keep her daughter's existence a secret from Cidus, which was not that difficult.

Cidus never set foot in the village. He did not care about his people. Every year, on Iridia and Evior's birthday, Cidus had a bag of gold delivered to her old shack in the forest. As far as Cidus knew, she still lived there because she had made it appear so.

"I have a matter to attend to. I will be back in a few hours," she told Evior and her daughter.

They did not question her. They were used to Tabeka going to see her clients regularly. "Evior, you will stay here with Iridia?"

"Yes. I will look after her. How long will you be?"

"I told you. A few hours. Be sure to lock the door and do not open it for anyone."

Iridia frowned. "Mother, you did not tell us everything you saw. I feel it."

"Do not worry. Gather your clothes and whatever else you would like to keep. We will leave here late tonight. Evior, when I return, you must hurry to your home and pack your clothing. You are in terrible danger."

"Wait, Tabeka. I have a horse. How will you and Iridia travel? If I bring two more horses, my father will immediately be suspicious," Evior said, worry lacing his voice.

"I will buy horses and a wagon. I must leave now."

Tabeka picked up her bag containing her herbs and medical supplies and left.

There was no client, but a plan had come to her to obscure their escape. She hurried toward the forest, knowing the way well. Each day, she spent time in the forests around her home and her old shack to gather herbs and roots for her medicines and potions. She knew the woods like the back of her hand.

Hurrying across the veld, she almost ran to the forest at the base of Dreaded Peaks, the wilderness where she had spent five and a half years. She did not stop to look for herbs. She headed straight for her old shack.

It always surprised her that it still stood after so many years. Grimacing, she decided she must have done a decent job building it. It had been her safe haven, her refuge away from people. The villagers avoided the forest fearing the reported monsters within, though she had never seen any except the natural wildlife. She had seen the black dragons often, but they had not harmed her, and then suddenly they were gone. When she had lived in the shack, her clientele had been scarce. Most did not dare to enter the darkness of the trees.

She stood looking at the humble abode for a moment. It held so many bad memories, ones she had buried deep within her heart. Digging in her pocket for her key, she unlocked the large padlock, then opened the door. It smelled musty inside. She lit the oil lamp and set it on the floor. First, she lifted the frayed mat that lay in the center of the room, then her fingers sought the loose floorboards that were hidden beneath it.

Lifting two of the wide boards, she groped for the bag inside the cavity. Briefly, she opened the bag and gazed inside. Twenty years of saved gold coins glistened and sparkled within.

Except for what she had received the first year, she had never used any of it. Her land and cottage were paid for, and she had been able to earn enough to give Iridia and herself a decent living. Now, it was time to take her fortune and leave. They would make their home in Cront.

Before leaving the shack, she sat at the rickety table, set the oil lamp on it, closed her eyes, and concentrated.

Goddess Rania, can you hear me?

Yes, Tabeka.

I am about to sever all connection to Wildevein.

I know of your plan. It is a good one. Cidus will believe you have gone to the realm of dreams. At least, he will believe it long enough for you to escape to Cront.

He does not know of Iridia.

Not yet. But he will.

How?

I cannot tell you more than what the book of knowledge allows. Evior is in danger. Zohmes plans to tell Cidus that Evior is not his son.

The vision showed me, but Evior is afraid of his father. I am worried he will change his mind. He promised to escort us but wants to return to the manor.

He also loves Iridia. You know they are destined to be mated. He will not let her go without him. I will watch over you in your travels to Cront.

Evior cannot go back. Will we be safe there?

You cannot avoid what is to come as a result of what you set in motion so many years ago, Tabeka, but in Cront you will be under the king's protection. He and his team will assist you. Evior will stay with you and Iridia.

Rania's voice faded.

Tabeka stood, grabbed a small shovel from the corner of the room, a blanket, and her two bags, then she went outside and placed the bags under a tree, far from the shack.

Running through the woods, she headed for the stream that ran through the forest not too far from her shack. Long ago, she had found the remains of a young woman. It looked as if someone had attacked her. She had tried to find out if there were any more missing women in Wildevein but came up blank. No one had gone missing, so the poor girl had probably been a traveler. Strange then that her family or friends had not searched for her.

Tabeka had buried the corpse beneath a tree near the stream and placed stones upon the grave to protect it from animals. By all rights, she should have burned the body, but she did not have enough oil to do that at the time. The regular method of burial had not been an option. Plus, if she had heard of a missing woman later, she could have directed the family to where she had buried her.

After removing the stones, she dug until she unearthed the skeleton. The clothing was torn and mostly rotted. Strands of brown hair still clung to the skull. She took the bones out of the grave and placed them in the blanket. When she was finished, she hurried back to the shack. Laying the blanket on what used to be her cot, she arranged the bones on it.

Emptying the container of oil over the skeleton, the meager furniture, and the floor, she took the oil lamp, ran out of the door, then threw the still lit lamp inside. She ran for the cover of the trees and stood back while flames engulfed the shack.

Satisfied with the results, she picked up her two bags and hurried to the village near her home to purchase a wagon and horses.

"Tabeka, we rarely see you in the village. What can I do for you?" Jogano, the owner of the stable asked.

"I would like to buy two horses to pull a wagon, and I also need a pack horse. Will you help in choosing them? I require tack for all three horses, and whatever else is necessary for them to pull a wagon."

"Are you going somewhere?"

"My services have been called upon in Nimegen. I will be gone for several weeks, plus the journey there and back."

"I see. News travels of your healing abilities. I will choose strong horses for you." Jogano disappeared into the stable.

While he was gone, Tabeka took a hand full of gold out of her bag and stuck it in her pocket.

Jogano returned a short while later. "The horses are waiting out front."

She paid him, then, leading the horses, she went to the other side of the village. The people she ran into along the way greeted her and looked at her curiously. For them to see Tabeka in town, especially with three horses, was unusual. She only went there when it was necessary to buy a few necessities. Their food she usually purchased at the smaller market closer to the farms nearby.

Vogul was the local carpenter. He built wagons, tables, chairs, and many other things. He, too, was surprised to see her. She told him the same story and hoped Cidus would not question anyone in the village.

Then again, why would he? He would send his men, as usual, if he suspected anything. No... In a few weeks, when he would have the yearly bag of gold delivered to the shack, the messenger would report it burned, her skeletal remains among the ashes. He would think her dead. She only hoped she could fool him long enough for them to get to Cront. Cidus never showed his face in the village anyway, so her worry was probably needless.

Vogul helped her to harness the horses and attach the wagon. "Safe travels, Tabeka."

The suns had begun to set when Tabeka pulled up in front of her cottage. "It is me. Open the door," she called out.

Iridia opened the door. "Mother, I am glad you are back. Why are you so dirty?"

"I fell while gathering a few herbs." It was as good an excuse as any. "Did you pack, Iridia? Evior, you must hurry to your home to gather your clothes and belongings. We will leave soon."

"I will escort you as far as I can, but I am still not sure—"

"I spoke with the goddess Rania. You *must* come with us. You are in grave danger from Cidus and Zohmes. That is all I can tell you. Tell your father you are going hunting. Make sure he does not see you taking your things. When you return, you can help us load the wagon."

Iridia still stood in the doorway. "You actually went and bought a wagon and horses! And a pack horse, too!"

"Yes, girl. Now help me gather enough food to last us for a few days. The next village is several days traveling."

Evior kissed Iridia on the cheek, then left. Tabeka gazed after him as he mounted his horse and rode in the direction of the manor. He had become Iridia's friend when they were very young, and they had soon become inseparable.

Tabeka had become quite fond of the youngster in whose life she had played such a big role. It was almost as if the gods had directed the two children to meet and become close. And lately, that friendship was fast growing into something else. Tabeka saw it in the way they looked at each other and their interactions.

The boy had grown into a fine young man, and he was incredibly handsome, too, with his shoulder-length, blond curly hair and blue eyes. Looking at him, no one would ever guess he was not Cidus' son.

"Mother, what if he does not come back?" Iridia twisted her hands nervously.

"He will, child. It is written in the book of knowledge."

"Sometimes I *do* wish I had your gifts. How is it that I did not inherit the abilities?"

"The gifts can be a blessing or a curse. Be glad you do not have them," Tabeka said, though deep down she had a feeling that Iridia had gifts waiting to surface like her aura showed. "Now come and help me gather supplies."

CHAPTER TWO

Tabeka knew Evior would go with them. Rania had told her he would. Still, seeing him return, calmed some of the worries she was feeling.

"There you are, Evior. You packed light. We are ready and packed, though we will need to buy more supplies at the big market in Nimegen. We need waterskins, wineskins, enough food that will not go bad, bedrolls, and tents.

"I could have bought some of it in Wildevein, but it would have looked suspicious. Your father never goes to the village, but his servants go there to get supplies. If anyone talks, all they will know is that I have gone to another village to help in a healing."

Evior nodded. "Yes, I did not dare to pack much. It is going to be a long journey. The wagon will slow us down, especially through the mountains. I am glad it is spring. The journey would be impossible in winter. I will buy whatever else I need at that market. I did not want to raise my father's suspicions."

"What did you tell him?"

"That I was going on a hunting trip with some friends and would be away for some weeks as you suggested. I hunt often, and my father knows I am sometimes gone for weeks, so it was not strange to him."

"Lighten your horse's load and put your belongings in the wagon. I will need you to drive it. After I bought it, and Vogul harnessed the horses to it, I had trouble getting the animals to walk," Tabeka told him.

Evior chuckled. "I can teach both of you. Then we can take turns. I will tie my horse to the side of the wagon, although Iridia could ride it. She rides very well."

"You have taught her much. Next, you will be telling me you taught her swordsmanship."

"Yes, I did. She wields a sword better than some of my friends."

Tabeka remembered her own young training days. Her parents had left her weapons behind with her belongings when they had abandoned her, but she had not used the sword since. When she lived in the shack, she hunted using her bow and arrows. After so many years, her fighting skills were rusty, to say the least.

"Iridia can have my sword, and the bow and arrows. They are in the wagon."

Tabeka locked the door, made sure all the window shutters were closed and locked, then quickly turned and strode to the wagon. She climbed on, smiled at Iridia, and sat beside Evior, who settled in the center to drive the horses.

When they began to move, Tabeka did not turn back to look at the cottage. This was a closed chapter of her life now. She doubted she would ever see their home again. In a way, it made her sad. The years she had lived there raising her daughter had been happy ones. Not once had she ever regretted taking the infant. Iridia had brought much joy to her life.

Because they had traveled day and night, it only took them half the time Tabeka had figured to reach Nimegen. As they traveled, Evior had taught her and Iridia how to drive and handle the horses. They had taken turns sleeping in the back of the wagon, but there was only enough room for one person.

"One of us will need to watch the wagon," Evior said looking at the two women as he hitched the horses to a post.

"People do not steal in these parts. If they get caught, the penalty is heavy. You know that," Tabeka reminded him.

"True, but best be safe. Iridia, your mother and I will go and buy what we need. Can you stay with the wagon and horses?"

"I wanted to buy some things, like pants and a tunic. I hate traveling in this dress." Iridia scowled.

"I will take you to the market when we return," Evior promised.

They headed to the market and bought everything they needed. Evior had to make several trips back to the wagon to store their purchases. After they bought food, wineskins, and waterskins, filled them with wine and water, they returned to where Iridia awaited them impatiently.

"Your turn," Evior told her.

"Mother, can I have some coins?" Iridia asked.

Tabeka took a hand full of gold coins out of her pocket and handed them to her daughter. "Be careful. The traders like to haggle. Stay with her, Evior. Do not let them take advantage of her." She sighed.

Maybe she had been too overprotective of the girl all these years. In her heart, she knew she had to be. Iridia looked too much like Ivia for Cidus not to become suspicious had he seen her. Then again, he had his son, and Evior was blond, like Cidus. He had probably forgotten all about Ivia, as stone-cold as he had been when she had died. The poor woman had only been a means for him to have an heir, one that had titled heritage from both parents. His sexual pleasures, he found elsewhere. Everyone in the surrounding area knew of Cidus' prowesses. He coveted many of the young women from the village and local farms and had his way with many a wedded woman.

After Evior and Iridia returned, they decided to have a warm meal at the local inn. Evior went inside first to see if any of the customers were people that knew them.

"It is all clear."

Tabeka took hold of Iridia's hand. "Enjoy this meal. It will be the last full, hot meal you will have for a long while."

"Yes, the trek through the mountains will take weeks. We cannot travel during the night. It is too dangerous. The roads are narrow," Evior commented.

"You have been that far before, Evior?" Iridia asked.

"Yes, a long time ago on a hunting trip with my father and his men, and again when my father and I attended the king's joining celebration. My father decided to combine the journey with hunting. He did not like using the flyer much. We encountered morcougs along the way. The beasts killed two of my father's men."

"By the gods, I hope we do not come across them." Iridia shivered.

"It is spring. There is plenty of korobeast and harteox for the morcougs to hunt. I do not think they will bother us unless we bother them," he reassured her.

Now and then Tabeka glanced through the windows to make sure their wagon was safe. They had tied the horses to a post right in front of the inn.

"Tabeka, stop worrying. You reminded me earlier, there is very little crime on Ierilia. Well, except for Zohmes and his accomplice of course," Evior said.

Of course, Evior did not know that her bag of gold was hidden in the wagon. She could not very well carry it around. Neither could she tell him about it. How could she explain to them where she acquired such a treasure?

"Do you think the king and his team will be back in Cront when we arrive there?"

"When we are close I will try to contact his general, Brenn Mildash. Though the king contacted me personally, it just does not feel right to bother him with questions of no importance for him."

Tabeka nodded. "I was not with them long enough to know them all. I did sense some aliens among the group, people not from Ierilia."

"They are from a planet called Earth. I am sure they will all help us find accommodations, Tabeka. You worry too much."

The trek through the mountains was long and tedious. Often, they had to stop to remove debris from the path. Their food supplies had dwindled, but Evior hunted every few days to supply them with meat.

It somewhat surprised Tabeka that they had yet to cross paths with another person. The trade route seemed to be deserted, but it was not that long ago that Zohmes and Odoxon had gathered an army and used this pass to march against Cront.

Cidus had sent many of the men from Wildevein to their deaths in servitude to the malicious god, leaving quite a few women without a mate and children without a father.

She halted the wagon in a small clearing. They had been riding for hours, and the suns were beginning to set. All she wanted to do was wash the dust from her body and get some sleep. Iridia had crawled into the back of the wagon an hour earlier, but the road had been bumpy. Tabeka knew the child could not have slept more than a few moments.

"We will make camp here for the night."

Iridia slipped from the back of the wagon and rubbed her eyes. "I'll gather some wood for a fire."

Evior dismounted and tied the reins to a tree close to the

wagon. "We have a little meat left from the korobeast I killed. There should be enough for the three of us tonight and for breakfast." He grabbed the small bundle of meat from the back of the wagon and brought it to Tabeka.

Once Iridia returned with the wood, Evior started the fire. They settled around it, roasting their meat on sticks and sharing wine from a wineskin.

"We have made good time. We should reach Cront sooner than I expected." Tabeka took a bite of meat.

"I am thankful to hear that." Iridia took a deep swallow of the wine.

Tabeka took the wineskin from her daughter. "Do not drink too much wine, Iridia. It will go to your head."

Iridia scrunched up her face. "But I will sleep well because of it. My whole body aches."

Leaves rustled, and the sound of a limb cracking echoed in the quiet night. Something dropped to the ground in front of them. It was a creature like none Tabeka had ever heard of or seen. Its body was huge and covered in green scales. Half-man and half-reptilian, its face was grotesque. Its snout was large like a kora's, and when it opened its maw, Tabeka could see rows of razor-sharp teeth. The creature gnashed its teeth together and sniffed the air. Its yellow eyes trained on the chunk of meat roasting over the fire.

Tabeka and Iridia jumped up. "I do not have my sword!" Iridia shouted.

Evior drew his sword. "Stay behind me."

Suddenly the beast leaped toward the fire, its large clawed hand snatching the meat. Holding its prize close to its scaled chest, it took off running through the trees without giving them another glance.

Tabeka and the others warily took their places around the fire again.

"What *was* that creature?" Iridia shifted closer to Evior, her eyes wide as saucers, her body visibly trembling. "We need to leave. I cannot sleep here. What if it comes back?"

"It must have been one of Zohmes' creations. You know we cannot travel at night. It is too dangerous." Evior had lowered his sword, but he still studied the trees.

"The goddess Rania protects us. She told me we will come to no harm during our journey. I trust the goddess to keep us safe." Tabeka added more wood to the fire and stoked its flames. "Rest, both of you. I will keep first watch. We can take turns."

More than a month after they had left Nimegen, they arrived at the borders of Cront. Tabeka was awed at the beauty of the city. She had heard about it but could never have imagined it in her wildest dreams. "Have you heard back from the general?" she asked Evior.

"Yes. He gave me directions to his estate and invited us to be his guests until we find a place to live."

Tabeka looked at Iridia. "Girl, change your clothes before we present ourselves at the general's house."

"Why?"

"You look like a boy with very long hair," Tabeka growled. "Women do not wear pants. You know that."

"Tabeka, the women on King Biryn's team all wore pants. I saw none in a dress. Iridia looks just fine. I actually think she looks rather fetching," Evior argued.

Tabeka looked at her daughter. She had to admit, she did look charming. The pants and tunic accentuated her slim figure. Her long black hair was tied back in a braided ponytail, and her green eyes sparkled. For a moment, Tabeka saw Ivia in her mind. Iridia looked a lot like her mother, but not completely. Her face was softer, she had a dimple in her chin, and in her cheeks when she smiled, and her face was oval, whereas Ivia's face had been heart-shaped, and her eyes had been brown. The resemblance was there, nonetheless.

She ran her hands through her own fiery locks, now streaked with premature white strands. Her years of worry, hatred, and thoughts of vengeance had left their mark. She loved her daughter so much that the revenge she had planned — to tell Cidus that his heir was not his son and that Iridia was his real child — was now a distant plan. Iridia had become the child she had lost and was like her very own. She could never hurt the girl with such a truth.

Yet Rania had told her she had started something that apparently was written in the book of knowledge, and she had no power to stop what would be and was to come.

"We are here," Evior announced.

Tall gates opened automatically, and they drove through them. Tabeka gasped. The general's grounds were beyond beautiful, like a paradise. Trees in full bloom lined the drive to the home. Home? It was more like a manor, or even a palace. It looked huge.

A woman came down the steps to meet them. "Tabeka, I am happy to see you and your family made it safely through those mountains."

Tabeka had seen her briefly when they had met with the king, but she could not remember her name.

"I am Ciara, Brenn's mate. Please, come inside. Dinner is almost ready."

"You have met Evior and me, and this is Iridia, my daughter," Tabeka introduced.

Tabeka noticed Ciara gazing intently at Iridia. The woman had tiny, glistening, scales on her face. What was she? What did she know?

"We have rooms ready for you. I am sure you would like to refresh before you eat? I will have the servants bring your belongings inside, and I will show you to your rooms." Ciara led the way into the house.

"Is this a palace?" Tabeka stopped to admire the lavish entrance hall.

Ciara chuckled. "No. The palace is fifty times the size of this house."

"I have never seen such a beautiful house." Tabeka stopped before a tall mirror. "I look terrible."

"You can bathe and change your clothing upstairs. You have just arrived from a long journey. It is to be expected that you feel dusty and disheveled." Ciara led them to the stairs.

Tabeka, Evior, and Iridia followed behind her. Just as Tabeka lifted her foot to begin up the stairs, she stopped when she saw the man coming down toward them.

"It cannot be." Her heart beat a staccato rhythm, and dizziness almost overtook her. She grabbed the rail to steady herself.

Apparently, Cidus had used his flyer to get there ahead of them. But how could he have found out so fast? It had to be from Zohmes. Behind her, she heard Evior curse.

"Father? How in the gods' names could you have known?" Evior uttered.

Cidus continued to descend toward them with a confused look on his face. Tabeka stood frozen, her feet glued to the floor. He walked passed Ciara and stopped in front of Tabeka.

"Tabeka? Is that really you?"

She managed to get the feeling back in her body and took a step back, almost tripping and falling against Evior.

"We must leave. Father, you cannot make me return." Evior took Tabeka by the arm, then grabbed Iridia's.

"I do not understand. Tabeka, please explain? Is he my son? Please? I am dumbfounded."

Cidus' gaze held hers. She could not miss the question in his eyes as he hurried to join them. Ciara walked down the stairs and stood next to Cidus.

"Please, before you make hasty decisions, let us go to the

kitchen, and I will explain." Ciara began to walk toward the end of the entrance hall.

Tabeka hesitated. She had not been this close to Cidus in more than twenty years, not since the night of the birthing. Did she really want to be in his company now?

She looked at Evior. "Do you want to talk to him?"

"Why should I?"

Tabeka noticed the hatred in Evior's eyes. She looked at Cidus, saw the confusion on his face, the bewilderment in his eyes, and did not understand any of it. The man acted like he did not know Evior.

"Tabeka, please? Allow Ciara to explain? After so many years...I have dreamed of this moment...I have so longed for you..."

Were those tears in Cidus' eyes? And the words he uttered? Something was wrong here. Very wrong.

"Children, wait for me here. I will go with Ciara and Cidus to the kitchen to hear what they have to say but be ready to leave."

She followed Ciara and Cidus into a large kitchen but refused the chair offered to her. "I will stand. Thank you."

Ciara set three glasses on the table and filled them with wine. Tabeka gratefully drank hers, feeling it calm her. "So, what is it you wish to tell me, Lady Ciara?"

"Lady? Just call me Ciara. Tabeka, this is not the Lord Cidus you know. This man is the real Cidus."

"Real? What do you mean?"

Cidus cleared his throat. "Tabeka, the man you know as Cidus is really Jatron, my twin brother. The evening after we became betrothed, Cewrick switched us. He took me, imprisoned me, and put Jatron in my place at the manor."

Tabeka thought she had surely gone mad. Twins? Cewrick? "I am confused. How could Cewrick have your brother? How is it you did not know of this twin?"

"It was a secret my father took with him to the realm of dreams. Zohmes told me the whole story after he imprisoned me." Cidus looked down at the cup of wine in his hands. "Just after my mother gave birth to us, my father gave Jatron to Cewrick. Apparently, my father was in league with him. Cewrick knew my mother was carrying twin boys and he demanded to raise my brother to replace his own son. Jatron was kept a prisoner in his castle but apparently well cared for. Cewrick placed a spell on my mother, so she never knew she had given birth to two infants. When Zohmes left Cewrick's body, he took me with him, and I became *his* prisoner. The king and his team rescued me not long ago."

"Now I know I have lost my mind. This is a very confusing tale." Tabeka shook her head to try and absorb all he had told her. But now that she examined him closer, she noticed his blond hair threaded with silver strands. And his eyes. They were the eyes she remembered, eyes that were loving and warm. Now, they gazed at her with love. The icy expression was gone. There was a difference. It was slight, but nevertheless a difference from Cidus. Cidus? No, Jatron...

"I gave you a betrothal gift. A—"

Tabeka pulled the gold chain from beneath her blouse. "Though I grew to hate you, I always wore it. The man who gave me this was kind, goodhearted, and he loved me truly. We had three wonderful months together."

"And the young man with you is my son?"

"No. He is not. I lost the infant after you...well...your brother, accused me of being a whore, that the child was not his. I fled and stumbled over a root in the forest and fell hard. It caused me to lose the infant." She saw pain mask his features fleetingly.

"When I saw you and the young man, I had so hoped. He is Jatron's son?"

Tabeka's heart sang with joy. The man she had hated for so

many years, was not her Cidus. Yet how was she going to tell the real Cidus about Evior and Iridia?

"Tabeka has a daughter, Cidus." Ciara interrupted, then sipped her wine.

Cidus looked even more bewildered. "But you said you lost—"

Tabeka held up her hand to stop his words. "Iridia is adopted. She does not know."

What have I done? I have created a complicated situation. How do I explain it all?

Cidus stood and pushed his chair back. He kneeled before Tabeka and took her trembling hands in his. "My love, dare I hope? Did you give your heart to another?"

She could not stop the tears from spilling and shook her head slightly. "No, Cidus, my heart has always belonged to the man with whom I spent three wonderful months. My love had turned to hatred and bitterness against the man who betrayed me. Until now. Now I feel even more loathing for the man I thought to be you, for having done this to you, to us."

"I have never stopped loving you, Tabeka, and we have so many years to make up for. First, I must reclaim my inheritance. I was first born, so I am the true lord of the Sirona Realm and owner of Wildevein Manor. My brother is malevolent and in league with Zohmes. I must stop him and his heinous deeds."

"I think we need to call Evior and Iridia into the kitchen now. They must be wondering what is happening," Ciara pointed out.

CHAPTER THREE

Tabeka explained as best she could what she had learned when Evior and Iridia joined everyone in the kitchen.

Evior stared at Cidus. "So, you are my uncle? Your name is Cidus, and my father's name is really Jatron?"

"Yes. And if it were not for King Biryn and his team, I would still be rotting away in that prison in which Zohmes kept me. I do not like to tell you this, but your grandfather was in league with Cewrick. When Zohmes left Cewrick's body, your father joined in alliance with Zohmes." Cidus looked ashamed as he took a sip of his wine.

"Oh, I have known all that for a long time. I hate him," Evior growled.

"I plan to reclaim my inheritance. I do not know how yet, but they will all pay for what they have done," Cidus said.

Ciara sighed. "A god and a sorcerer are undefeatable. Believe me, Zohmes' son, Jonathan, has more powers than the god, and he has tried. Yet Zohmes lives on. Liana, my cousin, was able to send Odoxon back to Wuits Peak, but Zohmes released him again. We have been fighting the two of them for some time now."

"My brother must be punished. He is not undefeatable. I have most of my strength back and have been practicing my swordsmanship with Brenn. He gifted me with a new sword since I lost mine when Zohmes took me. Soon, I will challenge Jatron." Cidus pressed his lips together in a grim line.

Tabeka placed her hand over Cidus'. "When I first saw you, my heart almost stopped. I thought Cidus...I mean Jatron...had found out about our plans and had taken his flyer to be here before us."

"Cidus...sorry, Jatron knows, and he knows where you are. You cannot flee from him. Zohmes knows everything. There is no place for you to hide from them. At least you are with us now, under our protection, and Rania watches over you." Ciara sighed. "Tabeka, you must all be tired from your journey and would perhaps like to bathe. Let me take you to your rooms." She stood and began to walk toward the door.

Cidus also got up off his chair. "Tabeka, can we talk later? After lunch? We can find a private place in the gardens."

Tabeka felt heat flood her cheeks. After all these years...the deep love she had for him surfaced in full force. Her heart felt whole again. Yes, she longed to be alone with him, to rekindle the fire between them, to feel his lips on hers, and to have him hold her against his chest.

"Yes, I would like that," she said softly.

They followed Ciara up the stairs. She opened the first door she came to. "Tabeka, this is your room. You will all find clean and suitable clothing in your wardrobes. After you have met with Cidus, if you do not mind, I would like to speak with you privately."

Tabeka felt a lot of power radiating from the beautiful mistress of the house. And the tiny scales on Ciara's face and neck still mystified her, what was she?

Ciara patted Tabeka's arm and gave her a warm smile. "I am a jewel dragon, Tabeka. We will talk later."

Iridia squealed. "A jewel dragon? A real one? Truly?"

Ciara laughed at Iridia's delight. "Yes, a real one. And I am also a sorceress."

"Mother, did you hear that? And why do you need to meet with Cidus? I have the impression you have met in the past."

"Yes. We were betrothed once. Before Jatron took Cidus' place." Tabeka looked at her daughter's stunned face.

"You need to tell me more, Mother." Iridia frowned. "Your heart holds too many mysteries, as I've said so many times."

"Go bathe and change your clothes, girl."

Tabeka quickly entered the room and closed the door before Iridia could ask more questions. She leaned against the door for a moment. The truth would come out. There was no way she could stop it. Would Iridia hate her for what she had done? And Evior—his real mother and his brothers and sisters were alive somewhere. She tried to still the fear in her heart, the dread of what was to come.

The luxurious perfumed bath relaxed her. She could have stayed in the water for a while, but they would be waiting for her...Cidus would be waiting. She washed herself and her hair, then got out. After drying her hair, she stood before the mirror to brush and braid it.

Suddenly, she was interested in her appearance. Her body was still that of a young woman. Her face a bit older than when Cidus had known her, but now the luster was back in her black eyes, and her cheeks were flushed. He had thought her beautiful then. Would he still desire her?

She braided her hair with care, then opened the wardrobe. There were several lovely dresses for her to choose from and they all looked like they would fit her. How could Ciara have known?

She chose a pale-yellow dress edged with white lace and embroidered with white flowers and leaves. It was beautiful. She had never had such an expensive piece of clothing. After putting on the white sandals she found, she hurried out of the room and down the stairs to the kitchen.

A woman was busy cutting bread. "They are in the dining room," she told Tabeka. "I will show you where to go."

She had tarried too long. Everyone was seated at a large dining table, and Tabeka noticed Brenn sitting at one end.

"General Mildash. How nice to see you again. Thank you for your hospitality. Ciara, thank you for loaning us these lovely clothes. We will be careful with them."

Tabeka had taken in her daughter's dress in a glance. Iridia looked so beautiful. Her hair was braided into a coronet atop her head, and her dress was a lovely mauve with purple embroidery and deep purple lace. She looked like a princess.

"The clothes are yours to keep, Tabeka. Now, take a chair and join us." Ciara loaded her plate.

"Evior tells us your journey was smooth with no incidents. I am glad you arrived here safely. You are welcome to stay as long as you need." Brenn gave her a big smile.

Tabeka did not know what to say. "Th-thank you, thank you both," she stammered.

She had never known such generosity, not even when she still lived with her family. Though her father was the ruler of the Hakania Realm, they had lived a simple life as traders, like the rest of the Hakanians.

Cidus stood and pulled out a chair for her. "You are as beautiful as I remember you, Tabeka," he whispered. "I always dreamed I would hold you in my arms again. Thinking about you is what kept me alive."

Heat rushed to her face. It was as if the years had fallen away. She felt like a young girl again. Iridia's curious glances did not escape her...or Evior's.

After they finished eating, Tabeka turned to Cidus as he thanked his hosts and excused himself and then took her hand. He led her out of the house to the gardens. When they were away from prying eyes, sheltered by the giant wraggia trees in the orchard, he stopped and gathered her into his arms.

They stood like that for a long time. Tabeka drank in his male scent that she remembered so well. She drew back a little and looked up at him. His eyes were closed. A lone tear trickled down his cheek. Standing on her toes, she kissed him on that spot, his tear now on her lips. He kissed her, gently, then hungrily.

He finally drew back and looked into her eyes. "After I claim my inheritance and exact my revenge, will you be mine, Tabeka? Will you join with me and be by my side forever?"

"Yes, oh, yes," she whispered. "But Cidus, there must be complete truth between us. There is something I must tell you. Let us sit."

Leaning against the trunk of a tree, his arm around her, she began to spill that which she had kept locked away in her heart for so long. "After I lost the infant, my hatred for the man I thought was you grew into a festering wound in my heart. I wanted to take revenge but knew not how. After five years Jatron approached me. Ivia, his wife, had lost one infant after another. Jatron wanted a son, an heir. He offered me gold to assure Lady Ivia carried the child to term. He told me to kill it if it was a girl and to make sure Ivia conceived again. I was to do this until he had his wish."

Cidus tilted her chin. "You did not—"

"Gods, no! I could not kill anyone, much less a babe. I knew the infant was female, so I plotted. There was a widow in Wildevein who was due to deliver her child around the same time as Ivia. I bought the boy with a bag of gold. When Ivia delivered, I swapped the infants. Evior is not Jatron's son. I had planned to tell Jatron that he had no son when the boy came of age. That was to be my revenge for what he did to me."

"Iridia?"

"Is his daughter."

"The boy and girl do not know, I presume."

"No. I love Iridia as if she were mine. I could not hurt her, and I have become very fond of Evior. It would destroy them to have knowledge of this. But now, everything has changed. You will exact your vengeance for what was done to you, and Jatron will receive his punishment."

"What happened to Ivia?"

"She traveled to the land of dreams right after the birthing. Jatron did not care. He had his son. He was happy. Oh, I detest him so. Do you hate me for what I did, Cidus?"

"How could I? I love you too deeply. But the boy deserves to know he has a mother. Yet, how you can tell them this tale without revealing all, I do not know. As for Iridia, I am not sure. Should she know she is the daughter of a monster? Jatron might be my brother, but he is evil to the core, just like Zohmes."

"It is hard to imagine that your twin is so opposite from you."

Cidus sighed. "Look at who raised him. First Cewrick. Well, Zohmes in Cewrick's body, and then Zohmes himself for a short while." He paused for a moment and frowned. "It is odd. I remember something strange now. When I was his prisoner, Zohmes told me he was our real father. I thought it was some kind of mind torture to tell me such things."

Tabeka pulled away from him and sat back, staring at him. "How could that be?"

"He said he had taken on the appearance of my father and had his way with my mother."

"Sorry for the intrusion." Ciara approached them from among the trees. "So now you know the truth. Both of you."

"You knew everything?" Tabeka asked.

"The goddess Rania revealed all to me. I know about Evior and Iridia. And yes, Cidus. Zohmes told you the truth. He is your and Jatron's father. You have inherited your mother's nature. Jatron is just like Zohmes. That is why Cewrick wanted one of the twins. Actually, Zohmes was in possession of Cewrick's body at the time. As it turned out, he got the boy that was most like him. Your father knew Zohmes was the real father. Your mother did not, and she did not know she had twins. Zohmes blackmailed Lord Seron Milhella into serving him by threatening to tell your mother everything. After she passed to the realm of dreams, Zohmes threatened to harm the boy he had taken. That is how it all started."

Tabeka stared at Cidus. "He knew you were also his son, yet he imprisoned you. The man is worse than a monster."

Ciara sat near them. "He is a god. A fallen god. Cidus is like Jonathan. He is good and kind. That is not what Zohmes wants. He has no use for that in his miserable existence. He did the same to one of the women from Earth, named Julia." She cringed but continued her story. "Zohmes took on the form of Julia's lover and had his way with her. Her true lover died shortly after. Zohmes wanted the infant and abducted the young woman. We saved her, but we feared Zohmes would try again. The gods and goddesses intervened. Julia's infant came to us from the future. Jonathan is her son, and he is also your brother, Cidus."

"By the gods, this is all too inconceivable," Cidus cried out.

"It is. But like Jonathan, you are a demi-god. You have hidden powers, only you do not know it yet. We will need to take you to the Clyss so your powers can surface."

"The Clyss?"

"A magickal pool in the Crimson Realm nestled within the mountains. It is a beautiful place watched over by the gods and goddesses."

"This is all too much to ingest in one day," Tabeka said.

"Tabeka, the truth will come out," Ciara informed her. "You must tell Evior and Iridia. You do not want them to find out from Zohmes or Jatron. But wait until after tomorrow's festival."

"They will hate me." Tabeka sighed deeply.

"No. They will be shocked, but they are both strong and will deal with the truth. You will not lose the girl you love like your own daughter. Do not be afraid. Come, let us go back to the house and we will talk more. There is much you both need to know and learn."

CHAPTER FOUR

Tabeka had a restless night. Her imagination of Iridia's reaction to what she had to tell her, played overtime. She realized she needed to trust what Ciara had told her and put it aside. She also had faith that the goddess Rania would look out for her.

Instead, she decided to concentrate on all that was good — her happiness that Cidus was back in her life and wanted to join with her. It was strange that she had not seen any of it in her visions. Then again, they were not allowed to know everything. The book of knowledge was written, and life would play out the way it was recorded.

Ciara had given her and Iridia a beautiful dress to wear to the festival. Tabeka was really looking forward to the day. It was the Festival of Restoration in remembrance of Ierilia's liberation from all the wicked sorcery and wars of so many centuries ago. Once a year, it was celebrated far and wide.

She had not attended a celebration after that fateful day in the past, and had forbidden Iridia to, just in case Cidus...Jatron...would attend it. This would be the first festival she would attend since the Festival of Light when she had met Cidus. She looked out of the windows at a clear blue sky, the suns already sending their slanted rays down to the world below them.

After pulling the dress over her head and tying the laces, she stood before the tall mirror. The dress was magnificent. The bodice was corset style in a deep orange. Two bands crossed her shoulders. The sleeves were sheer in the same orange hue and flared out just below her elbows. The skirt started snug around the waist and toward the hips in the same color as the bodice. Then a wide gold band hugged her hips. From there the silky cloth was draped with graceful folds in several panels down to her ankles, the hems of each panel forming a V. The panels were in various colors of brown, green, yellow, crème, and deep red. She twirled around, feeling so spoiled and grateful. She put on the orange sandals and hurried downstairs to the dining room.

Just as she walked in, Iridia came in behind her. "Mother, look at this dress! It is absolutely breathtaking."

Tabeka turned to look at her daughter, and how beautiful she was. Her dress was red and white. The blouse was sheer white, the sleeves puffed to the wrist. At the wrists was a wide, laced-up red band, with a white ruffle just covering the top of her hands. The bodice was red with laces in front from just above her breasts to the waist, and wide red straps over the shoulders. The red skirt fell in pointed layers to just below the knees. Below that, a full white skirt draped to the ankles. Iridia had braided some of her hair into a crown and twirled it on top with the rest cascading over her shoulders and down her back.

"It is beautiful, Iridia. You do look like a princess."

"She is *my* princess," Evior said when he came in. "Iridia, you take my breath away."

"We have Ciara to thank for all these lovely clothes." Tabeka walked to the table and greeted Ciara and Brenn. "Thank you again, Ciara. You really need to stop spoiling us like this."

Ciara smiled. "I love spoiling people. You both look so lovely."

"Thank you. I love your dress, too." Ciara wore purple, which really brought out her mauve eyes. Her dress was similar to Tabeka's, except in various shades of mauve and purple. Brenn, she noticed, was dressed in his official uniform.

"I am so looking forward to this day. I cannot remember the last time I attended a festival," Tabeka said. "Actually, I can. It was when Cidus approached me for the first time at the Festival of Light in Wildevein. That was so long ago…"

She startled when Cidus dropped a kiss on top of her head.

"That it was, but now we start again. Everyone, I would like to announce that Tabeka and I are betrothed. After I deal with my brother, we will join."

Iridia rushed to embrace her. "Mother, truly? You and Cidus are joining? When?"

"After he has reclaimed his rightful inheritance, child. For now, we are betrothed, and I have not been so happy in years."

"Good morning, Cidus. Tabeka, I have informed the king of your arrival. He would like all of us to join him and the queen for lunch tomorrow at the palace," Brenn said and dropped a kiss on Ciara's cheek.

Tabeka smiled and nodded. Inwardly, she cringed. Meet with the king? Why? Had Ciara told Brenn about Cidus being Zohmes' son? "I need to speak with my daughter and Evior first," she said. They knew nothing yet. She needed to tell them before going to the palace.

"Why, Mother? What is wrong with going to the palace? I am so excited. I will get to see the little prince and princess."

"There is something I need to tell you both," Tabeka said.

"Tabeka, there are no secrets in this house. Brenn and I know what we discussed yesterday. You and Cidus know, so you may as well tell them now that Cidus and Jatron are really Zohmes' sons."

Tabeka noticed the little frown on Ciara's face and a slight shake of her head. The biggest secret would not yet be revealed.

Evior set his glass down on the table. "My father is Zohmes' son? How is that possible?"

Ciara explained it patiently. She finished with, "Do not worry. You have not inherited any of Zohmes' evil traits."

Evior wiped his forehead. "That is a relief. I cannot imagine being related to him."

The conversation went back and forth between the betrothal and the twin brothers and the Zohmes scenario. Tabeka found it difficult, and she noticed Ciara had problems answering some of their questions. Fortunately, they soon finished eating their breakfast, and it was time to go to the festival. All would be pushed to the back of everyone's mind that day. But tomorrow, she would have to deal with telling Evior and Iridia the truth.

At least Evior could be glad he was not related to that evil god, but Iridia, unfortunately, was. She was his granddaughter. Until recently, she had never felt any powers emanating from Iridia. Yet it was just the other day she had wondered about it, had seen the aura that surrounded her, and had felt something radiating from her daughter. Maybe she escaped inheriting a lot of his DNA? All she could do was hope.

Cront was alive with music and adorned with banners, flags, and floral garlands. The streets were filled with dancing people and visitors from other realms. Stands on the sidewalks offered delicious foods for sale and memorabilia. Tabeka had taken some gold coins from her treasure bag and put them in the pocket of her dress, hidden under the many layers of cloth.

"You can dance better than that," she told Iridia as she watched some girls dancing.

"I am not going to dance, Mother."

"I am not asking you to. I am just complimenting your

dancing abilities." Tabeka grimaced. Young people were sometimes hard to deal with.

The market was something else. The traders all had their wares marked down and were outshouting each other trying to get people to buy. By the time they left the area, Tabeka had acquired a number of things for Iridia and herself that she would never have bought normally.

"It is time to go to the arena," Brenn announced.

"We had better hurry then to get back to the house," Ciara answered.

"Where is the arena?" Tabeka wondered.

"Just outside of Cront. You all will go there in my flyer. I will ride Atom to get him warmed up," Brenn said.

Ciara suddenly turned and pointed out a small group of people. "Look! Taylith and Liana are here." She hastened to meet them.

The rest of the group followed Ciara. Tabeka recognized the people as members of the king's group she and Evior had met with near the Dreaded Peaks. There was only one she had not met—the young woman holding Lord Henderson's hand. She must be the woman they had saved.

"Are that man and woman dragons, too? They have scales just like Ciara," Iridia asked.

"Girl, button your mouth. That is very rude," Tabeka admonished.

Brenn chuckled. "Oh, the young. Yes, Iridia, they are both dragons. Taylith and Liana are Ciara's cousins."

Iridia did not look the least bit sorry. Luckily, the dragons did not appear to be offended by Iridia's questions.

They followed the group back to Brenn's estate. The power radiating from the people in front of them prickled Tabeka's skin. They had fought Zohmes and could not defeat him? She could not stop the shiver that wracked her body. How was Cidus going to defeat Jatron if Zohmes protected him? It was a pity. Two brothers, one good, the other one corrupted by Zohmes. If all had been normal, she was sure Cidus would have shared his inheritance with his twin.

Tabeka was relieved when they had finally made it back to Brenn's estate. She did not really wish to attend the games, but it would be rude to their hosts if she declined. She could not help the sense of foreboding that had overtaken her. She knew something terrible was about to happen, but the goddess was silent, and no vision was forthcoming. She sighed and followed the others into the flyer.

Tabeka had seen flyers, but she had never flown in one. Such a luxury was reserved for the more affluent, and though her parents could have afforded it, they had never been interested much in modern technology.

The experience was exhilarating. She gazed out of the little window and looked down. Her stomach rolled for a moment but then settled. It was quite something to look at the festivities from above. But the journey was all too fast. They arrived at the arena in just minutes.

Hundreds of colorful flags, one for each realm, waved gently in the summer breeze. Banners with each realm's crest hung on the walls. Large, pastel-colored balls floated above the arena and the fields surrounding it. They glowed, almost as if there were a candle inside them.

The arena was crowded. The structure was crammed with people watching some of the early games. Others milled around outside, slowly taking their places behind the yellow ribbons marking the race course. Two tents with refreshments on tables stood on either side of the arena entrance. A large group stood near the starting line of the horse race. When she looked up, she saw the king and queen sitting on a platform, the little prince and princess on their laps. Excitement filled the air around her, but she just could not shake the sense of doom that filled her soul.

Cidus squeezed her fingers and gazed down at her. "What is it, my heart?"

She shook her head. "It is nothing…" She gestured to the riders and horses lining up at the starting line. "They are about to start the race."

A horse reared, swiveled around several times, the rider desperately trying to calm the nervous animal. He finally managed to get the horse under control and back in line.

The king's voice rose above the noise of the crowd. "Let the race begin!"

A loud horn sounded, and the horses shot forward. Tabeka's heart pounded in her chest. Something was not right. She knew it. She hated her gifts at times, and this was one of those moments.

Taking a deep breath, she pushed the anxiety aside, then focused her attention on the race. Brenn and Lord Henderson rode close together. From her experience during her younger years, Tabeka knew they were biding their time. Their horses needed most of their energy and speed for the last leg of the race.

She knew how exhilarating it could be to ride at such a pace. When she was young, before her father had disowned her, she had pushed her mare to the limits. The feeling of freedom was astounding. It did not take too long before she could not see the racers anymore.

"Let us get some refreshments," Ciara suggested. "The course is quite long, and it will be a while before we see them return to the finish line."

Even the cup of wine did not calm her sense of foreboding. *Rania, talk to me… I know something is wrong, but what?* The goddess did not answer her. Whatever was going to happen, had to be written in the book of knowledge. Tabeka knew the goddess was not allowed to reveal everything. After eating some of the delicious pastries and some fruit, they ambled back to take their places near the finish line.

Tabeka saw the cloud of dust in the distance and heard the thundering of hooves. The horses that were racing for first place had sped up now, and it did not take long before she could see them clearly. Brenn had the lead with Lord Henderson close behind. A third and fourth were several lengths behind but advancing fast. It would be a close finish.

There was a skirmish. She saw Brenn pull hard on the reins and swivel, then he spurred his horse to a full gallop and chased after Lord Henderson's mount.

"Oh, my God! Oh, my God!" Julia shot forward onto the race course.

"Julia, watch out!" Taylith yelled as a horse approached and barely managed to avoid her.

Tabeka's blood chilled in her veins. Lord Henderson had been unseated but was somehow caught. His horse spooked and raced toward the open field dragging the man along, oncoming horses trampling him and getting spooked as well.

The area became a mass of snorting horses, riders desperately trying to calm their animals, then dismounting and quickly leading them away from the scene, and people running onto the course. Her stomach churned. Was this the sense of doom she had felt? Surely the man could not survive this. She was horrified. Why did the gods not give her the vision! She could have stopped the accident. Was this truly meant to happen?

Cidus gripped her hand and pulled her forward through the throng of spectators that milled around the scene.

Brenn took charge. "Please, give us room." When they did not listen, he called for assistance. "Guards! Remove all these people. The race is over. There is no winner!"

Several guards rushed to his aid, and between them, they quickly cleared the area, then went to help corral the spooked horses.

Tabeka now had a clear view of Lord Henderson. Julia sat on the ground, tears flowing freely down her cheeks. Lord Henderson's lifeless body lay beside her, and she cradled his head in her lap. Blood covered the ground beside Julia. Tabeka saw a massive wound on Lord Henderson's head. It looked as though his skull was cracked. His clothing, hanging in shreds, was caked with flaps of skin, blood, and sand, exposing large areas of muscle where the gravel had flayed his skin.

Laura kneeled on the ground beside Julia, trying to calm the hysterical woman down.

Tabeka joined the others as they formed a circle around the trio, blocking them from view. As a healer, she knew there was nothing they could do to help Lord Henderson. He had gone to the realm of dreams, she could feel his departing spirit, and her heart ached for poor Julia.

Suddenly, a power so pure it made Tabeka gasp, crackled in the air around them. It came from Laura. How could that be? The woman was not from Ierilia, yet there was no mistaking the source. Laura had been blessed by the gods in some way.

Light, so bright Tabeka had to shield her eyes, emanated from the young woman. She peered from between her fingers. Taylith, Ciara, and Liana had stepped forward and placed their hands on Laura's shoulders. Jonathan held Julia in his arms while Laura worked her spell. The luminous blaze enveloping Laura and Lord Henderson grew brighter. Tabeka closed her eyes against it.

Just as suddenly as the magick had flared around them, it dissipated. Tabeka slowly opened her eyes.

Lord Henderson took a deep gasp of air, coughed and sputtered, blood dripping from his mouth down his chin. He opened his eyes and sat up. A raspy inhaling of air, spluttering, bloody mucus dripped from the man's mouth. He opened his eyes and blinked a few times. "Wh...wh... what...h-happened?"

Incredible! She could not believe what she had just witnessed. Tabeka had seen these types of injuries before. Nothing she knew of could bring a soul back from the realm of dreams. Yet Laura had brought the man back from the brink of death. That had to be the only explanation.

Tabeka watched in awe as Julia pulled away from Jonathan, her tears like a waterfall as she bent to rain kisses on Lord Henderson's bloodied forehead. "Baby, you're alive. You're okay. Laura healed you!"

He sat up and took Julia's hand. "I don't remember exactly what happened. One minute, Brenn and I were racing to the finish line, I felt the saddle shift a little, and the next...well, that's kind of hazy."

Tabeka watched as Brenn approached the couple. "Glad to see you are fine again, Bernie. Thank the gods for the healing powers they gifted Laura. But we need to investigate because I discovered that Bernie's saddle was sabotaged. The straps were cut. This was no accident."

"Zohmes," the king said softly.

Brenn brushed his hand through his hair. "We do not know that yet. Trevain and his unit are on the way to inspect the stables to see if we can find any clues as to who did this."

King Biryn crouched beside Lord Henderson. "Bernie, you gave us quite a shock. How could this have happened?"

Tabeka had not noticed the king joining them.

"I don't know. I felt my saddle move. The rest is all hazy."

Brenn returned leading York and carried the saddle. "Your horse appears to be fine, Bernie."

"Mother, that man's spirit was gone. How is this possible?" Iridia, standing beside her, asked softly.

King Biryn rose. "Cylena is returning to the palace with the twins to be safe. I have to remain for the duration of the games, but I will not chance something happening to the queen and the twins. Hirsuta and Cewrick have gone back with them and will remain at the palace with the queen." Biryn took a deep breath. "I will make an announcement that Bernie is fine, but there is no winner. The race is disqualified. We will hold it again at the next festival."

Tabeka watched the king stride back to the arena, followed by his guard detail. She listened to the interaction between Lord Henderson, Julia, and Julia's sister, Laura.

With Julia and Laura's help, Lord Henderson stood. A bit wobbly at first, but then he was fine. "I think this is the last horse race I'll ever participate in," he muttered.

"Why would Zohmes do this to Bernie? For what reason?" Julia uttered.

"I think I'd like to go have a bath and get into clean clothes," Bernie said.

"Maybe you should rest a while, Bernie," Laura advised.

"I feel fine, and I thank you for saving me. I'm forever in your debt."

Julia looked at him. "Are you sure you're okay?"

"Yes, we don't want to miss the rest of the activities, do we? Let me hurry home to change. We haven't had this much fun since we got here."

Julia poked him. "You're fucking kidding me! You call this fun? If you insist on coming back to watch the games, I'm going with you to get some clean clothes as well. My dress is just a tad stained."

Tabeka watched the others walk away, then turned to Iridia and Evior. "The magick among these people is all-powerful. They are truly blessed by the gods."

"I just heard him say he wants to go and bathe, get a change of clothing and then continue watching the games in the arena. After what he just went through?" Evior rubbed his chin.

"Evior and I are going back to the arena, too, Mother. Are you coming to watch the last games?" Iridia asked.

"Yes, child. I am right behind you two." Tabeka followed them. The feeling of dread still festered within her. The lord's accident had not eradicated it. What else was to happen? As if this was not enough.

Tabeka was glad when the games master announced the last event, the major game of the day — the obstacle course. There were quite a few participants, at least ten to each of the six teams. The people from Earth had their own team. She knew a few of them. Erica, Laura, and a young lady Brenn pointed out as Isabella, the queen's childcare assistant.

The horn sounded, and the game began. How they could manage some of the obstacles, was beyond Tabeka. There was a tall wall to climb with metal spikes poking out. If the participant grabbed hold of a wrong spike, it disappeared into the wall. Quite a few fell and tumbled again before they got to the top and dropped to the other side. Erica was the one that amazed her. She was such a tiny woman, yet she showed a strength and agility that belied her size.

There were many obstacles to conquer — to jump over, to climb, to slide. The last one was the most interesting and most difficult. It was a tall, round structure that rotated quite fast. It had small ladders hanging down, wheels surrounded it that rotated on their own, holes to climb through, and ropes to climb while spinning with the construct.

The last round was finally finished with Erica as the winner. Tanoth was second, and Ivran third.

The suns were setting, painting the sky a beautiful crimson. Lights turned on everywhere as far as she could see. They had just left the arena and were walking to the flyer when a young woman pulled Taylith aside.

Tabeka gasped in shock. It was Zandria. She knew the king and his team had saved her but had never expected to see her in Cront. She looked healthy and well taken care of, but she seemed to be agitated about something.

Taylith returned with Zandria and addressed Brenn. "Zandria has information that will be useful in the investigation of the accident." They moved a distance away from the team. Lord Henderson joined them.

"What do you think is going on?" Julia questioned.

Ciara leaned against the flyer. "We will find out when they return."

Zandria returned before the men and went straight to Laura. "Taylith told me I am to stay with you and Liana. He does not want me to return to the estate alone."

Tabeka could not help but notice the girl still looked unsettled. Whatever information she had to tell Brenn had to have been important. She took Zandria's hand. Surprise registered in the young woman's eyes when she faced her.

"Tabeka! But how?"

"It is no longer safe for us at Wildevein. Iridia and Evior are here as well." Tabeka gestured to the young couple standing near the edge of the flyer.

"My family? Are they safe?"

"Your family will be fine, child." She patted Zandria on the shoulder. "Iridia will be overjoyed to see you."

They were interrupted by the return of Brenn, Taylith, and Lord Henderson. Tabeka could feel the tension radiating from them.

Brenn opened the door of the flyer. "Come, I will take you all to my estate where we continue celebrating this day. After I drop you off, I need to leave for a short while, but I will join you all later."

CHAPTER FIVE

Tabeka could not believe how quickly Brenn and Ciara's staff had decorated the estate. It was magickal. Garlands of colorful flowers lit up by strands of twinkling lights, were strung from tree to tree. The whole courtyard was bedecked in celebration of the festival. It reminded her so much of when she had met Cidus the first time when their camp had been decorated in a similar manner.

Many of the guests were outside in the gardens celebrating. An orchestra played on the verandah, the music echoing throughout the property.

Iridia tugged Evior's arm. "Come, I want to dance."

"I think I'll go with Brenn and Mark," Lord Henderson said as they made their way to the front door.

She still could not shake that sense of unease from earlier in the evening and one accident for the day was enough. Someone obviously wanted the man dead. Tabeka grasped his shoulder from behind. "Stay here, Lord Henderson."

"Why, Tabeka?"

"Tabeka, did you like the games?" Julia asked.

Tabeka shook her head. "I do not like anything to do with danger." She turned to Lord Henderson. "I had a feeling of doom, but the goddess did not grant me a vision, so I could not warn you. I am so glad you are healed, Lord Henderson, but I still feel that something else will happen. The premonition has not left me."

"Please, Tabeka, stop it with the lord stuff? Just call me Bernie?"

"When I was a young girl, my parents taught me to address people by their titles. After they abandoned me, I lived a secluded life for many years. The old teachings are still present."

"Bernie from now on, please."

She watched him leave with leaden eyes, the feeling of unease dissipating. It was not Bernie anymore who was in danger. Then why still the sense of pending doom within her?

Cidus threaded his fingers with hers. "Would you care to dance with me, Tabeka?"

She nodded and smiled up at him, squashing her shadowed thoughts. "Of course."

Cidus led her to the dance floor. Tabeka's heart raced, and blood rushed to her face when he pulled her into his arms. Gods, she felt like the young girl she used to be when he held her thus. So many years had passed her by. Years full of pain and anguish… Of hate.

Cidus swirled her around the dance floor. "You are still a beautiful dancer."

She gazed up into those kind blue eyes. Eyes filled with so much love, it made her ache. How could she ever have mistaken Jatron for the man who had stolen her heart? "I am sorry I was so blinded by hate that I could not see the truth."

"Let us forget for a few hours what has been done to us, my heart. What has been set in motion will invade our lives soon enough."

"You are right. Let us enjoy tonight." Tabeka pushed all thoughts of Zohmes and Jatron from her mind. Cidus was correct. The events set in motion would play out, and she did not want to think about it. Before she knew it, several hours had passed.

Both winded from the lively dance they had just finished, Cidus led her to the sidelines and into the ballroom. "I will get us some refreshments."

Tabeka approached Julia, Bernie, Brenn, and Ciara. The tension surrounding them was palpable.

"It's only a few days until our wedding. I have so much to do, and—"

"You are betrothed." Tabeka could not help joining the conversation. Love was something that should be celebrated, and after Bernie's accident, the couple needed something else to focus on.

Julia's demeanor visibly changed. Her eyes sparkled, and a bright smile lit her face. "Yes. We will be joining in a few days. Would Cidus, you, and your family like to attend the wedding? The joining ceremony will be held in Henderson, at the Temple of Fertility, and the celebration will be here. Brenn and Ciara are hosting it."

The happiness on their faces was delightful, but then suddenly, pain pierced Tabeka's skull. Her vision blurred, then went dark.

A man of great power, who Tabeka knew not.

Young and viral, his countenance was handsome. Long dark hair, a strong chin, such perfect features.

He opened his almond-shaped eyes and pinned her with a stare.

Glowing green, the pupils were slits...so cold, like a serpent.

A shudder wracked her body as his laughter echoed around her, pierced her soul.

It was evil, triumphant.

The vision faded. Tabeka's eyes blurred and then focused. For a moment, she felt disoriented, then she remembered. She was in a ballroom on Brenn's estate. Dancers swirled across the floor, and the haunting sound of a slow Ierilian tune filled her ears.

Who was the man she had just seen in her vision? She had met so many people this night, but not him. Was it Zohmes? No. From what she had been told, Jonathan looked like his father. The god had red hair. The man in the vision was obviously someone they needed to watch out for, a man who meant harm.

"Tabeka, what is wrong? You are so pale." Cidus handed her a cup of wine and a small plate filled with fruit, cheese, and pastries.

"Nothing, I am fine. Just a bit tired." Should she tell him? Yes, there should be no secrets between them. She shivered. Yet she still needed to divulge the biggest secret of all, one that caused her stomach to roil and her heart to knot in fear.

"Iridia, is your mother all right?" Julia asked.

"Yes, this happens when she has one of her visions. She will be fine. Come on, Evior, I want to dance again." The young couple headed back to the courtyard.

Tabeka was thrilled when Julia had invited them to attend the joining. She wished every day could be filled with happy events. Alas, what the goddess had just shown her, spelled some kind of calamity. But what?

"What worries me, you had your vision right after I told you about our joining. What did you see, Tabeka?" Julia wanted to know. "Was it about our wedding? Does Zohmes have fun stuff in mind?"

"No, do not worry, Julia. It had nothing to do with your joining or Zohmes."

Tabeka smiled when Julia sighed in relief. "Are you almost ready? Your gown?"

"Yes, and it's gorgeous! Our seamstress from Earth, Olivia, designs breathtaking clothes. Wait till you see it. Ask Ciara to show you images of the king and queen's clothes they wore at their joining. Olivia had a big hand in designing and making all the clothing with the help of the royal seamstress."

Several people joined them. Tabeka had seen them all when she and Evior had met with the king at Dreaded Peaks. Jonathan's name she remembered well because of his hair and relationship to Zohmes. It suddenly dawned on her—the young man was Cidus and Jatron's brother, and her Iridia was related to them, too. Jonathan and Cidus were her uncles. Oh, this was becoming all too tangled.

She greeted everyone with a smile she did not feel. They talked back and forth for a little while, some of the couples dispersing to dance again.

Tabeka looked up at Cidus. "I am really tired. Would you mind if I go to my room? I understand if you would like to stay a while."

"I am tired, too. It has been a long day, and I have not experienced so much activity in many years. I will walk you to your room." Cidus took her arm and led her to the stairs.

Tabeka opened the door to her room. "Cidus, would you care for a glass of wine? I am not ready to be alone after today's events."

Cidus made light of it, though she noticed the worried expression in his eyes. "I will not ignore an invitation into a lady's bedroom."

"Please, take a seat." She gestured to one of the chairs near the windows.

"You look serious, Tabeka. What is troubling you?"

"Having to tell everything tomorrow."

"I understand your fear. Tabeka, what Jatron wanted you to do is monstrous, barbaric. Kill an infant just because it is not a boy? I cannot believe that man is my brother, my twin, that we are a divided cell and developed together within my mother's body and share the same blood."

"Evior has a mother somewhere on Ierilia, and brothers and sisters. The woman moved away right after I paid her the gold. He will hate me for this secret, and so will Iridia."

"A woman who would sell her child is not worthy. Evior, after he recovers from the shock, will think that. Iridia, when she thinks about it all, will be grateful you decided not to take on the task Cidus demanded of you, and she did not die at birth. But it will be a lot for the two of them to take in. Iridia is Jatron's daughter, my niece, and Zohmes' granddaughter. She is going to need my protection."

"The woman who birthed Evior already had five young ones, no mate, and was very poor."

"No excuse to sell your child. With the amount of food my estate produces, an extra mouth to feed should have made no difference for her. Their needs should have been met."

Tabeka gave him a troubled glance. Of course, he would not know of the changes at Wildevein. Under Jatron's rule, the estate no longer provided for the needs of the people. The realm was dying. No longer was there abundant wildlife in the forests, their harvests meager, the crops diseased, and the people suffered greatly because of it.

"So much has changed since your captivity. Wildevein is not the place it once was, the Sirona Realm changed dramatically. Your brother fills his coffers with gold while the people in Wildevein struggle to feed their families."

A flash of anger crossed Cidus' face. "My brother has much to atone for, but I know this is not what is troubling you. Does all this have to do with the vision you had at the celebration?"

"Yes. I saw a vision of a man I have never met. He was very handsome, tall, long black hair with a perfect body. His eyes were what scared me. They were a glowing greenish yellow with slitted pupils, like a serpent. And he laughed, an evil triumphant laughter."

When Cidus gathered her into his arms and held her tightly against his chest, she felt so safe. She never wanted to leave his side. "Cidus, stay with me?"

He tilted her chin and tenderly kissed her lips. "I never thought I would hold you in my arms again. This is but a dream, and I will wake to my living nightmare."

She wrapped her arms around his neck and whispered against his lips, "Oh, Cidus, if this is a dream, we are sharing it, and I do not want to wake from it."

He captured her lips, kissing her as if he were a man drowning and she was the very air he required. And she returned the kiss like a woman starved for his affection. His mouth blazed a trail of fire across her from her jaw, down her neck, his hands seeking the ties to her dress.

When he loosened the corseted top, her dress slid down her shoulders, exposing her breasts. He lowered his head, sucking one beaded nipple into his mouth, his fingers teasing the other. Her blood was on fire and need pooled in her belly. Each nip of his teeth and soothing caress of his tongue seared her skin, building the sweet ache within her.

Cidus swept her into his arms and carried her to the bed, laying her gently on the downy comforter. He yanked his tunic over his head, dropping it to the floor then rid himself of his pants and boots. Gods, he was just as handsome as the first time she had seen him. She clasped his hand and pulled him down to her, aching for him to fill her. She opened her thighs to allow the hard ridge of his erection to brush against her aching core. It had been too long since she had felt the heat of his touch.

He groaned when she slid her hand between their bodies and grasped his cock, guiding it to the slick opening of her vagina. "Gods, Tabeka. I will not last. It has been too long since I have felt your touch."

She gazed into those deep blue eyes. "And I have been with no other man. Please, Cidus…I need you, now."

He leaned down, seeking her lips, and with one thrust of his hips seated himself deep within her core. It was exquisite, that pleasure-pain, the feeling of fullness. She wrapped her legs around his waist, meeting each rock of his hips. Her body tensed, and a moan escaped her lips as the flames raged out of control, that sweet friction driving her over the edge of ecstasy bringing Cidus along with her.

Cidus collapsed beside her, both breathing heavily, he nestled her in his arms against his chest. "I love you, my dancing queen. I will always love you."

She traced her fingers down the hard planes of his chest. "Not much of a dancer anymore. I leave that to Iridia now. And I have never stopped loving the man I once knew, the man holding me in his arms again now."

"You will always be my dancing queen, and you will dance again, if only for me."

CHAPTER SIX

Tabeka absently raked a brush through her hair the next morning while standing in front of the bathroom mirror. Her mind was troubled by the coming meeting with the king. Hate had ruled her heart and her soul for so many years. The revenge she had started would play out, except not in the manner she had planned. There was no stopping what had been written in the book of knowledge, but how was she to tell King Biryn what she had done?

The lies she had perpetrated surrounding Iridia and Evior? Her heart ached for them, and she hated herself for the part she had played in deceiving them. How could she tell Iridia that her father had wanted her killed and Evior that his mother chose coin over raising another child? And in front of King Biryn and the queen?

A trial was going to be held that morning for those who had harmed Bernie. The two perpetrators that Zandria had seen, the Earth people, Liam and Barry, would be facing the king before lunch. She wondered what kind of sentence King Biryn would hand down. After all, the two had planned to kill the lord. Tabeka shivered. The group from Earth was not that large, and then for one's fellow travelers to betray you like that? Bernie had to be devastated by it all, and extremely angry.

A knock sounded at her door.

"Come in." She hurried out of the bathroom.

Cidus walked through the door and hugged her. He dropped a kiss on top of her head. "You look lovely. We should head down to the kitchen and have a quick snack. Breakfast was a few hours ago."

"Did I sleep that long?" She leaned against him.

"We both did. I am still recovering from my lengthy imprisonment, and you are not used to so much activity in one day. It is no surprise. But Brenn will send a flyer as soon as the trial is over to take us to the palace."

"I am so afraid."

"Did Rania speak to you about any of it? Reassure you that all would go well?"

Tabeka heaved a sigh. "No, the goddess is silent on this matter."

They went downstairs to the kitchen and had a quick cup of tea and a pastry. After they finished, they went to the landing pad to wait for the flyer and found Iridia and Evior already there.

"Mother, what took you so long? I cannot wait to meet the little prince and princess. This is so exciting." Iridia bubbled over with anticipation.

Tabeka felt her stomach knot at the knowledge that her daughter's exuberant happiness would soon be clouded, and that of Evior. She walked up to Iridia and hugged her. "You know I love you more than life itself, right?"

"Yes, Mother. Why are your eyes filled with tears? Stop being so emotional." Iridia kissed her on the forehead, then turned her attention back to Evior.

Tabeka returned to Cidus who protectively held her against him.

When they arrived at the palace, Ciara was waiting on the landing pad to meet them. "Tabeka, step aside with me for a moment."

Tabeka wondered why, but she followed Ciara. When they were a short distance away from the others, Ciara laid her hand on Tabeka's forehead. "I have felt your fear. This will help you."

Tabeka felt her stomach settle, her quivering stop, and she felt completely calm. "Thank you, Ciara."

"Do not worry, Tabeka. Everything will be fine. The book of knowledge will not allow harm to befall those that do not deserve it, and nothing is written without a positive outcome, even if we do not always see it right away."

"I wish I had your powers."

"You are a healer, and you know your herbs, roots, and potions well. That is a rare talent. Not to mention, you have the gift of foresight, and the goddess Rania talks to you. Not everyone can be a sorceress or a sorcerer. The king and queen are waiting for us to join them. Follow me."

They caught up with the others. The palace awed Tabeka, Iridia, and Evior. If they thought Brenn's estate was lavish, the palace was breathtaking. When Ciara led them into the royal quarters, Tabeka curtsied, Iridia and Evior following her example.

"Please, come and sit at my table," King Biryn invited, holding up a goblet of wine.

They sat at the end of the table. The king broke the silence. "Please, eat. We will talk after we have filled our stomachs."

Brenn and Ciara sat opposite her. "What was the sentence imposed on the two people from Earth?" Tabeka asked.

"Twenty years in the mines for one, and the younger man was sentenced to ten years," Brenn told her.

She thought about the sentence for a moment. The people from Earth had gone through a lot, crashing on a strange planet, needing to learn new customs and language. The sentence seemed harsh, yet attempted murder was not something to just wipe away with a lighter sentence.

Cidus had loaded her plate without her noticing it. "Eat something, Tabeka. You had only a pastry earlier."

She picked at her food but did manage a few bites. Though she felt calm now, she was still nervous at what she was about to divulge.

"Now that we've all eaten, Tabeka, I would like to hear your tale. Please speak?" King Biryn said.

Tabeka began. She did not dare look at any of their faces while she talked, so she focused on Cidus beside her. She heard a chair scraping, looked up and saw Iridia starting to stand, her face drained of color, but Evior stopped her and made her sit down again.

"That is all of it, Your Majesty," she concluded.

The king ran his fingers through his hair. "That is quite a story. Cidus, your brother is a beast. Who in their right mind would kill a newborn infant?"

Cidus nodded. "I was just as shocked. If it weren't for Tabeka's intervention, her hatred, her wish for revenge, and agreeing to my brother's plot, Iridia would not be alive today."

Tabeka looked at her daughter. She looked very pale and sat not saying a word. Had she lost her? Could Iridia ever forgive her?

Evior stood. "I have nothing much to say. A woman who would sell her infant for a bag of gold is not worthy to be called my mother. I have no wish to find her or know her."

King Biryn agreed. "I understand how you feel, Evior. Perhaps one day you will feel different. I am sure Tabeka knows the name of the woman who birthed you."

"I do not wish to know it. And I am thankful to Tabeka because if it were not for her, Iridia would have been killed at birth." He turned to face her with a slight bow of his head. "Thank you, Tabeka."

"That means more to me than you can imagine, Evior," she said softly.

Cidus stood. "That means, Iridia, that you are my niece, and since my brother and I are Zohmes' sons, that makes you his granddaughter."

Iridia jumped up now, her eyes wild, an agitated expression on her face. "You are all out of your minds! I do not believe a word of this. Mother, tell me you did not lie to me all these years. Did you?"

Tabeka's heart ripped in two at her daughter's expression and words. "My sweet daughter, yes. It is all true. But you are like my own child. The vengeance I sought was never going to happen, not the way I planned it. After Jatron denounced me and I lost my own babe, I did not think I could ever love again, but you stole my heart. My sweet girl, if I had not agreed to Jatron's demands, the goddess showed me he would have found another healer, and you would have been killed at birth. Jatron would promise gold to whoever would do his bidding, and there are many that would have done the deed for a bag of gold."

"What was my real mother like? Can you tell me anything about her?" Iridia demanded in a shrill tone.

"Jatron manipulated the Lady Ivia. She was beautiful but submissive in nature. I felt sorry for her. She was nice, sweet, and believed anything and everything the man told her. I wept when she went to the realm of dreams after the birthing."

"And Jatron did not care? He got his son, and that is all he was interested in?" Iridia demanded.

"Yes. But from what I know, it was all written in the book of knowledge, and it has come to pass that you now know the truth of it all."

"A curse on the gods and the book of knowledge. Why does it have the power to dictate our lives?" Iridia shouted.

"Daughter—"

"Do not call me that." The look of anger on Iridia's face was like a dagger to Tabeka's heart.

"Iridia, you grew up knowing about the book and that it maps out our paths."

The king stood up and banged his fist on the table. "Calm down, everyone. Iridia, if it were not for your mother's intervention, you would not be here today. When you leave here, you think about that. Evior, I am sorry your mother decided to trade you for gold. But as Tabeka said, everything is mapped out for us in the book. We cannot argue with the gods.

"What I find interesting is, that somehow, we are all related and intertwined. Iridia is Zohmes' granddaughter. Cidus, you and your brother are Zohmes' sons. That makes you brothers to Jonathan...and my uncles. We have become a complicated labyrinth of family. I need to have my scribe begin a family tree."

"It is quite the entanglement," Cidus agreed.

King Biryn smiled grimly. "That it is. Now, can we continue this lunch and talk about the upcoming joining of Bernie and Julia? I, for one, am enjoying life for a change without interference from the two that would love to rain havoc on our city."

All Tabeka wanted was to reach out to Iridia, but as the group got up to leave the king's quarters, her daughter took Evior's hand and ignored her. Tabeka followed the others out of the rooms and back to the flyer. What would be next? When would Iridia speak to her again? Would she ever?

Ciara, who walked next to her, placed a gentle hand on her shoulder. "Tabeka, do not worry. Iridia will be fine. Give her some time."

"Come, walk with me, Tabeka," Cidus invited after they had finished dinner.

Tabeka nodded. Worry for Iridia gripped her so tight she could barely breathe, and she had not seen Iridia or Evior since their return from the palace, nor had they come to dinner.

Holding hands, she walked with Cidus through the orchard.

"You worry too much." Cidus squeezed her hand.

"Iridia has a stubborn streak. She may be Ivia's daughter, but she does not have her personality. It could be a long time before she will speak to me again."

"Come, sit here with me." Cidus pulled her down to a grassy spot beneath a wraggia tree. "Ciara told you not to worry, and Evior understands why you did what you did. He does not blame you."

"I know." She rested her head on his shoulder. "I love that girl so much…as if I gave life to her. I became more than fond of the boy because of my interference in his life, but also because I got to know him. He is an admirable young man."

"It is not too late for us to have a family. It was always balm on my wounds — the knowledge that you were raising our son or daughter. I am so sorry you lost the infant, for what Jatron did."

A noise startled them. Tabeka looked up to see Evior and Iridia walking toward them.

"Mother, can I speak with you?" Iridia asked. She did not appear to be angry anymore.

Tabeka jumped up eagerly. "Yes, of course." She hastened to join her daughter.

Iridia stopped walking and stood in front of Tabeka. "I am sorry for the way I acted and yelled at you. The shock of what I heard was too much to absorb all at once."

"I understand, girl. I would have been stunned, too. I wish I could have spared you."

Iridia took Tabeka's hands in hers and stared at her intently. "You saved my life, Mother. Jatron wanted you to kill me at birth. Through your plans of revenge, I am here today. Thank you. You are the mother I have always known, the one that raised me, fed and clothed me, wiped my tears, tended a wounded knee or arm, and held me if I could not sleep or had a bad dream. I love you, Mother."

Tears streamed down Tabeka's cheeks. "I am so sorry, child. Over the years, my plans for revenge changed. I did not ever want you to find out, and now to hear you are a direct descendant of Zohmes must be confusing your mind. I know it addles mine."

Iridia's eyes shot sparks. "I do not want to be related to that beast. Or the man who would have preferred me dead. My uncle is his twin. I would much rather regard him as my father."

Tabeka held her daughter in her arms. "Be at peace, my girl. You are much loved, and I am sure Cidus will be happy to regard you as a daughter after we are joined." The ache in Tabeka's heart eased as her daughter cried softly on her shoulder. "Come, let us join the men."

Hand in hand they walked back and sat near Cidus and Evior. Tabeka regarded the young man's strong face, his eyes, and saw nothing but strength and calm. "Evior, how do you feel now?"

"Exactly the same. A woman who would sell her infant for gold is not worthy to be my mother. Cidus just told me he will adopt me. I already bear the Milhella name and will continue to be known as Evior Milhella. I would be proud to call Cidus father."

"Your true father was a brave warrior. He passed to the realm of dreams fighting in the king's army before you were born."

"Do I look like him? Or the woman who gave me life?"

"No, you do not look like her or like your father. They both had very dark hair and brown eyes." She rubbed her chin thoughtfully. "You know, I have always thought you resembled Cidus…I mean you resembled Jatron enough that you could be his real child. It would not surprise me if your mother lay with the man. He was known to bed many women in the village. He only bedded his wife long enough to get her with child. You do realize you have three brothers and two sisters out there?"

He shrugged. "I do not know them, and they do not know me. I have no wish to search for them and upset the balance of my life, or theirs. You, Cidus, and Iridia are now my family, and the thought of even a drop of Jatron's blood running through my veins is abhorrent."

"Let us talk of more pleasant things. Bernie and Julia's joining is in two days. Did you see the dresses Ciara gave us for the occasion, Iridia? They are lovely."

"I did see mine. It is red with gold embroidery. A dress for a princess." Iridia grinned. "The dragon princess spoils us."

"It will be an interesting ceremony. From what Ciara told me, the ceremony will be a mixture of their Earth traditions and Ierilia's."

Cidus chimed in. "We need to buy them a gift tomorrow. I will ask Brenn for a loan, and we will go look for something nice and meaningful."

Tabeka shook her head. "No need to ask Brenn. I have all that gold Cidus…I mean Jatron, has given me over the years. It came from your estate. We can use some of it."

"Can Evior and I come?" Iridia asked eagerly.

"Yes. You can give us ideas on what to buy," Cidus answered.

Tabeka suddenly had a flash of insight. "How about a

beautifully carved cradle with a mattress, blankets, sheets, and everything."

"Mother! Julia is not with child."

Tabeka gave them a mysterious little smile. "A cradle will be needed in the near future."

Evior sighed. "She has had another one of her visions."

CHAPTER SEVEN

"That was the most touching and beautiful ceremony," Iridia said as they left the temple.

"It was. I cannot wait for the day I see you dressed like that." Tabeka glanced at Iridia and saw her flaming cheeks. That day would come sooner than they planned.

"Never will you see me dressed like Bernie and his assistants." Evior chuckled.

"I am so looking forward to the celebration," Iridia said, and she sighed as she walked up the steps into the flyer.

Tabeka was glad when the dinner was over, and the dancing began. She ached to be in Cidus' arms as he led her to the dance floor.

"I am so happy that Iridia has made peace with you, love. She is a lovely girl. I find it hard to imagine she is of Jatron's blood," he told her as he swept her into a fast dance.

"She looks so beautiful in that red dress."

"Have I told you how lovely you look in yours?" Cidus dropped a kiss on top of her head.

Her own dress was teal. It had a scalloped neckline with silver embroidery around the edge. The dress was form fitting to just below the hips and then flared out. A silver coined belt rested on her hips and hung to the hem in the front. The sleeves came to the elbow, then flared out, also trimmed with silver with a braided silver cord wound around the tops of her arms. It was really beautiful. Tabeka could not believe Ciara's generosity. She needed to do something really nice for her and Brenn, but what? They appeared to have everything.

"Thank you. Ciara is too kind. She keeps giving us clothes, though I could afford to buy them myself."

"Maybe she enjoys it?"

Tabeka nodded. "Can we sit for a little while? My feet are getting sore."

They went outside to the courtyard. While Cidus was gone to get them a glass of wine and some snacks, she looked into the ballroom and watched the dancers, especially Iridia. She could hardly imagine that the girl had been so upset a few days ago. She was now again full of laughter and appeared to be having a really good time.

"A glass of wine for my lady and some fruit." Cidus handed her a glass and a small plate.

"I think these red fruits from Earth are my favorite. They are so succulent and sweet. Oh, there are Julia and Bernie. Come, we will go and speak to them." Tabeka set her plate down on a table and took Cidus' hand.

They joined the happy couple who stood chatting with Jonathan and Liana.

"Julia, Bernie, thank you for inviting us to share this special day in your lives. Julia, your dress was breathtaking," Tabeka complimented.

"I hope, when I join with my lifemate, I can have a dress like it," Iridia said.

"Thank you, but I couldn't wait to get out of it. This dress is a lot more comfortable, especially for dancing. Iridia, are you having fun?"

Tabeka could not help gazing at Jonathan. It was hard to

imagine he was a brother to Cidus and uncle to Iridia, yet if she imagined the red hair away, there was a facial resemblance between the three.

The four young people grouped together and chatted. Julia turned to her. "Tabeka, have you found a home yet, or are you still staying with Brenn and Ciara? What the hell…"

Suddenly all the lights went out, and the candles snuffed pitching the ballroom into semi-darkness. After a second or two, the lights came back on, and so, mysteriously, did the candles flicker on again.

"Okay… That was weird," Julia said.

"Must have been a momentary glitch in the electrical system," Bernie commented. "Though how the candles can snuff out and light automatically again, is beyond me."

"Where did Evior and Iridia go?" Liana asked. "They were talking to us. There was hardly time enough for them to walk away."

Tabeka looked around, gazed over the crowded courtyard, but did not see them anywhere.

Bernie chuckled. "They are in love. We can all see that. They took the opportunity to scoot off for some privacy."

Jonathan disagreed. "No. They didn't have enough time. We would have still seen them. The lights were off for a second, no longer."

"Maybe they are in the ballroom?" Liana suggested.

"I will go and look," Cidus said and took off to the ballroom.

Tabeka was about to search for them when her head ached, and she knew she was about to have a vision. She sank down on an empty chair nearby. The vision did not last long. She opened her eyes to a concerned Julia and Bernie. "It has happened. My feeling of doom and my vision has come to pass. Someone or something has taken them."

"I'm going to tell Brenn. I'll be back shortly." Bernie left in search of Brenn and Ciara. He returned fast, followed by Ciara.

Tabeka trembled from head to foot. Ciara joined them, immediately placing a hand on Tabeka's forehead and instantly she felt calmer. "Come with us to the study. We will have privacy there."

Cidus took Tabeka's hand, and they followed Ciara, Julia, and Bernie to the study.

"Now tell us exactly what happened," Ciara said.

Tabeka felt tears threatening to spill, "Some time ago, I had the vision. I saw Iridia and Evior with blood dripping from their bodies. A realm permeated by evil. A man, I think it was Zohmes, with blazing red hair. Another man, very very old. I can still hear their evil laughter. The one with red hair pointed at Cidus, then at Evior, and shook his head. His eyes spit fire. Then I saw two men in a sword fight, their faces bloody. I think it was Cidus and his brother. I think Zohmes has spirited Iridia and Evior away."

"Tabeka is correct. But it was not Zohmes. Odoxon took them. Rania informed me, but that is all the goddess said." Ciara took Tabeka's hand and clasped it between her own.

"What would that sorcerer want with them? Rania said nothing else?" Tabeka asked.

"No, nothing."

Brenn entered the study, his face set in a grim mask. "We can find no trace of Iridia and Evior. Due to the circumstances, Biryn and Cylena have returned to the palace with the twins. I have arranged a meeting with the team in the morning in the royal chambers." He turned his attention to the newly joined couple. "Bernie and Julia, you should return to the celebration and mingle with the guests. There is nothing more that can be done this evening."

After the couple left, Ciara pulled Tabeka up from the chair. "Come, Tabeka. Try and enjoy the last of the celebration."

Tabeka shook her head wildly. "How can I enjoy myself when my daughter is in danger? For what reason would that sorcerer want to take her? Evior I can understand. If Zohmes has told Jatron where we are, maybe he sent Odoxon for the boy. But why Iridia?"

Ciara embraced Tabeka for a moment and chanted softly. Tabeka immediately felt completely calm.

"Now that you are calm, remember, Iridia is Zohmes' granddaughter. By now he knows everything. Tomorrow we will have the meeting and rest assured, the king and his team will rescue them." Ciara nodded to Cidus.

"Come, love. I will get you a drink." Cidus placed his arm around her shoulders and led her to the refreshment tables.

Tabeka sipped from the eldalas spirit he handed her. Between Ciara's calming spell and the eldalas, she felt completely at ease now, but worry still gnawed at her heart. What would that god and sorcerer do to her daughter and Evior? The vision would not leave her mind now, the children covered in blood, the two men fighting and their blood-covered faces...

"Have another, love. If anything, it will help you sleep tonight." Cidus handed her another glass of eldalas spirit.

She drank it fast, too fast. It took effect, and she swayed on her feet.

Cidus just managed to catch her. "Come, let us go to our rooms. We are not the important guests. No one will miss us." Taking her arm and supporting her, he led her up the stairs.

CHAPTER EIGHT

Tabeka woke up before sunrise. For a moment she lay in bed feeling disoriented, then full memory of the previous evening returned. She choked back a sob and sat up.

Cidus pulled her down and against him. "My love, you are awake too early. The meeting at the palace is not until after sunup."

"I am worried."

"The king and his team will save them. Go and have a nice hot bath. It will relax you."

"Nothing can relax me now until I see Iridia's sweet face again." But she listened to his suggestion. Placing a kiss on his cheek, she went to the bathroom and turned on the taps to fill the tub.

After relaxing in the fragrant water for a while, she felt better, though her heart still felt like a heavy stone in her chest.

Cidus entered the bathroom as she was drying off. "Do you feel better now? The suns are beginning to rise. I will bathe quickly, and then we had better go downstairs. The king expects us to join him for breakfast."

"I feel much better, but the hot bath did not cleanse my

worry and troubled heart. I will wait for you," she said and went to the bedroom to get dressed.

As they walked down the stairs, Tabeka was amazed that the whole house appeared back to normal. The household staff must have worked all night to get it cleaned up. Brenn and Ciara were already in the kitchen waiting for them.

"Morning, Cidus. Tabeka, how are you? Were you able to sleep a bit?" Ciara looked concerned.

"Morning, Brenn, Ciara. Yes, I did get some sleep. Your calming hand and the eldalas spirit Cidus had me drink later helped."

"Morning. We cannot tarry long. The king does not like to be kept waiting," Brenn said.

They sat at the table. Gieth, Brenn and Ciara's cook, set large silver cups filled with aromatic tea on the table for them.

"No more visions this morning, Tabeka?" Ciara asked.

"Nothing. Has the goddess spoken to you?"

"Not yet, but do not fret. Rania protects all of us. We will find out what we need to know soon enough."

They finished their tea and followed Brenn and Ciara to the flyer.

The king and most of the team were already at the table when they entered. Though the food smelled appetizing, Tabeka felt no desire to eat. Dunmore pulled out chairs for them. Cylena was not there, Tabeka noticed. She was probably busy with the twins, and she would not go along on a mission.

"Let us eat first before we talk," the king said as servants began to bring in trays of food.

Tabeka picked at her food. Her throat felt as if it had a huge lump in it and she was not hungry at all.

"Tabeka, you need to eat," Cidus encouraged her. "Take a drink of juice with your food. It will help it slide down easier."

King Biryn wiped his mouth with a napkin. "Now, tell me, what exactly happened last night? Ciara?"

"When the lights and candles went out briefly, Odoxon took Evior and Iridia. Rania told me Zohmes had nothing to do with this." Ciara took a drink from her tea.

"Odd that Zohmes is not involved in this latest stunt." A perplexed look crossed the king's features. "Is that all we know?"

"Yes. Rania told me no more."

King Biryn toyed with his leftover food. "How are we supposed to find them if we do not know where to look?"

No one said a word until Taylith grasped his head.

"Taylith, a vision?" Ciara asked, but he did not answer.

Tabeka watched his hands grip his temples, his eyes glowed eerily. She waited impatiently. Was the vision about Iridia and Evior? Gods, she hoped so. Images of Iridia and Evior covered in blood flashed in her mind. She knew they were in danger and it ripped her to shreds that she did not know where they were or how to help them. They had to find them before it was too late.

They waited in silence, the only sound in the room the occasional scraping of a fork on a plate.

Tabeka grasped Cidus' hand. Taylith's vision seemed to take forever, but it was probably only minutes before he removed his hands from his head and sat up straight. He looked disoriented, and his hand shook slightly when he took a drink of water from his glass. She understood the disorientation. Sometimes her own visions felt as if an ax had cleaved her head in two.

"We must take Cidus to the Clyss. After that, he must defeat Jatron before we can find Iridia and Evior. The fight will be fierce. I Am showed me a tall pillar of fire descending on the two men fighting, Zohmes' face hovering above. Jatron's men will fight by his side, along with Zohmes' beasts.

Zohmes will do everything in his power to prevent Cidus from winning. The whole team must go except for Cylena. The four swords will be needed. After Cidus has control over Wildevein and the Sirona Realm, I Am will show me where we must go to rescue Iridia and Evior. Iridia cannot be killed, but Evior is in danger." Taylith took a deep breath. "I will call on the dragons to come and guard the queen."

Tabeka raked her fingers through her hair. This was all so much to take in, and still, they did not know where her daughter was being held. "What do you mean Iridia cannot be killed?"

"That is all I Am showed me for now."

"Thank you, Taylith. Tabeka, you will remain at the palace with Cylena," Brenn told her.

"I want to go with you!"

"No. There is nothing you can do to help," Ciara said gently. "Stay here where it is safe. Cidus, are you ready to face your brother?"

"More than you know," he replied grimly.

"Zohmes will expect the attack. He will warn Jatron to be prepared," Aldis commented.

King Biryn rubbed his chin. "Aldis is right. If Taylith's vision is any indication, we will face a small army."

"This battle will be more than a mere skirmish. Aldis, notify Captain Ryston to ready his men and a stealth ship for their use. We leave for the Clyss within the hour," Brenn commanded.

The king's flyer awaited them, the door already open and the steps resting on the pavers of the landing pad. Cidus examined it for a moment before ascending. It was sleek, unlike Brenn's, which was a bright yellow, Biryn's flyer was as if it were made of pure gold. The king's crest was engraved on the flank.

Tabeka had mentioned Jatron having a flyer. It would be his after he defeated his brother. He wondered vaguely what it was like—as sleek and beautiful as Brenn and Biryn's? He had a flyer before his capture, but it was nothing like these.

Cidus' thoughts drifted to the Clyss as he sat and fastened the belts. He had heard the legends of the valley. A fearsome creature hid within the basin. A monster. One that Cewrick...or Zohmes in Cewrick's body had tried to capture but had never been successful. The Clyss was protected by the gods, and so was the creature bound to the magickal pool.

They arrived at the Clyss in no time. The valley was incredibly beautiful. Lush with trees and plant life. Birds fluttered in the air above, and colorful flowers dotted the edge of the water and the velvety carpet of grass. It reminded him of the secret oasis he had taken Tabeka to so many years ago.

Cidus studied the shimmering water of the Bottomless Basin. Did the monster still reside beneath the water?

Astiana joined him by the pool. "No, she does not. That monster was Ciara's dragon. Brenn freed her from her bonds, and together, with Icaras, they defeated Cewrick and removed Zohmes's influence over him." She grabbed his arm. "There is so much you do not know yet. Come. We must make haste. Izarus will join us soon."

Astiana led Cidus to the clearing by the waterfall. The other magick users had already formed a circle waiting for them to join the group. He joined hands with Astiana and Ciara, and the soft sounds of a chant filled the silence.

Izarus appeared within the circle in a flash of fire and light. His long white hair billowed around his head as if blown by an unseen force and an aura of power crackled in the air surrounding the god. His piercing stare leveled on Cidus.

"Cidus, the task the gods have placed before you will be rife with danger. Jatron will be difficult to defeat. Zohmes and Odoxon have leached their poison throughout the Sirona

Realm and will assist your brother in keeping his hold on Wildevein. Jatron cannot be killed. You must banish him to Garissa Island. There, he will remain throughout eternity. The survival of your people depends upon the goodness of your heart and the strength of your will, for if you fail, Sirona will be lost and so, too, will Iridia and Evior."

Izarus raised his staff and pointed it at Cidus. A fierce wind howled through the Clyss, and a bolt of lightning crashed down, striking him hard enough to cause him to stagger. If not for the grip Astiana and Ciara had on his hands, he would have stumbled to his knees.

"You may now enter the pool to fully activate your powers." Izarus eyed the group of magick users. "Go forth, my children. The blessings of the gods and goddesses are with you."

Cidus shielded his eyes from the bright flare of light in the wake of Izarus' disappearance. If the god had activated the magick within him, he did not feel it. There was not even a burning sensation in the spot the bolt of lightning had struck him. He quickly shed his clothing and waded into the pool of water.

The water made his mind whirl, almost as if he had consumed too much eldalas spirit. Warmth suffused his body. It permeated his skin, flowed through his blood, and with each beat of his heart, power rushed through his veins. He closed his eyes against the bright glow that surrounded him.

Moments passed, but it had felt like hours. The light dissipated and Cidus opened his eyes, feeling a little woozy. Gathering his bearings, he swam to the shallows and joined the others at the edge of the water.

Jonathan handed him a towel.

"Thank you." Cidus dried and quickly dressed. Odd that he did not feel any different now. It was as if it had been a dream. The power faded as quickly as the intoxicating effects of the water. "I don't feel any different."

"It's bloody weird when you are in the water. Then you don't feel a damn thing," Jonathan told him.

Cidus gave the young man a sidelong glance. "I do not know how to use this magick. If I cannot feel its presence. How do I call upon it?"

Jonathan clapped him on the shoulder. "I'm still waiting for the answer to that."

Liana chuckled. "Says the one that faced off Zohmes and won." She glanced at Cidus. "The gods will guide you, just as they do Jonathan."

Brenn leaned against the flyer and motioned to the door. "Load up. Captain Ryston and his troops will be waiting at Dreaded Peaks."

They boarded the flyer. Cidus took a seat and strapped in, a feeling of dread pooling in his stomach. When they reached their destination, he would have to fight his twin. Izarus had said Jatron could not be killed. Even if he had the power to do so, he could not slay his brother. He would not allow hatred to rule him, for that was a shadowed path that would lead him straight into the clutches of his father, Zohmes.

He shuddered at the thought. How could his father— *well…not my father now*—have allowed Zohmes to be intimate with his mother? The mere idea that he was the spawn of an evil god was abhorrent and caused his stomach to churn.

"We will land in the same location at the base of Dreaded Peaks. You know the coordinates, Dunmore," Aldis said, then turned to the others. "The dragons will fly us to Wildevein Manor. We cannot chance them seeing us. A surprise attack is essential. The stealth ship will land just outside the manor's walls. The soldiers will wait until our arrival."

As they approached the Dreaded Peaks, it appeared Zohmes expected them. Opposed to the glorious blue skies and sunshine they had left behind, ominous black clouds hung low, hiding the forest from view. After Dunmore broke through the thick layer of clouds, the landscape below looked dark and gloomy. It matched Cidus' mood. Would he be victorious?

"Have faith, Cidus. Believe," Astiana, sitting beside him, said softly.

Astiana told him the flyer had landed in the exact spot the team had camped in previously. After they stood on solid ground, Ciara, Hirsuta, and Icaras, chanted. "The flyer is invisible now except to us," Ciara said.

"Dunmore, you will wait for us here," Biryn told his aide.

"Are we ready?" Brenn addressed all of them. "Got your weapons?"

Cidus merely nodded and fingered the fleet pistol, then adjusted his sword. While on the flyer, Aldis had shown him how to use the phaser. He still wondered about the powers he was supposed to have now. Jonathan had said the gods would guide him, but he felt very unsure.

He watched in awe as Ciara, Liana, and Taylith, shifted to their dragons. They were something to behold and made a magnificent trio.

Splitting up into three groups, they climbed onto the dragons. Cidus sat behind Jonathan, and soon the dragons leaped and surged up, then flew above the forest. They landed not far from Wildevein Manor. Cidus spotted Jatron's minions surrounding the manor and on top of the wide stone walls.

While they were on the flyer, Brenn had informed him about the soldiers under his command. Some of them were Ierilian, but others were engineered. He did not quite understand the concept of it all, except the engineered soldiers felt no pain and had no feelings. Ierilia's technology was amazing. The soldiers looked Ierilian, yet they were not. The engineered soldiers joined the team, and they headed toward the walls.

Out of nowhere, a small army of half human, half-reptilian soldiers appeared and headed straight for them. Cidus drew his sword, his fleet weapon in his other hand, as the creatures charged.

Through the clanging of swords and firing of fleet weapons, Cidus heard the creaking of the tall metal gates. More of Zohmes' minions joined the fight. These had the head of what looked like a lion, except the faces were kind of deformed. A wild mane surrounded their heads. They had claws that were the size of a man's foot, and their bodies were covered in coarse black fur.

Cidus heard a growl beside him and turned quickly. To his surprise, Brenn was in the process of changing into a large lion, and so were Laro and Ivran. The three lions were magnificent in their splendor. They charged the creatures while Liana, Jonathan, Icaras, Taylith, and Cewrick held their hands out and fire shot from their fingers. The team annihilated the multiplying creature-soldiers in bunches.

Erica, the little woman from Earth, amazed him. He did not have much time to watch her, but each time he spotted her, she fought right alongside the others, swinging her golden sword, and killing many. As did Biryn. When he saw Erica again, she and Laura were fighting back to back. These women from Earth could hold their own and were as good warriors as the soldiers, if not better.

The fight seemed to go on forever, though Cidus realized it probably was not that long. They broke through the open gates to meet up with more of the soldiers and creatures. Where did they keep coming from?

They are hiding everywhere. Cidus startled. A voice had spoken in his head. He was going insane. Now he could hear voices?

The battle was still raging in the center of the courtyard

when a man walked toward them. Cidus took off a monster's head with one swipe of his sword as it approached from his left. He then turned and gazed upon his twin.

Jatron uttered an evil laugh. "Ha, ha, you cannot defeat me, brother. It is nice to meet you at long last. I will give you a chance. One last choice. Join our father and me in our battle to gain control over the throne."

Join them? The man had to be jesting. "Never!" he shouted and using his full body weight, lunged his sword at Jatron.

Their swords clashed. They sparred, Cidus drawing blood. Jatron managed a blow to Cidus' leg, but he hardly felt it. He dodged the next few thrusts, then he felt Jatron's blade slice his forehead. Blood dripped steadily, blinding him. Using his free hand, he swiped at it. A rush of adrenaline caused him to thrust and parry faster, to swiftly avoid Jatron's stabs.

Suddenly, a strange power surged through him—so great, it almost threw him off balance. This man was his brother, his duplicate. Fighting Jatron was like fighting himself. Yet he felt no connection to this evil creature. It was as if, while in the womb, good and evil had separated and formed two infants—all good into one child, evil possessing the other.

Loud laughter resounded throughout the courtyard. Cidus glanced up briefly. A hideous face, surrounded by flaming, wild hair, hovered above them.

"Meet your father!" Jatron shouted. "Zohmes will make short work of all of you! Including this weakling of a son!"

Fury, uncontrollable rage, pooled throughout Cidus' mind and body. His brother hardly resembled him anymore. Jatron's blood-covered face wore a grotesque mask of hatred, distorting his features.

Around them, Cidus heard the others battling, Cewrick and the other magick users were chanting, but it faded completely as his wrath overtook everything else. He raised his sword high above his head, pointed it at the sky, and uttered a howl that came from deep within his soul. It was a heartwrenching cry at everything Zohmes and Jatron had done to him and Tabeka, a roar at the loss of their child.

A pillar of fire the width of a man descended from the black clouds and enveloped Jatron. Zohmes' face still hovered above, but he was no longer laughing. Instead, his eyes spat lightning fire down. From the corner of his eyes, Cidus saw Jonathan blocking the fire bolts, and retaliating by sending just as much fire back to that face.

Strange sounds came from Cidus' lips. The pillar of fire seemed to consume Jatron, and he disappeared slowly, the sword falling to the ground.

Zohmes was suddenly gone, and the pillar of fire had disappeared. The battle was over. Cidus fell to his knees, tears scalding the wounds on his face. "It is over. I killed my brother," he mumbled.

"No, Cidus. You sent him to Garissa Island. We can only hope the gods will keep him there." Ciara dripped some liquid on his face from a tiny flask.

Cidus shook his head. "How can you be sure. He just vanished."

Ivran handed him the sword that had fallen when Jatron disappeared. "I believe this belongs to you."

"Look around, people," Brenn said.

Cidus pulled himself together and stood. He looked up. The black clouds had dissipated. The suns bathed Wildevein and the surrounding landscape in their light, Polarium sending its rays upon the manor.

"The Dreaded Peaks are gone," Astiana said. "We are now gazing at Astanica. Look how beautiful it all is. It is once again like I remember it." The courtyard and the ground beyond the walls were strewn with bodies. "We need to clean up this mess, Taylith. Liana?"

Taylith stepped over a dead creature. He nodded. "Yes. We

will do that, but I Am has just told me that we will discover the answer to finding Evior and Iridia, and the grimoire and black gem, within those mountains. I Am also warned me that our quest will be endemic with danger and we will not have success overnight."

Jonathan clapped Cidus on the back. "You did well, brother."

Cidus managed a smile. "As Liana told me, I do not know how I did all that."

"We will learn. I'm glad you're my brother, and like you, I don't acknowledge that evil bastard whose name starts with a Z."

"I still do not understand what games Zohmes is playing. To trick my mother and impregnate her…and your mother as well."

Aldis interrupted them. "Quiet, everyone. After this mess has been cleaned up, we will need to regroup and fetch supplies from the palace. I Am told Taylith this mission will take longer, so we need our backpacks, food, bedrolls, and other equipment."

CHAPTER NINE

At the palace, Cidus was impressed with how quickly the team got ready. They could not postpone the mission until the next day. Evior's life depended on it, and even if Iridia could not be killed, Odoxon could cause her grievous harm and make her suffer.

Biryn had called ahead to have supplies readied for their departure. While they refreshed and changed clothing, the staff loaded food packs, waterskins, and wineskins onto the flyer. Taylith and Ciara's dragon friends had arrived to guard the queen and the twins, and Dunmore would also stay behind with the queen. A small team of engineered soldiers would accompany them on their quest to find Evior and Iridia. They awaited them at the base of what was once the Dreaded Peaks.

Cidus comforted Tabeka when he said goodbye. "We will bring them back, my heart."

She gazed up at him, a troubled expression crossing her features. "Why do you have to go?"

"I cannot stay behind knowing that I have the power to help save Evior and Iridia." He kissed her gently.

"Come back to me, Cidus. Save my girl and Evior and bring them home."

He hugged her tightly, then released her and watched as she safely entered the palace. Reaching down, he grabbed the strap of his pack and hefted it onto his shoulder, then joined the others in the flyer, seated himself, and buckled up.

Cidus gazed out of the window of the flyer. So much had happened since the king and his team had freed him from Zohmes' clutches.

His stomach dropped when the flyer took a sharp decline and descended to the valley. From the window, Cidus could see that Captain Ryston and his men were already gathered at the base of the mountains.

"All right, everyone. Grab your gear and your weapons. There are proton phasers stored in the weapons hatch." Aldis opened the door.

Cidus fetched a phaser from the rack, then followed the others outside. The landscape was so much different now. Instead of the jagged foreboding spikes, the mountains were lush with trees and plant life, their peaks so high they would be hidden if there were clouds. If he had not seen the miraculous change with his own eyes, he would not believe this was the same realm.

He studied the group of women that were part of Biryn's team. Even though Cidus had seen the women fight and hold their own in battle, he still had a hard time understanding why the men would risk their safety.

"How do we know where we will be going? The mountain range is vast. It could take weeks, even months to find where Odoxon may have taken Iridia and Evior."

Liana placed her sword in its sheath, then holstered a fleet weapon. "Do not worry. I Am has shown Taylith were we must go. He will lead us to them."

"That easy huh?" Erica grabbed a proton phaser and handed it to Laura. "We just play a game of follow the leader, and Doxie will just hand them right the fuck over?"

Liana gave Erica a sidelong glance. "I banished the old bastard to Wuits Peak once. I can do it again."

Laura giggled at Liana. "Jonathan's language is really rubbing off on you." She nudged Liana's shoulder. "The trick is to bind him *permanently* to Wuits Peak. You figure that out, then you can have bragging rights."

Ciara chuckled. "She has a point, Liana."

Cidus turned his attention to the men. "Are you sure it is safe for the women to accompany us on this mission?"

Biryn clapped him on the shoulder. "Do not underestimate them, Cidus. Without their assistance, our mission will fail."

Aldis approached them. "Captain Ryston and nine of his soldiers will join us on this quest. The rest will remain here to guard the flyer and the mountain pass."

"May the gods and goddesses protect us. Let us move out." Brenn hoisted his pack on his shoulders. "Taylith you have the lead."

Brenn followed behind Taylith, along with Ciara, Cewrick, and Hirsuta. Cidus joined Icaras and Astiana at the back of the group.

Taylith set a steady pace into the trees and to the mountain pass. Birds fluttered in the limbs above and every now and then Cidus could hear a small animal scurry about in the underbrush.

Astiana exclaimed when they exited the pass. "Just like it used to be. Look at the abundance of flowers. After this mission, I would like to go to my old home. I hope the temple was restored to its former beauty, too. If it was, I will live there once again."

Biryn shook his head. "That would be risky, Astiana. Zohmes is very familiar with that temple. You would not be safe as long as he is still around."

"There is another pass we must go through before we reach the place where we will find Evior and Iridia. We will not get there before nightfall," Taylith called from the front.

"Surely, Zohmes and Odoxon would not have another of their temples hidden in these mountains?" Cidus wondered.

"Who knows. Rania said this is all Doxie's doing. The old goat apparently has an agenda of his own." Erica marched to the front to join Taylith.

"So far, our journey has been easy," Cidus remarked. "All I have seen are birds and small animals and a few korobeast."

"I don't trust it," Laura responded. "The evil wizard, or *old goat* as Erica calls him, never makes things easy."

The pass was lengthy. By the time the suns began to go down, they had not yet reached the end.

"Let us camp here for the night," Brenn called out.

They were up at sunup, quickly ate, packed their bedrolls, and continued. Though the mountains were now verdant with vegetation, there were still steep cliff walls.

The Astanica Mountains were some of the highest on Ierilia, besides Wuits Peak. No mountain was as high as Odoxon's former prison.

They walked for a few hours until Taylith stopped next to a sheer cliff face. "We need the four swords now."

Biryn, Taylith, Erica, and Brenn, drew their swords and joined him.

"I do not see anything except hard rock," Brenn said.

"Look harder."

"I see something," Biryn shouted. "Look, it is a small circle with an eye in its center. The colors of the rock make it difficult to spot."

The other three looked to where Biryn pointed. The four stood together and touched the tips of their blades together at the center of the engraving. They jumped back when a huge oval appeared emitting a brilliant light.

"What the fuck is that?" Laura shrieked.

Cidus shielded his eyes for a moment. The light dissipated, and in its stead was a field of moving plasma. It almost appeared to be liquid as the red and purple mass swirled and moved, with what almost looked like an eye in its center.

"Some kind of force field?" Aldis asked.

Hirsuta stepped close to it, then turned to face them. "We must step through it."

"What if it fucking zaps us?" Erica muttered.

"Yes, and what the hell is waiting for us behind it?" Laura said.

"There must be a cave or something behind it," Icaras suggested. "Maybe we have found another temple."

"If no one else is brave enough, I will—" Liana got no further as Jonathan pushed her aside and stepped through the swirling mass.

Cidus watched in consternation as the plasma seemed to eat Jonathan. He disappeared completely.

"Jonathan!" Liana shouted. Before anyone could stop her, she stepped through the field.

One by one they stepped through it. Cidus followed them, wondering if they had all seen their last moments.

He experienced a rush. His body felt as if he were in some kind of shaker as he tumbled over and over through what seemed like a long plasma tunnel. He closed his eyes against flashes of red and white light, like small lightning bolts. His breath caught, and his chest felt tight.

He fell to the hard ground with a thud, just in time to hear Erica exclaim, "You've got to be fucking kidding me. We're back in Dreaded Peaks. That motherfucking thing threw us back in time!"

CHAPTER TEN

Cidus looked around. The verdant valley and mountains were gone. Instead, they were surrounded by the dark, craggy Dreaded Peaks. "It appears the portal took us back to the past. Did you not say that Zohmes had a temple here? Maybe Odoxon also took Evior and Iridia back in time to that place."

"That is possible." Icaras stroked his chin thoughtfully.

The soldiers came tumbling through one by one, all looking just as shocked as they inspected the surroundings. Cidus still had a hard time distinguishing the engineered soldiers from the real ones unless the engineered soldiers talked—their speech was monotone, without expression.

Aldis took out his datapad. "We are not far from where the temple is. Let us move on. Taylith, will you be able to find this entrance again?"

"I Am will show me. But the god told me there is no temple here. We need to leave the portal and follow this path to where the flyer should be."

"No!" Cidus shouted. "We need to find Evior and Iridia."

"Let I Am lead us," Taylith told him. "We will find them."

"If I recall, we fought some cute, cuddly monsters somewhere around here," Erica mumbled. "What if we run into them again?"

"We defeated them once and will do so again if necessary. But if the temple is not here, neither will those creatures be." Biryn stomped his foot on the ground. "By the gods, this is all too strange. Nothing like our other missions. What if we are stuck in this time and place?"

Astiana took Biryn's hand. "Have faith. I Am sent us here. He will get us out."

"Taylith, lead us out of here and back to the flyer," Aldis ordered. "Stay alert, everyone. Eyes front, back, and sides. Be prepared for unexpected attacks. We are back in Zohmes territory."

"No, we are not," Ciara stated. "I do not know where he is, but we appear to be safe, at least from him."

"How do you know?"

"Laura, you would ask *me* that?" Ciara frowned.

"Sorry. You communicated with Rania."

"Yes. She is watching over us, too. Lead on, Taylith."

The team began to make their way along the rocky path back to the flyer, everyone watching out for craggy peaks jutting up from the ground, and anything that could be lurking in crevices between the jagged cliffs. Somber clouds darkened the sky causing it to seem like dusk within the peaks. Cidus wondered how far back in time the portal had taken them. He could not remember the peaks ever quite looking like this. Something had changed, but he could not put his finger on it.

"We will not make it back today," Brenn commented.

"Do we really want to camp here?" Cidus asked.

Taylith stopped dead in his tracks when several beasts jumped from above and landed in front of them. Cidus felt a ripple go down his spine as he looked at them. They stood very tall but were grotesque monstrosities.

Their grayish fur blended in well with the craggy stone of

the peaks. Cidus had not spotted them while they traveled the path before entering the portal, nor had anyone else. Did these creatures belong to the past?

Two long arms jutted out from each shoulder of their muscular bodies. They had hands shaped like a man's, but the fingers were tipped with lengthy claws that looked hard enough to gouge rock. Four long yellowed saber-like teeth curved from their protruding jaws. A row of small yellow eyes ran the length of their oblong heads to the side of their stubby snouts. The beasts jumped and pounded the ground with their fists so hard it made the ground beneath their feet tremble.

"What in the hell is it with this damn planet! First, we meet wookies on our previous quests, and now deformed fucking gorillas!" Erica drew her sword.

One creature, larger than the others, leaped from an outcropping of rocks and landed on the ground between the team and the colossal beasts. It reared up on its hind legs and pounded its chest, then released a loud roar.

Chaos ensued. More of the creatures appeared from thin air, or so it seemed to Cidus. Sword in hand, he sliced at the beast in front of him. It lunged forward, trying to grasp him in its long arms. A claw snagged his shirt. The monster held him with two fists, its other arms raised in the air ready to pounce on Cidus' chest. He dropped his sword, snatched the fleet weapon from its holster and shot the creature in the throat. It stumbled backward, still holding onto Cidus. A loud battle cry rent the air. A sword's blade protruded from the beast's chest, then was yanked out. Blood poured from the wound, coloring its hide a bright murky yellow. Its grip loosened and Cidus pushed the monster forward. It fell to the ground with a loud thud.

Erica stood in front of him, her sword at the ready but there was no movement. No fighting. Cidus gazed at the carnage.

Odd, that the gorillas, as Erica had called them, would just stand down. Several of the beasts lay slain on the ground, yellowish-colored blood pooling beneath the bodies. At the front of the group, the largest lay against a large outcropping. Its severed head had rolled several feet from its body, the eyes glazed over and its tongue protruding from the gaping jaws.

As suddenly as they had appeared, the creatures climbed the stone walls and disappeared into the jagged, rocky peaks.

Cidus picked up his sword from the ground and sheathed it. "I have never seen the likes of such creatures."

"Mutant gorillas with big fucking teeth. That's what they were," Laura muttered.

"Why did they stop fighting?"

Erica patted his shoulder. "Taylith killed the big one, is my guess. It had to be the leader."

"Move out, people. I do not want to hang around and wait for another attack. Light your glimmer sticks," Brenn called out.

They trudged on through the night as fast as they could traverse the hilly pass, stepping over rocks and crags, and never stopping to drink or eat. Cidus was sure he felt eyes watching their every move.

The suns should have been peeking over the horizon when they exited the pass and hurried to the flyer, but there was no sun, just a blanket of dark gray dotted with some black clouds.

"Since we've been on Ierilia, I've never seen such a sky," Erica commented while looking up.

"Maybe Zohmes is brewing up a storm," Laura said.

"I already told you, we need not fear Zohmes this time," Ciara reminded her.

When they cleared the pass and entered the valley, the flyer was gone, and there were no soldiers in sight.

"What in the bloody hell is going on?" Jonathan pushed his

way to the front of the group. "The flyer, the hovercraft…the men. Zohmes has to have taken them. But for what purpose?"

"Fucking Zohmes, up to his tricks again," Erica muttered, forgetting Ciara's words. "Maybe it's an illusion. The ships are here, but we just don't see them."

"The four of you, scout the woods for the other men." Captain Ryston gestured to the soldiers that had accompanied them through, then pulled his communicator from his pocket and flipped it on. "Lieutenant Zenarhi… Lieutenant! Answer me!" He shook his head and stuffed the communicator back in his pocket. "Nothing. Not even the slightest static. It is as if they have vanished into thin air."

"I tried to contact Dunmore, but he is not answering." Biryn turned his communicator upside down and sideways, examining it.

"Let me try," Aldis offered. "Nothing. Maybe it is the brewing storm interfering with communication?"

"I do not think it is the storm." Brenn fiddled with his communicator, then his datapad.

Cewrick gazed at the group, a troubled expression on his face. "We need to return to the palace. We have enough magick between us to reach it."

Taylith gestured to Liana and Ciara. "We will change into our dragons and fly all of us to Cront. There is something very wrong, and I for one do not want to just appear in the palace."

Liana nodded. "We will use our magick to shield us from view."

"Agreed." Brenn turned to the captain. "Ryston, you and your men remain here. Guard the pass."

Taylith, Liana, and Ciara moved a distance away from the group and called out their dragons. Even though the suns were hidden behind the clouds, their scales still sparkled like jewels.

Cidus climbed on Ciara's back, along with Brenn, Astiana,

and Biryn. Cidus held on tightly to Ciara's scales when she lunged her huge reptilian body into the air. The speed at which she ascended was quite disconcerting. She was much faster than a flyer. It did not take them long to reach Cront.

Biryn chuckled. "It takes a bit of getting used to but do not fear, Ciara will not allow us to fall."

Cidus gazed at the city below. It did not resemble the Cront he knew. The houses and buildings looked neglected. The people walking on the street looked poor, and some even looked sickly. The dragons flew low, back and forth several times. There was no palace.

"Where is the palace? It has to be there, but we just don't see it." Biryn sounded agitated.

"It could not have just gone missing. Ciara, fly to our house," Brenn suggested.

The dragons circled once more, then flew in the direction of Brenn's estate. Where the estate should have been, now stood a number of dilapidated cottages. Grimy children played outside them. Women were hanging washing on lines strung from cottage to cottage.

"Land a distance away from those homes," Brenn ordered.

Taylith, Ciara, and Liana landed in a clearing close to the woods that flanked what should have been the orchard. The abundant rows of fruit and nut trees were not there. Instead, there was an overgrown forest of twisted trees. Dark, thorny vines crept up the tree trunks. Clumps of slimy moss hung from branches that were devoid of leaves. Beneath the trees, the shrubbery, if one could call it that, was dense. It was as creepy as the trees. Thorny, with webs and slimy substance scattered throughout, it was going to be difficult to navigate. After the dragons had shifted, the team, being careful to avoid the thorns, slipped behind the trees to hide from prying eyes.

Aldis scanned the area. "I am going to investigate. Brenn? Come with me. The rest of you stay put."

The two men left the safety of the trees and hacking through the thick bushy vegetation, headed toward the cottages. Cidus waited impatiently for them to return. And when they did, their faces were pale. Both men were visibly shaken. "What did you find?"

"Me. Working in a garden behind a cottage. Ciara is one of the women hanging clothes on the line," Brenn said grimly.

"What do you mean?"

"That we ran into duplicate versions of Ciara and me."

"How is that even possible?" Jonathan raised his eyebrows.

Cidus asked, "Did they see you?"

Aldis shook his head. "No. We hurried back here. Something is not right."

Biryn looked as though he would be sick. "We need to go back to where the palace should be."

The dragons shifted, then knelt to allow the team to climb on their backs. Cidus again flew with Brenn, Astiana, and the king. The dragons made swift work of the flight back to Cront. When they arrived at what should have been the palace grounds, they landed in an area where they could not be seen easily.

"I am going with you this time." Biryn slid from Ciara's back and headed for the open field.

Cidus and Taylith joined Brenn, Aldis, and Biryn. They hurried to some hovels. Held together by boards, they could be nothing more than shelters. They approached hesitantly.

A woman came flying out of one of the hovels. "Biryn, where have you been all this time? Are you drunk again? Did you spend the pennies you earned shoveling the stables? You are a good for nothing..." She attacked Biryn and began pummeling his chest.

"Cylena? What is going on here? Where are the twins?" he shouted.

"You mean those two whiny, snot-nosed infants you

saddled me with?"

Cidus and Brenn managed to get the woman away from the king though she continued to scream, kick, and yell.

"Biryn! Run! Hide!" Aldis shouted.

Cidus looked in consternation at a Biryn replica approaching. The man was drunk out of his mind, swaying all over the place and singing at the top of his lungs.

Taylith grabbed Cidus by the shoulder drawing his attention. "Cidus, we need to leave. The answers we seek are not in this place." Cidus nodded after he noticed the others had already started back toward where the rest of the team had hidden. He hurried after Taylith.

They returned to the shelter of the forest. "Now what do we do?" Cidus queried.

"While you were gone, I spoke with Rania. We did not travel through time, and we are not in the past. We are on an alternate version of Ierilia, one created and ruled by Odoxon. Before he was exiled to Wuits Peak, the sorcerer created this planet, which he named Odoxus. He duplicated nearly everything except those parts of Ierilia he did not want, like the palace and the other realms. And there are no dragons or lions. After his escape from Wuits Peak, he has been steadily replicating people. Through his magick, anyone born or moving into Cront, and the realm, duplicates automatically now. He rules the planet from his castle that stands on an island in the middle of a large lake called Stealz Depths." Ciara leaned against a tree and took a sip from her waterskin.

"And where do we find this lake?" Cidus asked.

"Rania did not say. I suggest we go into Cront, if it is even called that here, and mingle with people in the taverns. Someone might be able to enlighten us."

Jonathan took a chunk of bread out of his pack. "Good plan. We'll need to leave our swords and backpacks here but hide your fleet weapon in a pocket. We don't know what we're going to run into."

Erica shook her head. "There is no way in fucking hell I am leaving my sword. I've had it stolen once. I don't want it disappearing here!"

"Erica is right. The four swords are too important. Their loss would put Biryn in jeopardy. I have a feeling they can be used against Jonathan and Cidus as well," Ivran reminded them.

"Hide them in here." Icaras pointed to a hollowed-out tree trunk on the ground. "We will place a protection spell on our equipment and the swords as I did outside the village of Yeavoth. No one will be able to breach the spell."

The team stuffed their packs and swords within the tree trunk. Cidus hated parting with his sword, but they had no choice. After he placed his gear with the others, the magick users joined hands and chanted, the trunk and all the contents disappeared.

"Now that the sword issue is taken care of, we need to head out to the city."

Brenn nodded. "Yes, but we have to be extremely careful not to get close to any of our duplicates. We might not frequent the taverns and inns normally, but who knows what our alter-egos are like. Look at Biryn. Our poor king is a drunk here."

"Okay, after this I need a frigging drink of wine." Erica opened her wineskin and took a long gulp. "Doxie has been playing fucking games all this time. For God's sake, an alternate Ierilia? Duplicates of all of us? The old fart is one sick misbegotten mongrel!"

Cidus shook his head, baffled at Erica's language. He knew it to be her birth tongue. He resolved he would ask Jonathan for translation of all the foreign words he, Julia, Laura, and Erica often uttered. However strange the words sounded, he sensed that Erica had not called Odoxon a nice name.

CHAPTER ELEVEN

They entered Cront on foot. Ciara, Taylith, and Liana changing into their dragons was not an option. There were no open areas for them to land and if they were seen it would cause an uproar in Cront or whatever the city was called here.

Cidus walked alongside Liana and Jonathan. "I just had a thought. Odoxon's magick would have created duplicates of Iridia and Evior when they arrived in Cront. So why would he abduct the real ones?"

"Maybe he is doing it for Zohmes?" Liana suggested.

Ciara turned around. "No. In fear of repeating myself once again, Rania told me that Zohmes has no part in all of this. This planet has no magick, it has no gods and goddesses. The people here worship nothing except their ruler. Namely, Odoxon."

"So, everything is not exactly the same as on Ierilia," Hirsuta said.

They stopped when they got close to the city center. Astiana sighed audibly. "This is not the Cront we know. Look at it all."

"Father, you need to hide your staff," Icaras told Cewrick.

Cidus watched the staff disappear. The magick around him

still astounded him, and now he had such powers as well? After they returned from this mission, he really needed to talk with Cewrick and Hirsuta, and maybe Astiana. He was going to need a lot of their wisdom.

He looked at the main street of the duplicate Cront. None of the buildings were the same. The street was paved with uneven rocks. The buildings were high and appeared to be built into sheer cliffs on both sides. Homes protruded from the cliff walls with wooden plank bridges that had rope handrails connecting to the other side. It appeared the shops were built on top of each other. Everything was brown, black, or gray — dark and gloomy. A lot of people milled about, some crossing the bridges up above. It had become quite dark. He guessed it was evening. It was hard to tell without suns telling them the time of day. At the end of the street stood a tall craggy tower.

"I wonder if he copied Henderson, too?" Laura said.

"Maybe. We don't have time to find out unless we're led in that direction." Erica began to walk down the street, followed by Icaras, Laro, and Ivran.

Cidus hurried to catch up to them. "Hey, we need a meeting point," he called out.

"Right here," Brenn said. "Split into teams of four, and remember, if you see your double, run. Do not turn around. Do not look at them. Get out of there as fast as you can."

Liana, Taylith, and Laura, were in his group. Cidus headed to what looked like an inn or tavern. It had a crooked sign hanging from two metal chains. It read, The Ruthless Sword. "Fitting name for an inn on such a dark world. Should we go in?" he asked.

"Looks like a tavern." Laura resolutely pushed the door open and stepped inside. Cidus followed with the others.

Cidus waved a hand in front of his face. "What is all that smoke in here?"

"Oh my God! They're smoking cigarettes and cigars," Laura exclaimed. "How would they even know about those? Are they even real?"

"From the Earth people." Taylith found a small table with four empty chairs. "I do not understand these people sucking on a stick and blowing fumes from their mouth."

"It's a bad habit on Earth, kind of like an addiction. It's very hard to stop it after you smoke for a while. I guess there were some smokers among us. I've never really thought about it," Laura said.

A topless waitress approached them. "Mead?" she asked.

"Yes, four, please." Taylith handed her a gold coin, raising his eyebrows at the bare breasts.

"Real gold?" the young woman asked while turning the coin several times and holding it up to inspect it.

"Yes. Is it enough?"

Cidus watched the woman stuff the coin into her little apron as she left to get their order.

"We had better watch what we eat and drink here. Everything is so filthy, and who knows what they used to make their mead and alcohol," Taylith warned.

"Yeah. Makes me wonder what it is they're smoking, too. From the vegetation I've seen so far, nothing much looked edible, and nothing resembled tobacco leaves." Laura sniffed. "Actually, it kind of smells like pot."

"A pot? What do you mean?" Liana asked.

Laura giggled. "Marijuana. It's a plant, but it's also a drug used and abused on Earth that makes you high. Some people used it for medicinal purposes, for pain."

"And it smells the same?"

"Sort of."

The waitress returned with the mead, placed the mugs on the table, and quickly left.

Taylith took a sip from his mead and pulled a face. "It is

horrible. I am not drinking this."

"Laura, honey! What are you doing here? Why are you dressed like that? And Taylith. I thought you two were going away?"

Cidus was shocked to see Julia's double approach them, dressed in what he suspected was Earth clothing. Not too far behind was Bernie.

"Hey, you guys. What are you up to? Did Odoxon send you here? Are you going on some kind of mission for the old bastard?" Bernie asked while he pulled up a chair. "Where's the rest of the team?"

"We're just relaxing for a few hours. Hey, how do we get to Stealz Depths?" Laura asked.

"You lost your fucking memory? You practically live there, for God's sake." Julia pulled a face. "What's with the clothes?"

"It was a joke," Laura pushed her chair from the table and looked at Taylith. "I think we need to go."

Cidus stood up and turned, almost causing the waitress to fall. She dropped her tray laden with more metal mugs of mead. It crashed to the floor, the mead causing large foaming puddles.

"Sorry," he mumbled, stepping gingerly back from the naked breasts she was almost pushing against him.

Taylith handed the waitress another gold coin to compensate for the spilled mugs of mead.

"Why don't you guys come and sit with us? Why are you leaving already?" Bernie yelled and held up his drink.

"We have to run, sorry," Laura told them.

"Aw, come on. Don't be fucking spoilsports. Have some fun, spend time with us. I don't see enough of you, sis," Julia shouted.

It was hard to get away from the duplicate Bernie and Julia, but finally, they let them go. Once outside, Cidus breathed a sigh of relief.

"We are working for Odoxon? I think I've seen and heard everything now." Laura stepped over a puddle of sludge in front of the doorway.

"I hope the other team members have more success in finding out how to get to that lake," Cidus muttered.

They backtracked back to where they had to meet the others. There were so many people on the street, they almost had to push and shove their way through the milling crowd. Cidus heaved a sigh of relief when they reached the outskirts of the city. They waited impatiently. Thunder sounded, and lightning rent the black sky. Within seconds, there was a downpour. They hurried to a nearby building and tried to shelter behind it, but the pelting rain was relentless.

As sudden as it had started, it stopped. They rushed back to the meeting place to find Cewrick, Hirsuta, Brenn, and Ciara waiting for them, soaked to the skin.

"Any luck?" Brenn asked.

"All we discovered is that apparently, our team is working for Odoxon here," Cidus told them.

Icaras, Ivran, Laro, and Erica ran toward them, followed closely by Astiana, Biryn, Jonathan, and Aldis. "Did you guys find out where that dumb lake is?" Jonathan asked while shaking the water from his hair.

The street behind them had turned into what almost resembled a shallow river. The throng of people had disappeared to find shelter, but now they began to appear again. They waded through the ankle-deep water, apparently used to such downpours.

"One person drew a map for me." Astiana pulled a napkin from her pocket that had miraculously stayed dry.

"I already said this, but some of you were not here yet. Our duplicate team is apparently working for Odoxon." Cidus grimaced at their expressions.

Erica laughed. "Right. So we're Doxie's team now? What

about the king's double? He was shoveling manure in the stables. Sorry, Biryn."

Biryn chuckled. "Quite a drop from king to stable boy. Odoxon must have created this Biryn that way on purpose."

They studied the little map. "If the landscape is similar to Ierilia's, where we need to go is beyond where Initiation Genesis is back on Ierilia. We will need to fly there," Brenn said.

"Oh, I forgot to tell you. In the tavern we went to, we ran into Bernie and Julia. After we asked where the lake was, Julia asked if I lost my memory. She said I practically live there. We got out of there in a hurry." Laura wrung her hair out, then shook her head, sending water splattering at Taylith standing beside her.

"We need to return to the forest and gather our things, then head for Stealz Depths." Aldis ran his hand through his wet hair, brushing it out of his face. "There is no telling what Odoxon has planned for Evior and Iridia, but it cannot be good."

They walked quickly to the forest and the hollow log containing their gear. Cidus was surprised when Astiana appeared to be touching air, and the log suddenly appeared. It would take him a long time to get used to the magick of the team, which he also now had.

He grabbed his pack and slipped it over his shoulders, then sheathed his sword. A strange feeling suddenly overcame him, like ice spiders crawling along his spine. Time was passing, and they still had no clue where Odoxon had taken Iridia and Evior.

"I fear for what Odoxon may have already done to Iridia and Evior. I cannot return to Tabeka without them."

Hirsuta squeezed his shoulder. "We will find them."

Taylith, Liana, and Ciara moved to the clearing and called out their dragons. Cidus climbed onto Taylith's back, along with Laura, Erica, Laro, and Icaras. When Taylith lunged into the air, he wondered vaguely if they just disappeared into thin air like the log in the woods. He knew the dragons were using their magick to shield them from view.

They flew back to where Brenn's estate should have been. Genesis on Ierilia was located very close to Xynnar and was separated from the Xynnar Valley by a ridge of mountains.

Cidus peered down at the landscape below. The sensation of flying upon the back of a dragon made him uncomfortable. It was so much different being in the air than riding on the back of a horse. On a dragon, there was a much longer drop should you be unseated. He shuddered at the thought.

"Holy hell! That looks nothing like Genesis!" Laura leaned far and looked down at the ground.

Cidus grabbed her by the shoulders and pulled her back. "Be careful! You do not want to slip."

Erica chuckled. "She'll be fine, Cidus. Taylith won't let her fall. The dragons use magic to keep us seated."

"If you say so." He was still skeptical but leaned a little further to gaze at the terrain below. Laura was right. Nothing looked the same. Instead of a verdant valley, the plants looked diseased. The farmland was dry as if there was a drought, yet it had just poured. Maybe it had only rained in Cront. What was a pristine beach on their Ierilia, was littered with garbage and the carcasses of dead fish and animals.

"Oh my God! They are ruining this place, just like Earth!" Erica sounded agitated. "What in the hell is wrong with them!"

"Starshine, that is not the Genesis you know. Your people have not ruined it," Laro tried to reassure her.

"No, this is Odoxon's creation and looks like it is a different village," Icaras said.

It was a sobering thought that Odoxon had the power to create a dimension and planet of his own. *He has the ability to create life, to clone us.* That idea chilled Cidus to the bone. The old man had duplicated many of the people from Ierilia into his own vast world.

When the dragons flew beyond the Genesis location, they slowed. The air suddenly became thick. Dark, murky clouds engulfed them. Cidus could barely see two inches in front of him. His stomach flipped when Taylith took a sharp decline.

"What is happening?" Cidus called out.

Laura looked back at him. "Taylith said they will have to fly closer to the ground. The clouds are obscuring their view."

The descent seemed to take forever, but finally, they burst free of the black clouds.

Treetops. So close, Cidus was afraid they were going to crash into them. His heart pounded in his chest when Taylith banked hard left, his wingtip almost brushing the leaves below them. Cidus felt his stomach creep up to his throat.

The dragons spotted a clearing and landed. Cidus took a deep breath and slid off Taylith's back. Thank the gods. His feet were on solid ground again. He would gladly take a flyer over dragon flight any day.

"Damn, that was a hell of a ride!" Erica grinned at Cidus. "See? I told you they use magic to keep us from falling."

"Though we can see very far and through almost anything, I did not see the lake," Liana said.

"I hope the directions were correct. We will need to travel through the woods on foot." Aldis headed toward the dark outline of the forest.

"Maybe Doxie has it hidden from plain sight," Erica suggested.

It was inky black within the forest. The trees were like none on Ierilia. Their foliage was almost as dark as the trunks. Leaves, if one could call them that, were wide, and draped from gnarled branches. Some of the huge, craggy tree trunks almost looked as if they had faces. Strange insects scurried away from the invaders of their domain. The ground was soggy and covered with a strange spongy moss that was almost the same color as the soil beneath it.

Cidus' feet sank into the substance, sometimes up to his ankles. It made walking difficult. Several screams from behind caused him to swivel. Roots appeared from the ground, trapping Erica, Jonathan, Icaras, Astiana, and Liana. The round appendages were gnarly, like the branches, and wrapped around their bodies, slowly lifting them while squeezing the air out of their lungs.

Cewrick raised his staff and chanted. Green lightning shot from it, aimed at the roots. One by one they shriveled, the captured falling to the ground, gasping for air.

Laura and Ciara hastened to them, but they were already recovering.

"We need to bespell the ground for us to continue." Icaras looked at his father who nodded.

"Yes. I know which spell to use. Odoxon used a very ancient incantation, but I know the counterspell. Link hands. Cidus, you, too." Cewrick held out his hands.

Somehow the words came to him, though he had no idea what the gibberish all meant. The flow of ultimate power channeling from the hands he held almost overpowered him. It radiated throughout his body. He wondered if Jonathan felt the same and told himself he needed to have a one-on-one talk with the young man who was now his brother. Well, half-brother, but nevertheless a brother. That reminded him of Jatron, and a piercing pain shot through his heart. The thought that his twin was forever rotting on Garissa Island and that he had sent him there, gnawed at him.

"The ground is safe to walk on now," Cewrick told them and headed to the front. "I will lead."

The forest was endless. When night fell, it was so dark, they had to light their glimmer sticks. "We do not want to camp in these woods," Brenn called out. "Speed it up, everyone."

A loud howl echoed from deep within the forest. Cidus shivered and wondered what kind of animal could bellow so loud. He did not have to wonder long. The sound of heavy steps, growls, another howl, and suddenly creatures surrounded them. The one closest to Cidus had its maw wide open. Sharp teeth and long fangs glittered white. A lengthy, greenish tongue flicked in and out, and yellow saliva dripped to the ground. He drew his sword. The beast ducked its head showing huge antlers almost resembling trees on its head. It was much taller than him, and he felt dwarfed. He stepped back hearing some of the magick users begin to chant. The thing's eyes lit up as if it had a switch inside its head to turn them on and off. They shone brightly, emitting an eerie glow.

The chant did not work. Cewrick stepped in with his staff, but he could not damage them either.

Erica shouted, "These are fucking deformed wolves. We're their next meal! Or, hey, they look more like gargoyles!"

"The swords," Taylith shouted and sprang toward one of the varmints swinging his sword. He jumped up and pierced it between the eyes. The animal fell to the ground so hard, the ground shook beneath Cidus' feet.

Erica, Biryn, Taylith, and Brenn made quick work of the brutes. "Move on," Brenn shouted.

Almost jogging now, they made their way through the darkness, at times hacking at branches that almost seemed to reach out for them.

Cidus nearly fell on top of Taylith when everyone in front of him stopped dead. "What is it?"

"We are at the lake. There is no shore. These woods border the water—if you can call it that. I do not see an island," Cewrick said while planting his staff firmly on the ground.

"I need to go to the little girl's room," Laura said and hid behind a tree, Taylith on her heels to guard her.

"And I'm starving," Jonathan growled.

Aldis walked a little way along the waterline. "There is no place for us to camp."

"What are those low hanging clouds in the middle of the lake?" Liana pointed at black clouds that seemed to almost touch the surface.

"That is where Odoxon's island is," Ciara said calmly. "Rania just told me."

CHAPTER TWELVE

Cidus stood staring at the black cloud, worry for Iridia and Evior nearly overwhelming him.

"Zap us over there, Scottie," Erica joked.

"Indeed. We have no choice. We cannot stay here." Astiana held her hands out.

"Oh right! Just bloody pop over there without knowing where the hell we are going." Jonathan shook his head. "We could end up in his dungeons…or worse."

Ciara joined hands with Astiana. "I will lead us there. Rania has shown me where we need to go."

They joined hands and began to chant. The magick flooded Cidus' veins, the words of the spell easily falling from his lips. A whirlwind surrounded them, whipping his hair around his face. He felt as if he were spinning, his body sucked into a vortex. He had no sense of the others, just the rapid whirling motion of his body, then suddenly everything stopped, his feet hitting solid ground. A wave of dizziness passed through him, and he blinked several times, trying to bring the world back into focus.

Jonathan grabbed his shoulder to steady him. "The first time is always a bitch. Don't worry, the weirdness will fade."

When his vision cleared, he realized they had made it to

the island...or at least he hoped they did. The land was densely forested but directly in front of them was a path that cut through the woods. It looked to be well-traveled, but by who or what? He shuddered to think of what may be lurking within the trees.

"It is getting late. There is enough of a clearing here to set up camp." Aldis scanned the treeline.

"Cewrick, shield the area. I think all of us can use a little rest." Brenn dropped his pack and bedroll to the ground. "We will have to make do without a campfire. I do not want to alert the inhabitants of this island to our presence. That is if there are any besides Odoxon. He may have his minions roaming the grounds, though."

The ground was dry, despite the damp air, so they did not bother to set up tents, choosing instead to lay their bedrolls on the ground.

"Even with Cewrick's shield, I do not trust this place. I will take first watch." Taylith took a drink from his waterskin.

"You and me both. I will take first watch with you," Biryn said.

After Cidus had laid his bedroll out, he pulled a packet of dried meat from his pack and joined the others in munching on their meager rations. They had no idea how long they would be stuck on this alternate Ierilia. They would need to be careful with their provisions until they found drinkable water. Everything was so different, including the vegetation and plant life.

Cidus lay on his stomach resting his head on his arms and gazed at the murky forest. Not far from where he lay he saw some strange plants. It almost looked as if they were eyeballs growing from the ground. They were grayish, sort of transparent, with small red veins leading to a red circle on top. He wondered what they were. There were whole patches of them.

Unlike the abundance of colorful vegetation and flowers of his home, this land had virtually no color anywhere. How could Odoxon have created such a somber planet? If this was supposed to be an alternate Ierilia, what had happened to the beauty of his home planet? Then again, from what he had been told, Odoxon was centuries old, the oldest sorcerer living, and looked very ancient. Maybe this place mirrored his corrupted soul.

He stared at the treeline and spotted several tall apparitions. They had round ribbed stems, were very dark in color, and stood half the size of the trees. An oblong, bulbous flower crowned the top of the stems — if one could call it a flower. It had diamond-shaped leaves flaring out from its top. A row of gray dots almost seemed to glare at him from the bottom of the bulb. Long spikes jutted out from beneath the bloom, and its roots lay gnarled upon the ground as if it were ready to run away.

Closing his eyes, he rested his head on his arms and thought about Tabeka. How was she holding up? She had to be worried sick. Picturing her sweet face in his mind, his heart stirred. Was it really possible after all this time? Or was he still Zohmes' prisoner and everything that had happened was just a hallucination? After twenty-five years of imprisonment and torture at the hands of the demented god, had his mind finally cracked? Gods, he hoped not, because if his mind was playing tricks, the truth of it might break him.

Cidus startled when some of the team began to stir, get up, and walk around. Disoriented for a moment, he sat, then remembered where they were. He got up and quickly packed his gear, then joined the others.

They ate a simple breakfast of dried fruit and smoked meat, washing it down with water from their waterskins.

He studied the treeline while he ate. The forest still looked as dreary as it had when he had finally fallen asleep. A place of nightmares. Odoxon would not make it easy for intruders to infiltrate his castle but there was no movement, no sounds. It was as if the place was devoid of life.

Laura scanned the trees and wrinkled her nose. "This place really gives me the creeps."

"I am ready to get this mission over with." Ivran stood and brushed the dirt from his pants. "If the duplicate Biryn and Cylena are any indication of the people here, I do not want to run into a Reana copy."

The thought of an evil version of himself and Tabeka gave Cidus the chills. "Yes, the sooner we get to Iridia and Evior the better."

Cewrick hoisted his pack on his shoulder and grabbed his staff. "I will take the lead. We do not know what magick lies within these woods."

Cewrick led them to the path Cidus had seen the previous night.

Cidus scanned the trees as he followed the team into the woods. Even though the path was well-trodden, the only thing to catch his attention was the strange plants he had noticed before sleep had overtaken him. He shivered. Large patches of eyes seemed to stare while they progressed further into the dense forest. Mixed within those patches were the much larger plants, their large bulbous flowers towering over the smaller cylindrical bulbs.

"What in the hell is with the eyeballs!" Jonathan stepped over a mass of roots growing into the path. "The bloody things seem to be watching us."

They trudged forward. The path seemed to disappear beneath the overgrowth of roots and vegetation. Many of the plant stalks rose above their heads.

A loud bursting noise startled Cidus, then another, and another. Suddenly the forest was filled with the sound of mini explosions, and a sludgy, greenish liquid rained down from above, coating their hair, skin, and clothing. Cidus' stomach rolled. It smelled like rotting flesh, and they had no way to wash the stuff off.

"This is fucking disgusting!" Erica slung some of the sludge from her clothing.

"Disgusting isn't the word for it. I smell like roadkill." Laura yanked at one of the large diamond-shaped leaves of the larger plants. "We have nothing to wash this crud off, but at least the leaves will help get most of it."

To Cidus' consternation, the large bulbous flower at the top of the fat stem hurdled down from above, the petals opening to display a row of very sharp thorns that looked like teeth. He yanked Laura out of the way while Taylith sliced through the base of the plant. It fell to the ground with a loud thud.

All around the team leaves rustled, and thorny vines slithered across the ground. The thick gray stems of the plants shifted and turned, the bulb-like flowers hovered above them waiting to strike.

"We need to get moving. Fast! There are more of these plants, and I think we just angered them," Aldis warned.

"Odoxon has a bloody, twisted mind." Jonathan started walking forward, but Icaras held him back.

"Let my father take the lead. He is the most experienced with the magick used in this place."

"We stink of rotting morcoug. The stench of dead flesh alone will attract predators," Laro added.

Cidus held his sword in one hand and his fleet weapon in the other. If Taylith could kill the plant by slicing through it, then he wanted to be ready.

They moved forward, and the carnivorous plants moved to attack, but to Cidus' surprise, the beasts stopped short. An invisible wall protected them from the gaping mouths of the flowers and the rows of thorny teeth.

"How—"

"Icaras is shielding us," Erica said.

"Of course," Cidus mumbled, then jumped to the side when one of the bulbs slammed hard against the shield. The bulbous head and gaping mouth could easily fit half of the team within. Cidus grimaced. They were protected…for now. At least Icaras could call upon his magick to assist the team and keep them safe. Cidus hated the feeling of uselessness. Why would the gods grant him such abilities but not the knowledge to use it?

Astiana walked beside him. "You worry needlessly, Cidus. As I have told you a few times already, when you have need of your magick, the gods will show you what you need to do, just as they have Jonathan."

Cidus grimaced. It was disconcerting that Astiana could read his thoughts. Besides her beauty, her normal appearance, it was easy to forget that she was a goddess. "It does little good to have such power but have no understanding of how to call upon it."

They had been walking for quite some time when Cidus noticed the plants had stopped their relentless attack.

"There is a small clearing up ahead. We will rest there, then continue on," Cewrick called out.

The clearing was bigger than Cidus had expected. Several large boulders lay clustered together that they could sit on to rest, and there was a small pool of water about the size of the fishpond in Brenn's gardens. The water was clouded and murky, but he was very tempted to use the filthy liquid to cleanse the malodorous grime from his skin.

Erica peered down at the water. "That looks just about as nasty as the gunk covering me."

Laro pulled her away from the water. "I would not get too close, love. There is no telling what may live in it."

Liana strode to the pool. "I think I would be more afraid of the water than what lives in it." She wrinkled her nose. "I think the stench of that water is worse than what is wafting off us right now."

They rested for a little while, hydrated, using their water sparingly, then continued on. The vegetation became more clustered and shorter in size, and the trees were starting to thin. The only spots of color Cidus could see in this black and white world were the crimson dots of the strange eye plants. Luckily, they were far enough away that if they burst, the team would not get showered with their ooze.

After walking another half hour, they finally broke through the trees. Cewrick stopped and pointed his staff. "Behold. Odoxon's castle."

Cidus looked at the replica of Biryn's castle, except instead of beautiful marble and gold towers, this palace, if one could even call it that, was dark and somber, like the rest of Odoxon's creation. The towers were enveloped by low hanging black clouds, and a moat surrounded its walls, edged by strange shrubbery. Thick branches with thorny black vines wound around them, dark spiny clusters of leaves. Within the bunched foliage he saw large red masses that resembled a flower bud. The center glowed bright, then dim, much like an electrical impulse. The way the flowers moved, Cidus could not shake the feeling that they were being watched.

"Watch out, Cidus!" Liana pushed him out of the way.

Several winged dragons swooped down. Dragons? No, nothing like Ciara, Taylith, and Liana. These were more like phantoms, specters. Their wingspan was huge, their bodies transparent. They had a long reptilian body and even longer forked tail. Their head resembled that of a snake with two glowing blue horns protruding from it. Cidus was sure he could see veins pulsing through the translucent skin. Liana had not moved fast enough. One of them had her in its claws and prepared to swoop up.

A roar issued from its mouth, its tongue flicking in and out and spitting blue streaks of fire as Liana called out her dragon. Instead of a helpless female, the apparition had a real dragon to deal with.

Ciara and Taylith called out their dragons and joined Liana in the fight against the phantoms.

"All of you, gather together. I will shield us," Cewrick told them.

The team gathered close to Cewrick. He raised his staff, the crystal glowing brightly. After his chant was done, he lowered his staff and studied the creatures the dragons were fighting. "Odoxon plays with power only the gods themselves should wield."

"They remind me of the wraiths we encountered near that stream. Remember?" Erica said, looking at Laro and Icaras.

"Let us hope they do not multiply like the soulless howlers did," Laro said.

It did not take long for the three dragons to defeat the wraith-like dragons. They landed in the clearing, none the worse for the battle they had just fought. Cidus watched them change back into their humans. It still amazed him that they could shift forms. All he had known were the dragons Cewrick...or Zohmes had captured and changed centuries before. The black dragons. And they had not been able to change. "What is next I wonder?"

"Maybe somebody can magically get this stench off us? Odoxon will smell us coming." Erica complained.

"She has a point," Jonathan agreed. "Liana, Ciara, and Taylith are no longer covered in this grime. Help the rest of us to get rid of this obnoxious crap."

Liana grinned. "Shifting to our dragons does have its uses."

Astiana grabbed Cewrick's arm. "They are right we could also attract more beasts. Let us perform a cleansing spell." She motioned to the team. "Gather together."

After the team stepped close to Cewrick and Astiana, they joined hands and Cewrick raised his staff in the air. They chanted in unison, and a soft glow radiated from Cewrick's staff, surrounding them with light. When they completed the spell, the staff returned to normal, and Cewrick lowered it to the ground.

Cidus looked down at his clothing and inspected his hands, then ran his fingers through his hair. The smell was gone, and his clothing looked freshly laundered.

"Thank God!" Laura wiped her face with her hand. "My stomach was churning."

Aldis studied the vegetation surrounding a large mud-filled trench. "We need to cross that moat but be careful of that vegetation bordering it. Avoid the red buds."

Cewrick pointed his staff at the bushes. Fire streamed from its crystal head, burning a narrow path for them. They walked single file through the ashes. When they cleared the bushes, they had to move one by one along the edge of the water. The moat was so close, there was barely enough room for them to place their feet.

"There is no bridge," Ivran pointed out.

Behind the moat was a tall wall constructed of huge boulders. Cidus gazed down, but what should have been water, was thick black mud.

"Doxie baby has built himself quite the fortress," Erica said.

"Maybe he is afraid of his own creations and wishes to keep them out." Hirsuta stepped close to Cewrick.

"We will need magick to get into the castle." Icaras shifted his pack on his shoulder. "There is no other way."

They did not have time to form a circle. The mud stirred, and a row of humanoid forms appeared, dripping with sludge. As the muck slid slowly down their bodies, red, reptile skin appeared. They were huge. At least a dozen long spikes protruded from their heads. Their eyes glowed a bright orange and crackled as small bursts of flames shot from them. Sharp spikes also protruded from their shoulders, arms, and thighs and they had a thick forked tail. Their hands, if you could call them that, only had three digits, with long curved talons protruding from each finger. They had snouts and very thick lips.

Cidus looked at the others. They could not step back because of the bushes behind them.

"Of all the missions we've been on, we've never encountered so many strange creatures, one after the other," Erica said.

"Yanata. I seem to remember quite a few strange creatures there," Biryn muttered. "They were quite persistent."

Erica chuckled. "Oh yeah, our honeymoon from hell. Or should I say, honeymoon *in* hell! A memory that will remain with us forever. Those demons are just looking at us right now. They're not attacking."

"Not for long. Watch out," Brenn yanked her away and almost lost his footing as a long arm reached for her.

"There is no room to shift here," Liana said.

"No, but there is plenty of power between us," Astiana looked at the magick users. "Line up and hold hands. We can beat them."

"Doxie has been fucking busy," Laura muttered. "I wonder how he gets out of his hellhole."

Erica snickered, as she raised her sword. "He's a sorcerer, remember? He can just zap himself out of his castle, just like they're going to zap us into the place."

The chanters stepped toward the edge, their voices echoing around the castle. The words flowed from Cidus' lips. Would he ever know what the hell he was spewing from his mouth?

It took a few minutes, but then the guardians of the moat

and castle began to crumble slowly, until they completely disintegrated, their remains sinking into the mud. Cidus could not help but think that destroying the creatures had been way too easy.

Jonathan stepped back. "Now we can zap to beyond that wall."

Jonathan took Liana's hand and pulled her protectively against him. Cidus could feel a strong connection between the young dragon and his brother. Could it be? Were those two destined to be together? To become lifemates?

His attention was diverted as they grouped together to get ready to transport.

CHAPTER THIRTEEN

They landed safely behind the wall and faced a large courtyard. Everything seemed quiet. Too quiet for Cidus. He could not shake the feeling of foreboding that chilled his veins. There were no guards, no monsters. Steps led up to a set of iron doors, the main entrance to the castle.

"Do you think he knows we are here?" Biryn wondered.

"I do not think so. He is under the false impression that his castle is impregnable," Hirsuta said.

"If our doubles are all serving him, how many of our doppelgangers will be inside?" Laura frowned. "What if they see us?"

"They may not live in the castle. Only one of us should go inside first," Cewrick said. "Jonathan and Cidus, you are both demi-gods, your powers are the greatest."

"I do not know how to use mine," Cidus said.

"And I'm still green," Jonathan agreed.

"Green?" Liana asked.

"I'll explain later. Liana is older than Taylith and Ciara. Maybe she should go?" He rubbed his chin.

Cidus was surprised. The young woman was older than her brother and cousin? They looked the same age. He sighed. There was so much he did not know yet, and the dragons were a complete mystery. It was going to take a long time to learn the history behind it all.

"I will go," Hirsuta offered.

While they were still arguing about who would go inside the castle to investigate, Cidus suddenly realized that Cewrick had disappeared. "Where is Cewrick?"

"Inside, I presume." Erica pulled a face. "We were taking too long to decide."

Cidus waited impatiently for Cewrick to return. He hoped the sorcerer did not get caught within. Odoxon's power was immense, and with the grimoire and black diamond in his possession, it could make the old magick user invincible. It relieved his worries only slightly that the others did not seem concerned for Cewrick's safety.

Cidus let out the breath he was holding when Cewrick opened the entrance and motioned for them to come inside.

"There are no guards within, and I encountered no other people. The layout is the same as the palace. How Odoxon could have known the interior is a mystery."

The team cautiously entered the castle. It may have been modeled after the palace in size and layout, but that is where the likeness ended. As this alternate Ierilia mirrored the darkness of the old sorcerer's soul, so, too, did the home he had created.

Images of torture and great bloody battles were etched into the dark gray stone of the walls. Stained glass windows, the color of blood, cast an eerie red glow throughout the room. Sconces resembling gnarled hands adorned the walls, crimson candles clutched within their claws, the dripping wax resembling large droplets of blood. A large tapestry hung on one wall depicting the old sorcerer. At his feet, kneeling in supplication, was a woman, scantily dressed. A jeweled collar encircled her neck. The man fisted the chain that was attached to it. Cidus cringed. The woman could easily have been Ciara or Liana. He shook his head. Odoxon had set his sights on one of the dragon princesses.

He heard Taylith growl and watched him yank the tapestry from the wall. Odoxon was playing with fire if he thought to supplicate Ciara or Liana. The dragons would rip him to shreds.

Taylith's eyes began to glow, but Cidus could not tell if he was having a vision. There was too much rage radiating from the dragon.

"Twisted fucking bastard," Jonathan's voice held an edge of fury. "That was Liana's image on that piece of crap."

Liana shifted closer to Jonathan, a grim look on her face. "Do not let the old idiot's imagination anger you. I am no man's pet."

It was Liana then.

Cidus was sure now that Odoxon had duplicated all the people of Ierilia, including Liana. He had not been back long enough to know all the stories behind the missions, but he knew Liana had recently been found and that it was Odoxon behind her abduction. It was highly possible there was another Liana in this hellhole and that Odoxon had replicated her to suit his whims.

He shook the sickening thought from his mind. "This place is huge, how are we to know where Iridia and Evior are being held?"

"Follow me." Taylith stalked to the front of the group.

Taylith led them to the floor where the king's private rooms would have been located if they were in the actual royal palace. He stopped at an entrance to one of the suites. Cidus noted that the door was not one that would lead to the king's chambers.

"Liana, Jonathan, both of you stay hidden." Taylith silenced Liana when she was about to speak. "No. You will stay out of sight. Brenn, Erica, and Biryn, you must come with me. We will need the swords."

Cidus could have sworn that a secondary conversation between Taylith, Liana, and Jonathan had been taking place at the same time. Liana and Jonathan backed down and allowed the others to pass.

Cidus slipped into the room along with them. The luxurious chamber seemed to be the only bright spot of color within the whole castle. Decorated in whites and golds, the suite was fit for a queen. Thick white carpeting covered the floor, and an elaborate four-poster bed took up a large section of the room. His stomach turned when he noticed the woman lying on the gold comforter. It was Liana, her wrists in gold shackles, chained to the two posts at the head of the bed. The jeweled collar depicted in the picture on the tapestry encircled her neck.

In the corner of the room in direct view of the bed, stood a large gilded cage. It reminded Cidus of the small enclosures used to hold tamed nyctea birds, but there were no birds in this cage. Held within was a man, his head was bowed, and blood caked the hair that hid his face. Gaping wounds covered what little Cidus could see of him. He gasped when the man looked up at him, the man's piercing blue gaze pinned on Cidus. *Jonathan.*

"What do you want, brother. Come to gloat?" The Liana doppelganger spat out, drawing Cidus' attention.

"We are freeing you both." Taylith drew his sword. "We must use the swords on the chains."

Erica joined Taylith on one side of the bed, Biryn and Brenn were on the other. They touched the tips of the swords to the locks on the chains at Liana's wrists. The locks began to glow, then suddenly released. She sat up and rubbed her wrists, then gave Taylith a scathing look. "Since when has my captivity ever been a concern of yours?"

Taylith bristled. "Be thankful that I am helping you now." He lifted the sword to her neck. "If you would like the collar removed, stay still."

She lifted her chin, allowing Taylith and Erica to touch the lock with their swords. A relieved look crossed her features when the collar dropped to her lap, but when she looked back up at them, hate filled her gaze. "I am going to laugh when he tortures the lot of you for my escape. Do not think he will not know it was his pets that released me."

Taylith sighed and walked to the cage, then gestured for the others to follow. "Come. We need the swords for this lock, too."

They touched the tips of the swords to the lock on the cage. Again, the swords emitted a soft glow. The padlock disintegrated. The Liana doppelganger rushed to the cage, opened the door and helped Jonathan's double through the opening. Cidus saw Ciara take a vial from her pocket and rush forward. She applied some of the liquid to the young man's wounds. They healed instantly, just like his own had after his battle with Jatron.

The duplicate Liana looked at the group and sneered. "Do not think we owe —"

To Cidus' relief...and trepidation, the doppelgangers vanished. The Liana double certainly did not have the real Liana's personality. "I hope that it was one of you that transported them."

"I did. They are off the island and somewhere in Cront. How safe they will be, I do not know. Jonathan, Liana, you can come out now." Taylith said.

Icaras stepped into the room and stood beside Cidus. "Now to find Iridia and Evior. I do not want us to be in this place longer than necessary."

"They are being held in the king's chambers," Taylith told them as he brushed past them and left the room.

Cidus and the others followed. Just a few paces down the hall and they had reached the door to the king's chambers. Of course, they were not the king's rooms, but the location was the same.

Liana pushed to the front with Taylith. "I am the only one that has been able to banish Odoxon. I am going in first."

She rammed her shoulder into the door hard. The hinges burst free, and the door fell forward. Several spikes shot from the sides of the doorway, one piercing Liana's arm before Taylith managed to pull her out of the way. Blood streamed down her arm. Cidus saw several large drops floating in the air, then drift through the doorway into the room beyond.

Taylith, Jonathan, and Liana entered. Cidus followed along with the rest of the team. No sooner had they entered the room when metal bars shot through the floor around them. They pierced the ceiling, effectively trapping the team. The bars glowed eerily, and there were symbols etched into the metal. Some resembled serpents, others were some kind of hieroglyphics.

Cidus had a vivid memory of his prisoner days with Zohmes. Icy cold invaded his spine, his soul, as he gripped the bars. Imprisoned again. From what he had learned, the old sorcerer's magick was strong. Would any of the team be able to break the sorcery that held them captive?

Pulling himself together, he shook the memories away, and once his eyes became accustomed to the dim lighting from the black candles placed everywhere, he gazed at the room beyond. Shelves lined the walls, holding rows and piles of ancient books. Could the grimoire be among them? Wasn't it true that something hidden in plain sight was harder to find than something that was well concealed?

"We need to get out of here," Hirsuta said and began to chant. Cewrick and the others joined her, but nothing happened.

Manic laughter interrupted them. They stopped chanting and turned toward the sound. Odoxon, stooped, holding a knobby staff, walked toward the cage, a flask in his gnarled hand. His yellowish beard, streaked with gray and white, reached almost to the floor, his scalp had bare patches. Whatever hair was left, hung in scraggly strings down his chest and back. The only brightness of the figure was his eyes. They had a strange glow issuing from yellow-greenish depths, the green split by black slitted pupils. Cidus had to repress a shudder at the macabre figure. The man's skin was deeply furrowed and like ancient parchment.

"You can chant all you want. Nothing can break this containment spell." His croaky voice echoed toward them, seemed to bounce off the walls, followed by his maniacal laughter. "I have everything I need now!" he bellowed.

An area of the room behind the old sorcerer lit up suddenly. Cidus stiffened when he saw a naked Evior and Iridia strapped to tables. Bands secured their heads. Metal cuffs encased their wrists and ankles and wide straps fastened their bodies down. His stomach churned when he saw similar wounds, like the Jonathan doppelganger, on Evior's body. The young man's eyes looked glazed, and tears of blood trickled down his cheeks. His face looked deformed where large sections of skin were gone, his lips had been cut out, exposing his teeth.

Cidus' gaze drifted to Iridia. Like Evior, her eyes were glazed and bloody. Large areas of skin looked flayed off exposing tissues beneath. Blood covered her body from head to toe, her breasts gone, her lips removed. Both appeared to be unconscious and close to death

"What is that?" Biryn pointed to the drops of blood Cidus had seen hovering in the air, now floating slowly toward the sorcerer.

"That is Liana's blood from when she cut her arm. I saw the droplets slowly drift away," Cidus said softly. Not soft enough.

"Of course. I needed her blood to complete the potion. Once I drink this, she will not be able to resist me." He held the flask up and caught the droplets of blood.

"You old entrail sucking kurakelda! I never wanted you in the first place. Drinking my blood will not bend me to your will!" Liana shouted.

"And what is in the potion? What will it do?" Cewrick asked, his lips a tight, grim line.

Cidus felt Jonathan move closer to him. The connection between them was undeniable. Without looking at his brother, he could feel him, sense his moves.

"This is going to be work for us, Cidus. He cannot best demi-gods with his magick," Jonathan hissed near his ear.

CHAPTER FOURTEEN

The sorcerer stepped away from Evior and Iridia. Cidus noticed a very large, silver-shaped egg standing on a pedestal near the wall. A long, silver chain was attached to it. Odoxon raised his hand, and it opened, displaying the grimoire and the black gem. Brilliant red light surrounded the book and the diamond.

Odoxon lifted the grimoire out of the egg. He placed it on a table and opened it, then turned to fetch the black diamond. His gaze rested on Cewrick and Biryn, and he began to speak, his voice low and ominous.

"An untouched young woman's breast-skin and nipples, a god's daughter. A virginal young powerful male's muscle tissue. A lock of their hair. The mucous membrane from both their eyes. The skin of their lips. A scraping from their genitals. A queen's maternal milk. The Pratiha's venom. The blood from a Clymm horse. The juice from the oubanium plant. Petals from the dioica flower. As an added touch, blood from the woman I desire. Mix all this with the juice from the drappenate. There, Cewrick, the answer to your question. What will it do? I will show you now."

He held up the flask and gazed closely at the grimoire, then began to chant. Midway during the spell, he stood and drank the contents of the flask all at once.

Cidus watched in consternation as his muscles bulged, his body began to deform. It was as if an inner sculptor was at work within the old man. In less than a minute, they saw a young man where the old sorcerer had stood, his wooden staff discarded on the floor. Healthy black hair surrounded a handsome, clean-shaven face. He had a young, muscular body, and his old raspy voice was that of a young man's as he finished chanting the spell. The only resemblance to the old Odoxon were his eyes. They were the same strange green-yellowish glowing color and the black elliptical pupils.

"Unbelievable," Cewrick uttered.

Jonathan grasped Cidus' hand. "We have to act. Now!"

"I do not know—"

The grimoire and black diamond floated back to the silver egg. Its lid closed seamlessly once the grimoire and diamond were housed within, and then it disappeared.

"The grimoire holds no spell that can break this forever young enchantment," Odoxon told them. "And no spell can free you from your cage."

"Oh, that's where you are wrong, you bastard!" Jonathan shouted.

Cidus felt Jonathan's power flow through him.

"You will not have her, young whelp!" Odoxon shouted, his pupils now dilating to almost cover the whole iris. "She is mine now." He raised his staff and sent Liana hurling through the bars as if they were not there. She landed beside the sorcerer.

"I will never be yours, Odoxon. Not then, not now, not ever! Drinking my blood did not bind me to you. Nothing you do ever will!" Liana shouted, then held out her hands, bolts of red fire shot from her fingertips, her eyes were ablaze with a golden glow. Cidus felt the essence of her dragon wanting to break free. But besides some more scales appearing on her skin, Liana did not change.

It seemed to humor Odoxon. "I like a woman with fire. Nothing you do can hurt me, my love."

"Shut the fuck up!" Jonathan shouted.

Cidus felt the strength surge into him from Jonathan's hand. His body began to heat, becoming so hot, it felt as if he were on fire. His hair sizzled, his eyes burned. Shafts of red light sprung from his eyes. He could no longer see anything except the red streams directed at the bars of their cage. They melted, the metal dripping in globs to the floor. Jonathan pulled Cidus through the opening. They faced Odoxon. Together, they chanted. Cidus had no idea where the words came from, and Jonathan probably did not either, he realized, but they chanted in unison. He felt the lightning flashing from his fingertips and aimed his hands at Odoxon's dim figure.

The power radiating from within Cidus slowly depleted. When he could see clearly again, there was no Odoxon. "Where did he go?"

Jonathan laughed sarcastically. "I've got no idea where the fuck we sent him. Hopefully to a place from where he can't escape."

Cidus saw Laura rush to Evior and Iridia. They were damaged beyond belief. Evior was so still he appeared to have entered the realm of dreams. He had witnessed Laura's healing power before. Would she be able to heal them? Could Ciara? They had to find a way to help the two young people. His heart shattered at the thought of bringing them home to Tabeka, broken and blind, tortured in such an evil way.

No one said anything. All of them focused on the young couple and Laura as she placed a hand on Iridia's abdomen and her other hand on Evior's belly. Cidus saw her close her eyes and concentrate. A brilliant light surrounded her. Iridia and Evior's forms began to glow from head to toe. Astiana chanted softly. The light that emanated from Laura suddenly burst into such brilliance, Cidus had to shield his eyes. When he opened them again, the light was gone, and Laura lay unconscious on the floor, her head cradled in Taylith's lap. She stirred, then opened her eyes when Taylith brushed his hand across her cheek.

Iridia was healed, her eyes bright and clear, but Cidus saw marks on her arms, legs, and chest. They resembled hieroglyphs. She sat up and tried to cover her nudity. "Where am I? What happened?" Then she let out a piercing scream. Cidus knew her memory had returned. With the sound of her cry, Evior stirred and began to wake. Laura had healed him, too. There was not a wound left on his body, and his eyes looked clear, though with a bewildered expression in them. Like Iridia, he had the same hieroglyphics on his arms, legs, and chest. What were they? Had Odoxon put them there?

Erica grabbed a red tablecloth off a table and draped it quickly around the sobbing, shaking young woman. Ciara did the same for Evior.

"We need to get them dressed." Hirsuta kneeled beside Iridia and placed the palm of her hand to Iridia's forehead.

Cidus was thankful to see that Iridia had visibly calmed. He rummaged in his pack and found the extra set of clothing he had packed. Evior was taller and a little broader in the shoulders, but the clothing would have to do. He handed the bundle to Evior.

"I have an extra set of clothing in my pack that should fit Iridia," Laura's voice sounded weak, but Cidus noticed she was now sitting up.

Hirsuta and Astiana helped Iridia get dressed. Liana held the blanket up to shield her from view, while Cidus, Biryn, and Brenn assisted Evior. When they had finished dressing, Evior moved to stand close to Iridia.

"Icaras and I will remove the memories of the pain of the torture from both of you," Ciara told the young couple.

"I do not want to forget what Odoxon has done to us," Evior said heatedly.

"We will only take away the recollection of the pain of the actual torture. You will remember and know what Odoxon has done."

Cidus did not miss the flinch from Iridia when Ciara reached out to touch her face. Then she relaxed and nodded, allowing Ciara to place her glowing hand on Iridia's forehead. Icaras did the same to Evior. Moments later they removed their hands from the young couple's foreheads. Both had a look of relief on their faces.

"Ivran, Aldis, and I have searched the rooms for the grimoire and black diamond. Odoxon has taken them or hidden them well, but we did find these," Laro said. He held a black staff in his hand topped with a black skull, and Aldis and Ivran carried several ancient books.

Biryn looked at the staff in shock. "That is Odoxon's staff, is it not?"

Cewrick stepped beside him. "Yes, it is. One of them at least. I will destroy it." He took the staff in his hand and in seconds, it disappeared. "We need to leave. Now that we have Iridia and Evior, we can fly back to Dreaded Peaks. Did you see anyone when you searched the rooms?"

"No. The castle appears to be deserted," Ivran said while packing some of the books into his backpack.

Aldis quickly packed the other books he was carrying and opened the door. "All is quiet. Come. I will take the lead."

Cidus went to place his arm around Evior's waist, but he shook it off. "I am fine now. I can walk on my own. Iridia?" Cidus smiled as the girl hurried to him and grabbed Evior's hand.

They filed out of the room, grouped close together. Cidus did not feel at ease. A prickling sensation told him that eyes were watching them. He glanced behind, up, both sides, but saw no one.

Almost at the end of the lengthy corridor, a group of warriors appeared from around the corner. At first, Cidus thought they were guards, but when he looked closer, he saw they were facing their doppelgangers or at least some of them. A duplicate Ivran, Erica, Taylith, Aldis, and Icaras stood frozen as they stared at their alter-egos. Their clothing was old and worn. The material a coarse weave, much like a burlap sack. Their weapons were crudely made swords and daggers—nothing but a dull blade with animal hide wrapped around the base to form a hilt. Their weapons were raised, and they were poised to fight, but they looked so shocked, they did not attack.

Duplicate Erica took a step toward them. "What the fuck is this? Some kind of sick joke? I thought I'd seen everything on this godforsaken planet, but this is fucking out there!"

"The old sorcerer is playing tricks with our minds," Aldis' alternate commented.

Murmurs of agreement rose from the doubles.

Erica took the initiative and stepped forward. Cidus was amazed at how brave this small, petite woman was.

"You're not happy here," Erica stated.

"Would you be?" her double sneered. "Who the fuck *are* you anyway? And where the hell did you come from?"

"We need to get out of here, but to make a long story short, I am Erica Martinez from Earth. We live on the planet Ierilia. Centuries ago, Odoxon created this world, a mirror of Ierilia and called it Odoxus. It looks as if he duplicated many of the people living on Ierilia. Now, we need to return to our own home."

"The old man is using one of his magick tricks meant to addle our brains. We are not the doubles here." Taylith's clone pulled his sword.

Erica's alter-ego grabbed clone Taylith's arm. "Wait. They

might be telling the truth. Odoxon is an evil son-of-a-bitch. He sent us to kill them after all." She turned her attention back to Erica. "If you are telling the truth, take me with you."

"Erica! No! You have Laro and Tomas to think about! And your people," Ivran's double argued.

"Laro would want to know the truth, too."

"He would not want you to risk the danger of going alone," Cidus heard Ivran mumble.

"Where is your Laro anyway?" Erica asked her double.

"Odoxon sent him and the rest of the team on another mission... Well, except for Biryn. The fool is drunk again." Erica's double shook her head. "Odoxon talked of more intruders in the mountains. But how about it? If you're telling the truth, take us all with you?"

Astiana stepped forward to join them. "That is not possible. Were we to take you back with us, it could alter all of our destinies. What about your comrades? Do they feel the same way?"

"Yes. Odoxon forces us to work for him, but we do it with repugnance. If we don't obey him, he will punish us in ways you can't imagine."

"Oh, believe me. We can very well imagine just what he would do." Erica scoffed. "I suggest you work behind the scenes then to make this world a better place. Your future is here."

"So, we are stuck in this hellhole," her double muttered.

"That is the way it has to be. Do you think you can help us get out of here?" Brenn asked.

"Yes, but before we do, why did you come here? How?" her double asked.

"Odoxon captured two young people from our planet. He needed them to create a potion to make him young again. We got here through the portal he created."

Duplicate Erica scrunched up her face. "A young Odoxon?

A Portal? You've got to be kidding me."

"How often is he here?" Cidus asked.

"He does go away a lot."

Erica nodded and smiled grimly. "That's when he's on Ierilia causing havoc with Zohmes."

"Who is Zohmes? So, the old fool can travel back and forth between our worlds?"

"Zohmes is a god that is raining havoc on our planet, and he freed Odoxon from captivity to assist him. Of course, Odoxon can go back and forth between Ierilia and here. His sorcery is unlimited. And now that he is young again, his magickal powers have multiplied a thousandfold," Hirsuta said.

"Enough talk," Biryn strode forward. "We need to leave."

"We're the only ones here. Odoxon contacted us, said there were intruders, and gave the kill order, but we have no wish to kill you. You can safely leave. We will escort you."

"Odoxon knows you can't kill us, but we are able to harm you. He merely sent you here to cause a delay. He doesn't care if any of you are killed in the process. We don't want to hurt anyone, least of all people that are like our twins. It appears that when Odoxon created this alternate world, he made sure there was no magic and no shapeshifters. He wanted to be the ultimate ruler," Erica told them. "Just so you know, as fast as he created this planet, he could more than probably make it vanish just as quickly."

"Oh my God! We'd vanish along with it," other Erica shouted. "Take us, please!"

"We can't. As much as I've always longed for a sister or brother, it would mess with our world. Maybe there is a way in the future for us to help you." Cidus saw Erica look pleadingly at Ciara.

Ciara shook her head. "It pains us to leave you behind. Upon my return to Ierilia, I will speak with the goddess, but I cannot promise you anything except that we will not abandon you."

"Goddess? There are no gods or goddesses here. The only power is Odoxon, and he thrives on the hate and discontent of the people," Aldis' clone commented.

"The old bastard gets his rocks off by forcing starvation and a life of squalor on the people. Even my God has forsaken this planet," the Erica double brushed her fingers through her hair, a look of frustration in her eyes.

"Nevertheless, we cannot help you unless it is allowed by our gods and goddesses," Ciara said.

Disappointment clouded double Erica's face. "I can't ask for anything more. I guess we'll have to wait."

Cidus felt bad for them. He saw Ivran, Aldis, Icaras, and Taylith's doubles throw curious glances at their alter-egos and the rest of the team. They had not uttered another word and had let duplicate Erica do all the talking.

"Follow us," the other Erica motioned them to follow her and began to walk, followed by her team.

They led them to the entrance and the iron doors.

"How will you get over the wall and through the moat?" duplicate Erica asked.

"We don't need to. Thank you," Jonathan said.

They walked down the steps. Once in the courtyard, Ciara, Liana, and Taylith called out their dragons. Cidus heard loud gasps from the five standing on the steps watching them. He quickly climbed onto Ciara's leg, then onto her back, and though he preferred ground travel, he was glad to be up in the air amidst the black clouds.

CHAPTER FIFTEEN

It did not take them long to get to Dreaded Peaks. Cidus was relieved to see the encampment of Captain Ryston and the four engineered soldiers in the valley below. After the dragons landed in the clearing and allowed their riders to slide off their backs, they shifted.

"Gather close together," Cewrick called. "We do not need to travel the pass to go home."

The team gathered, along with the soldiers. Within moments of starting their chant, the magick users transported them to where the portal was supposed to be, but upon landing, it was not there.

"Where the hell did it go?" Jonathan muttered.

Cidus gazed around. There was no sight of the glowing portal. "Odoxon has hidden it. It has to be here."

"Maybe he destroyed it," Laura suggested.

"No. Even with his powerful magick, he needs that portal to go back and forth between the two worlds."

"Everything looks the fucking same on this mountain. Who's to say we didn't end up in the wrong location," Erica sounded frustrated.

Cidus had to agree, the sharp craggy rocks were hard to distinguish one from the other. If they had been thinking rationally when they came through the portal they should have left markings on the rocks to lead them back.

"We encountered those strange creatures after we cleared the—" Laro started to say.

"You mean the mutant gorillas?" Erica interrupted.

"Yes, the mutant gorillas. We can track the creatures, then follow the path to the portal," Laro said.

Cidus gave Laro a confused look. "And just how are you going to track those creatures?"

Ivran patted Cidus on the shoulder. "Laro, Brenn, and I are lion shifters, and lions have a great sense of smell."

Even though Cidus had seen them change during the battle against Jatron, it still amazed him that the three warriors could change into lions. He watched as they shifted, and three majestic animals took their place. They leaped away toward the pass.

While the lions were gone, the rest of the team sat and nibbled on whatever rations they had left. Evior and Iridia huddled together, his arm protectively around her, her head resting on his shoulders. What had happened to the two young people, though Evior put up a brave front, had to weigh heavy upon their heart and souls.

The lions returned. One of them, the largest of the three, had yellowish mucus all over its fur and mane. "Brenn! Are you injured?" Cidus watched Ciara run to the lion, but before she could examine him, he shifted.

He grinned. "I am fine. It was a gorilla's blood. Last time I looked my blood was not yellow."

"And?" Biryn queried.

"We are in the right place. The portal has to be here, exactly where we left it." Brenn pointed at where the portal had been previously.

"The old kurakelda has returned to Ierilia, and he cast a spell to hide it from us thinking to trap us here." Liana felt the rockface.

Cidus joined her search along with the others. Nothing looked out of place, and the stone felt just as it appeared—cold and unyielding. Before long, he heard a frustrated growl escape Erica, and the sound of metal slamming against stone echoed through the pass as she lifted her sword and struck the rock wall in anger. A large chunk of rock rolled to the ground.

Look!" Erica cheered.

Cidus stared at the stone in disbelief. Where Erica had struck the wall with her sword, a small portion of the portal had been revealed.

"Hurry, use the swords." Astiana stepped beside Cidus.

Brenn, Taylith, and Biryn quickly joined Erica in front of the portal. As one, they touched the tips of the swords to what should be the portal's center. Cidus shielded his eyes when the swords began to glow brightly, the rockface flaming crimson before disintegrating to dust, revealing the gateway.

"I want to go home," Cidus heard Iridia whisper.

Thank the gods Ciara and Icaras had the forethought to remove the memories of the young couple's pain. Cidus knew it would be a long recovery for them both, but at least their minds were not broken.

"Let's get the hell out of here!" Erica sheathed her sword.

"Captain Ryston, you and your men follow me. We will guard the portal on the other side. A couple of magick users will help secure it." Aldis took the lead, stepping through the plasma, followed by the engineered soldiers, Cewrick, and Hirsuta.

"Evior, take Iridia through now." Ciara gently nudged the young man. "It is safe on the other side."

Cidus saw Iridia look uncertainly at the portal and sought to ease her fear. "Iridia, this is how Odoxon brought you and Evior to this planet. You do not remember?"

"No. All I remember is waking up strapped to that table and that monster experimenting on us."

"It is safe. Believe me. We came here through it, and we are all in one piece. Cewrick and Hirsuta will protect you on the other side," Cidus tried to reassure her.

Evior placed his arm around Iridia's waist. "If it is harmful, then we both suffer. Come on, love. I am right beside you."

After Evior and Iridia stepped through, the rest of the team followed. This time Cidus was prepared for the strange rush and bright flashing lights within the plasma tunnel. When he got to the other end, he braced himself for the fall and landed on his feet in a crouch.

Instead of dark clouds and the sharp spikes of the Dreaded Peaks, Cidus now stood in the verdant woods of the Astanica Mountains. Sunlight filtered through the thick leaves of the trees, causing shadows to dance on the dirt path. Birds flitted above their heads, chirping merrily, and flowers bloomed in a myriad of colors nestled within the lush green of the grass. Every now and then a salora would flutter by, their wings painted like stained glass.

"Look at that gorgeous butterfly," Laura exclaimed.

"Butterfly?" Taylith raised his eyebrows. "That is a flying butoro?"

Laura giggled. "Not butter, or butoro as you guys call it. That is called a butterfly on Earth. We have them, too, or used to. Not as big, mind you."

Taylith shook his head in disbelief. "Your language does not make sense. Why call such a beautiful creature after butoro?"

Laura, Erica, Julia, and Jonathan burst out laughing.

"Now that we are all here, please hide the portal and place a spell that will allow no one to pass," Biryn ordered, overpowering the burst of humor.

Cidus watched as Cewrick stepped forward and raised his

staff in the air. He pointed it at the portal and began to chant. A heavy breeze swirled around Cewrick, then the crystal in his staff began to glow brightly. A sudden flash engulfed the gateway to Odoxus, and it disappeared. Cewrick stopped chanting and lowered his staff.

"This spell is only temporary. Once Odoxon escapes from whence Jonathan and Cidus sent him on Ierilia, he will break it."

Biryn nodded. "Understood. But for now, it will keep our people from accidentally stumbling upon it or the doubles from entering Ierilia should they discover the portal on their end." He wiped his brow and grinned. "Let us return to the flyer. I am ready to return to the palace to my family and a hot meal!"

Everyone mumbled in agreement. Cidus joined them as they formed a close circle with the engineered men in the center. Power—not so shocking now—flowed through him as he joined the other magick users in their chant. He closed his eyes, allowing the energy to flow through him. When he opened his eyes, they were in the valley at the base of the mountains. The king's flyer was parked safely in the clearing exactly where they had left it, and Captain Ryston's men had camped closer to the woods.

The soldiers were sitting around a campfire roasting meat. They jumped up when the team approached.

"Captain Ryston, we will send a fresh team of your warriors to where the portal is located. I am not comfortable leaving the entrance unguarded," Brenn informed the captain.

"Yes, General."

"You and the rest of your men can return back to the base. Take a few days furlough."

"As you wish, General." Captain Ryston grabbed his pack and joined the other soldiers at the campsite.

Cidus followed the team to the king's flyer. All he could think about was getting back to Tabeka and bringing her daughter back to her. Had he heard Odoxon right when he named the requirements of the potion? *A god's daughter? A powerful young male?*

Erica's voice interrupted his thoughts.

"No offense, Astiana, but I am ready to get the hell out of Astanica and go home," Erica brushed her fingers through her hair.

"None taken. Though I miss my valley and temple, I long to see the sweet faces of the little ones." Astiana's face lit with joyful anticipation.

News of their return had traveled ahead to the palace. Cidus' heart felt as if it would burst with love when he caught sight of Tabeka at the top of the stairs near the front entrance. Iridia flew up the steps and fell into her mother's arms, sobbing on her shoulder.

Cidus followed the two women into the palace when Tabeka turned to him. "I do not know how to thank you."

"It was a team effort," Cidus hugged her briefly. "We are to have lunch with the king before we return to Brenn's estate. There is much we need to discuss."

"Do we have to be there?" Iridia asked.

"Yes. Some of it involves you." Cidus wondered if the girl should be told of her lineage so soon after her ordeal. She had been through so much the past few weeks, he could not help but be concerned for her.

"Me? Why? How can it involve me?"

Tabeka took her daughter's arm. "If the king ordered it, we need to obey, girl. I am so thankful to have you and Evior back." She looked up at Cidus. "And you of course. I am happy you are all back in one piece."

"Come, the others have already gone to the king's quarters. I am so hungry, I could eat a korobeast all by myself," Cidus said while taking Tabeka's free arm.

Before entering, Tabeka let go of Iridia and Cidus and turned to Evior, then hugged him. "I am sorry you both had to go through this. Thank the gods and goddesses you are home safe and sound."

Cidus knocked on the door, and Dunmore opened it. They quickly hurried to the dining table already loaded with food. They were apparently the last ones to arrive.

Biryn tapped on his plate. "Now that we are all here let us have a moment of silence to thank the gods and goddesses for their assistance and bringing us home safely."

Cidus closed his eyes. He had given up calling on the deities a long time ago, thinking they had abandoned him to Zohmes. Now, he knew that everything had to take place as it was written in the book of knowledge, even his years of imprisonment. He could not help but question the book. How was it written? Was it I Am that ruled their destinies? Why would the god put them through such torture? Or was there even a higher force that had created the book and mapped out their lives?

Nevertheless, the gods and goddesses helped them all the time, and he had to be thankful and not question what was and was to be. He opened his eyes and saw Astiana gazing directly at him. Had she read his thoughts? The idea that so many of the team could read each other's minds was uncomfortable. Now that he was a demi-god, would he have that power as well?

"Let us eat first and toast to a successful recovery of the two young ones at our table." Biryn lifted his glass then took a sip of his wine.

Cidus watched the king lean toward Cylena and plant a kiss on her cheek. She smiled back at Biryn with a look of love brightening her face.

"The queen has informed me that all was quiet during our

absence. Please, everyone, enjoy the food and wine." Biryn heaped up his plate.

Cidus finished the last crumbs on his plate, then helped himself to some strawberries. The delicious red berries the Earth people grew had really grown on him. He noticed Tabeka and the others enjoyed them as well. The large bowls of fruit were soon empty.

"Now that we have finished our meal, I believe Astiana needs to speak first." Biryn nodded at Astiana.

Cidus wondered if Astiana would confirm his suspicions that Iridia was Zohmes' daughter. And the alternate world where the people were impoverished and suffering? Would the gods allow the team to assist the residents of Odoxus or were they trapped forever in their own version of Yanata?

Astiana's chair scraped against the floor when she stood. "The goddess Rania communicated with me during our flight home. When we rescued Iridia and Evior, Odoxon uttered some startling words. *A god's daughter and a powerful young male.* It puzzled me, at first, as I am sure it did all of you. Rania has clarified the sorcerer's statement. It appears Zohmes has been a busy man, procreating, and so has Jatron. Jatron allowed Zohmes to be intimate with his mate, Ivia. Changing his countenance to that of Jatron, he lay with Ivia. This resulted in Ivia finally being able to carry a child to term with Tabeka's help. As Tabeka can attest, that child was Iridia. Zohmes has known of Iridia's existence, but he has had no interest in a female. His plan was, and probably still is, to create mini versions of himself. He will use any means possible to accomplish this, including finding willing accomplices using trickery. He wants sons to fight by his side and help him reach his ultimate goal. The throne. Jatron bedded many women in Wildevein and played immoral games. Evior's mother did lay with Jatron, but she also lay with Odoxon. It is Odoxon's blood that runs through Evior's veins.

"Though Cidus did win the fight against him, Jatron was not defeated. Zohmes intervened, saving Jatron before his banishment was complete. Jatron's hatred has grown, and he will not take the loss of Wildevein lightly. He is with Zohmes planning another attack on the royal house and the throne. Iridia and Evior are not in any danger at this point, but she needs to know she is a god's daughter and a demi-goddess, and Evior must understand that Odoxon is his father. They, like the rest of you have done, must go to the Clyss. There, it will also be made known what the symbols on Iridia and Evior's bodies mean. They were not placed there by Odoxon, but by I Am when Laura healed them.

"It is of the utmost importance that we find the grimoire and black diamond. You have all witnessed what Odoxon can accomplish now that the book and the gem are in his possession. After the completion of the forever young spell, Odoxon's powers have grown beyond comprehension. However, he cannot best the gods and goddesses. Jonathan, Cidus, and Iridia, you must work hard to learn to use your gifts so you can assist the team in defeating Zohmes and Odoxon.

"As for the world Odoxon created, we need to step in and undo the evil he has wrought there. The planet cannot be destroyed. The people on it are as real as you and I, but they have no laws. Evil reigns supreme. Poverty is severe, and living conditions are not even good enough for animals. Like Ierilia, centuries ago, we must take our army and wipe out all that stand with Odoxon. The gods and goddesses will help us make the planet hospitable.

"Before we can do that, I Am needs to ensure that Odoxon is back on Ierilia and then the god will temporarily seal the portal. The sorcerer must never go back to Odoxus. I Am has promised to help us with that. The portal will be relocated and hidden well from the sorcerer ever locating it and entering it again. We must go back to retrieve the grimoire and the diamond. There is no time to waste. While Odoxon still has possible access to the portal, and therefore the grimoire and the gem, he can devise unmentionable spells and cause much damage to Ierilia and all of us." She sank down on her chair and heaved a sigh.

"To go back there, we need at least a flyer. I wonder if we could get one through the portal," Brenn said.

Iridia spoke, her voice shrill. "I do not believe this. It is bad enough being Jatron's child, but now that is not true? I am Zohmes' biological daughter and sister to Jonathan and Cidus? I have no wish to be a demi-goddess or to have powers. I just want to live an ordinary life, to join with the man I love and have his children."

"And I am the product of that old kurakelda?" Evior asked, shaking his head in disbelief.

"And so you shall, Iridia. And yes, you are, Evior. It is written in the book of knowledge that you and Evior will join. But the book of knowledge has also shown me other plans for you two, of which I cannot speak yet. You must accept that you are a demi-goddess and Evior a sorcerer. You must be infused with your natural powers," Astiana said patiently. "I realize this is a shock for you both, and for Tabeka, but it has all been written."

"Sometimes the book of knowledge changes what has been written," Tabeka said.

"Very seldom. Do not worry yourself of what is to come."

"Why has Zohmes' not taken Odoxus for himself?" Cylena inquired.

"If Zohmes wished to rule a replica of Ierilia, he would have created his own. I think perhaps it amuses him to allow the sorcerer to keep Odoxus and torture the inhabitants." Biryn motioned for Dunmore to refill his glass of wine.

Cylena scrunched her face. "Why would Odoxon even create such a place?"

"Because the bastard is obsessed with Liana. If the real woman would not have him, he thought to duplicate one that would," Jonathan growled.

"You are not far from the truth, Jonathan. He created Odoxus and a duplicate Liana because the real Liana had rejected him. I assume he replicated Jonathan, Taylith, and Ciara to try to control the Liana of that world, though he does not have the power to reproduce their dragons or the lions for that matter. There is no magick on that planet save his own. The people there are truly powerless against him," Astiana stated.

Cidus cringed. The idea was enough to unsettle his stomach. He wiped his mouth with a napkin, then set it on the table. "What about all the rest of the doppelgangers on that planet? Does everyone on Ierilia have a double there?"

"From what Rania has told me, Odoxon only created duplicates of those that reside in this realm. After his original creation of the planet, if an infant was born, or new people arrived in our realm to settle, they have duplicated automatically on Odoxus."

"So, the rest of the planet is wild? Uninhabited?" Ivran asked.

Astiana nodded. "Odoxon had no interest in duplicating all of Ierilia's inhabitants."

"Since we arrived in Cront first, before Initiation Genesis, were all the people from Earth auto-duplicated?" Erica placed her utensils on her plate.

"Yes. But you will find no double for Jatron because he is from a different realm. Or Tabeka, Cidus, Evior, and Iridia. If they settled here, they would automatically be duplicated. Unlike Sirona, Initiation Genesis was once part of the Crimson Realm until the king gifted the land to the people from Earth.

Odoxon's evil sorcery was in place well before Initiation Genesis became its own realm. And before you ask again, Zohmes had nothing to do with Odoxon's creation of Odoxus. The old man first constructed his *toy world* centuries ago, before he was banished to Wuit's Peak and Zohmes sent to Yanata. The two did not join forces until after Zohmes was released from Yanata, and he, in turn, released Odoxon from Wuits Peak." Astiana toyed with her wine glass, a troubled expression on her face.

Cidus did not fault her for her worry. The whole team looked disturbed. It seemed as if they lost twice as much as they had gained in the war against Zohmes and Odoxon. Each revelation bringing more trials, more quests and trouble.

He brushed his hand through his hair wearily and peered at Tabeka. The joy that had surrounded her before the meeting had dissipated. He clasped her hand and gently squeezed her fingers.

"I think this has been enough for today. We are all tired and need to rest. I am sure you all want to go home. We will discuss our strategy for recovering the grimoire and black diamond tomorrow." Biryn pushed his chair back and held his hand out to the queen.

Cidus was glad the meeting was over, and they could leave for Brenn's estate. The trials of the past few days had taken its toll on the whole team, and he, for one, was ready to relax with Tabeka in his arms. Now that Wildevein Manor was back in his possession, he wanted nothing more than to return to his home and begin a new life with Tabeka. Surely the team did not need him on the next mission?

CHAPTER SIXTEEN

After a more than welcome bath, Cidus lay in bed with Tabeka safely cuddled in his arms.

She toyed with a strand of his blond hair. "Do you think Evior and Iridia will be all right?"

He sighed and kissed her temple. "They have a lot to think about and absorb. At least the memory of the pain they endured was wiped from their minds. They have each other to lean on, my heart. Do not worry yourself."

She shifted to gaze up at him, her eyes filled with anguish. "I cannot help it. What are the symbols on their bodies that Astiana mentioned? Why would I Am put them there? What do they mean?"

"I do not know. They are hieroglyphics and appeared after Laura healed their wounds."

"Wounds? Were they badly hurt, Cidus? The vision I was given showed them covered in blood."

He did not think it wise to describe what Odoxon had done to them. "Laura healed them. They are fine now."

"Cidus, Astiana said the team must make haste to find the grimoire and gem, that they have to go back to that place. That does not include you, does it?"

"I do not know. I hope not. All I want is to take you to Wildevein Manor, join with you, and begin our life there. If the king orders me to go with his team, I cannot refuse."

Tabeka sighed. "I love you so much. Since we have reunited, there has been one upheaval after another.".

Cidus pulled her closer and silenced her with a deep kiss.

He drew away and whispered against her lips, "Enough talk for tonight. All I want to do now is love you."

"Then make love to me, Cidus." She slid her arms around his neck, then nipped his lip playfully.

Cidus groaned. That little bite sent a sharp pulse of need straight to his aching cock, scalding his blood and inciting a craving so great only Tabeka could slake. He shifted her to straddle his hips and pulled her head down, seeking her lips. He kissed her hard, possessing her mouth, his lips blazing a trail down her neck, to her chest. She gasped, arching into his mouth for him to taunt her nipples with his teeth and tongue.

Gods, the taste of her skin was intoxicating, like chairi wine, and he was more than willing to drink his fill. And he did. Each touch, each taste, fueled his need and set his soul on fire. He skimmed his fingers down her back and grasped her hips, nudging her to straddle his shoulders.

"Place your hands on the headboard, my love."

Cidus gazed at the paradise that awaited him. Her thighs parted invitingly, the nub of her clit peeking from soft red hair covering her mound. He slid his finger along the slick wetness of her core, pushing one, then another into her velvety softness. Her cries of pleasure filled his ears when he took her clit between his teeth and tormented the bundle of nerves with his tongue.

"Gods, please, Cidus. I need you..." Tabeka released the headboard and scooted swiftly down his body.

He sucked in a breath. The raw hunger in her gaze made his skin prickle. Her touch seared his skin when her hands trailed down his chest, her nails scraping along his abdomen.

She grasped his cock, guiding it to her slick opening and with one twist of her hips she impaled herself on his erection. She rode him hard. Cidus gripped her hips, meeting each thrust, allowing her to claim him. Because he *was* hers, body and soul, and he reveled in the splendor of it.

He could not take his eyes off her. Gods she was beautiful. Her head was thrown back, her body writhing in abandon. He reached out and rolled her clit between his thumb and forefinger. A low, keening cry escaped her lips, and her muscles clamped tight around his cock. Lights danced before his eyes as his orgasm ripped through him, spiraling them both over the edge into bliss. Tabeka collapsed against his chest. He wrapped his arms around her and held her until his heart stopped pounding and their breathing evened out.

She shifted to lay down beside him, her head resting on his shoulder. "Do you think we will ever be free of Zohmes and Odoxon?"

Cidus twined a strand of her hair around his finger. "I do not know, my love."

Zohmes had centuries to cultivate his plans. And those plans included taking over Ierilia realm by realm, either by corrupting the lords or by impregnating their mates. How many other realms had he infiltrated? How many other children had he fathered? He chased the thought from his mind and focused on the woman nestled in his arms.

"Sleep now, love. The meeting at the palace will come early."

Cidus sat beside Tabeka at the king's dining table. After a hearty breakfast, Biryn was ready to begin their discussion.

Tabeka had chosen to come with him, instead of staying with Iridia and Evior at Brenn's estate. Ciara had agreed that it would be better for the young couple to rest a few days. Cidus hoped that time would help Iridia and Evior accept who they truly were.

"I do not think the whole team is needed to retrieve the grimoire and black diamond." Biryn toyed with the mug set before him on the table. "Zohmes has no interest in Odoxus. It would be foolish of me to leave Ierilia, or my people, without protection."

Brenn nodded. "I agree. This could be just the opening Zohmes is waiting for to act on his plans."

Astiana set her fork on her plate and studied the group. "I agree with Biryn. Rania spoke to me last night. The team is to split into groups. On this mission, Cidus, Ciara, Taylith, Liana, Brenn, Icaras, and Jonathan are to retrieve the grimoire and gem."

"So, what, the rest of us sit here and twiddle our thumbs while they put their lives in danger?" Laura shook her head. "No! I am going with them! What if they need my help?"

"Sweetness, we will be fine. Ciara will be with us if we have need of healing," Taylith tried to soothe her.

Cidus could see the worry in Laura's eyes and again could not help feeling that a silent conversation was taking place between her and the dragons. Suddenly Laura's eyes widened, and her hand flew to her mouth.

"I'm… I'm…pregnant?"

"You are sure, Ciara?" Taylith slid his arm around his mate's shoulders, a look of wonder crossing his features.

Ciara nodded. "Rania has confirmed it. Laura carries the first baby our people have been blessed with after centuries of captivity."

"Holy shit! That fast? I bet you it's all because of that Temple of Fertility," Laura muttered. "You watch everyone else get pregnant now, too! Especially Julia, since she and Bernie got married in that place!"

Excited murmurs filled the room and congratulations were given to the shocked couple. Years ago, Cidus had felt the same shock, then immense joy when Tabeka had told him she was carrying his child. It pained him to know that because of Jatron, Tabeka had lost that infant. He gazed at the woman he loved. Would the gods choose to bless them a second time?

Once the commotion settled, Biryn tapped his fingers on

the table, drawing everyone's attention. "That settles it. Laura cannot go on the mission to Odoxus or any future quests, should there be any. She will stay here at the palace while you are away, Taylith. We will ensure her safety."

"But—" Laura began to protest.

"Biryn is right, sweetness. It would be safer for you to stay here. Or if you would like, you can visit my parents at Storming Enclave," Taylith suggested.

Cidus chuckled as Laura screwed up her face. "Oh, no, no. I will stay right here. I love your parents, but when they find out that I am carrying their grandchild, there will be no escape from that floating island!"

Liana grinned. "She has a point. No dragon will want to let her out of their sight."

"And that is why Tura will be guarding her." Taylith glanced at Biryn. "With the king's permission."

"Of course," Biryn agreed. "Now that we have established Laura's safety let us continue. Astiana?"

"Rania told me that the grimoire and black diamond are on Odoxus. Odoxon has hidden them within the lake that surrounds the floating island where his castle is located. Beneath the depths, under the island, you will find a large egg-shaped container. The book and gem are within that capsule. But first, we need to go to the Clyss and speak with I Am. The portal must be moved to its new location before the extraction team can go after the grimoire and black diamond."

"What about the people on Odoxus? We should go back fast. We promised my double that we would ask Rania if we could assist them. We can't just leave them in that hellhole waiting for help from us, to starve and be treated like animals," Erica reminded them. "The animals here are treated better than the people are on Odoxus. I wonder how their animals are treated. If they even have any."

"Astiana has already told us that the gods and goddesses

will assist them. Rania said that we should give suitable weapons to the small group we encountered in Odoxon's castle. We can take supplies for them, like decent food, medicine, clothing, bedding, and other necessities. When we arrive, we need to meet with the other Erica to discuss future assistance and find out how many followers they have that long for a better life. Before we can do that, though, we need to be assured that Odoxon is not on that planet and that he can no longer enter the portal. As I said earlier, our first journey is to the Clyss."

Biryn agreed. "While you are gone, we will ready emergency supplies, and when we have the location, we will transport it all to where I Am places the portal. Dunmore is already busy sniffing out the spy in the palace who supplied Odoxon with the queen's milk. We have much to deal with."

After Cidus had heard his name as part of the extraction team, his heart sank. He had so hoped to take Tabeka back to Wildevein, but it was not yet to be. Now that he was a demi-god, would he be a member of the team forever? How could he rule his realm and go on missions?

Tabeka's hand rested on his leg. He felt her disappointment radiate through him. But he had to obey the king. "How many of us need to go to the Clyss?" he asked.

"The ones that were chosen," Astiana told them. "We will return to the palace after I Am has instructed us how to proceed. The flyer and cargo transport will be ready and waiting for the seven that were picked for this mission."

CHAPTER SEVENTEEN

During their flight to the Clyss, Cidus wondered how they would transport the supplies through the portal and on the other side.

Ciara answered his unspoken thoughts. "You will be with three dragons. One of us can carry more than any cargo ship can hold. As for moving the supplies through the portal? We will use carts."

Cidus found the mind reading very disconcerting. "Do all of you have the ability to hear another's thoughts?"

"No, we do not. Only a true god or goddess can pluck a person's thoughts from their mind."

"If that is the case, then how did you know what I was thinking?"

"Because you broadcast your thoughts when you are agitated or worried." Ciara gave him a patient smile.

It makes them very easy for Liana, Taylith, and I, to hear them.

"So, you can speak to each other with your minds?"

Ciara nodded. *As can you. With time, you will learn how to shield your thoughts from us.*

Cidus hoped that time would come soon. He would hate for the wrong person to pick apart his thoughts.

The beauty of the Clyss would never cease to amaze Cidus. The air around them was heavy with the fragrance of the blooming trees and shrubbery. Birds twittered and sang their songs, and bright colored saloras danced around the group.

"Please join hands and stand in a circle? Ciara and I will call upon I Am," Astiana called out.

Cidus stopped drinking in the scenery and joined the circle. Tabeka had stayed behind. She was not a member of the team. He sighed. Since his presence was requested, it meant that Biryn now regarded him as one of them.

Roiling clouds obscured the sun. A fierce wind set up, blowing his hair around his face. Cidus wanted to reach up to wipe the hair from his eyes, but he could not. Jonathan on one side, Ciara on the other, held onto his hands tightly.

Lightning pierced the clouds, and a face and body became visible. The god's long snow-white hair whipped around him in the wind, his white robes billowing. When he spoke, his voice boomed around them and echoed through Clyss Valley.

"My daughter Rania has summoned me. She has informed me of your trials and tribulations and has requested my assistance. We know of this world Odoxon created many centuries ago. It is as dark as the sorcerer's soul and reflects the evil that emanates from him.

"It was written in the book of knowledge that the portal and planet would not be discovered until now. The book has mapped out the path for each of you. I am disappointed that the demi-goddess, Iridia, and her chosen mate, is not with you. You must bring them here soon so that we may grant them the powers that are rightfully theirs.

"Cidus and Jonathan, you are both the better part of Zohmes, and therefore close to my heart. It is written, together as brothers united, and with the help of your team and your sister, will in the future banish Zohmes and Odoxon forever. But the book does not tell us when.

169

"I will relocate the entrance to Odoxus, that we will rename Giethoren, and I will lock the gateway so Odoxon can never enter it again. Only you, my trusted ones, my children, and the others of Biryn's team, can know the location and will be able to enter the gateway.

"In what was once the Dreaded Peaks, now restored to the Astanica Mountains, there is a hidden sanctuary protected by the gods. Cidus knows of it. He visited it often in his youth. Unbeknown to him, he was the only one who could see it. It is only visible to gods and goddesses, and a few chosen. Behind the waterfall is a secret doorway. The key to it is located within the statue of Astiana. Touch and turn the crystal jewel held within the statue's hand, and a secret compartment will open.

"Beyond the doorway behind the falls is a tunnel. Follow it. At the end of the tunnel is a cavern that has two passageways leading from it. There are inscriptions upon the walls. Cidus will know the correct passage to take. When you reach the cavern where I placed the portal, press the jewel in the center of the crossed swords and the door to the hidden cavern will open.

"This secret must remain with you forever and cannot be revealed to anyone, not even your loved ones. It is imperative you find the grimoire and black gem or Zohmes and Odoxon will triumph. I will watch over you.

"Between you, Cidus and Jonathan, you can banish the darkness from the planet. You must call on your deeply hidden powers. After you recover the grimoire and the gem, you will find the spell within the grimoire that will enable and assist you to do so. The planet will become one of beauty and will thrive. I have spoken. This is my will, and so it shall be."

The god faded, the wind ceased, and the clouds dissipated. Cidus tried to wrap his mind around all he had heard. He and Jonathan were the ones to finally triumph over Zohmes and

Odoxon with their sister and the team's assistance? The book apparently knew the complete future. Why could it just not map out the final battle for them now? Tell them when that final conquest would be? Why put them through these missions? It was all too difficult to comprehend, but who was he to question the highest of all.

It did not take them long to return to the palace. A flyer had already been loaded with the supplies and equipment they would need to complete their mission. He smiled when he caught sight of Tabeka waiting for him in the courtyard. She hurried to him, hugging him tightly.

"You will return to me, Cidus. I could not bear it if I lost you again," she whispered in his ear.

He held her in his arms for a few moments, then gently caressed her cheek. "All will be well, my love."

She stepped back and wiped the tears that glistened on her cheeks. "You had better go. The others are waiting."

"He kissed her quickly, then joined the much smaller team at the flyer. Laura stood beside Taylith, along with another woman he assumed had to be Tura, Laura's new guard — she had tiny scales on her face, like Ciara, Taylith, and Liana.

"Do not worry, Taylith. Your mate will be safe. I will allow no harm to come to her." The dragon lifted her chin proudly.

"I'm right here you know. I can take care of myself," Laura sounded exasperated.

Liana patted Laura's shoulder. "Of course, you can. But Tura is a big bad dragon, and you are a puny little human. We don't want you to get broken."

Laura shook her head and chuckled. "You are lucky I put up with the lot of you."

"Yes, we are." Taylith leaned down and kissed her. "We will return as soon as we can."

Cidus watched as Laura and Tura joined Tabeka on the castle steps. He hated having to leave Tabeka again. It left his soul empty and his heart aching. He imagined Taylith felt much the same. Probably worse, as the mate he was leaving behind was now with child.

"Load up. The sooner we find the grimoire and diamond the better." Brenn opened the flyer door and motioned for them to enter.

After they landed at what used to be Dreaded Peaks, Brenn requested that Cidus lead them to the sanctuary.

"I am not a god. You will need to show us where it is," Brenn said.

Cidus had to look for a few moments to find the crevice that led to his secret place. Everything was so changed now that the mountains were restored to their former beauty, but it became obvious the gods or goddesses were helping him. A bright light surrounded a crevice between two mountains. He quickly headed for it, followed by the team.

His small sanctuary had not changed. Cidus stood looking at where he had spent so many hours with Tabeka. The oasis was still as verdant, alive with birds and flowers, the waterfall cascading into the crystal-clear pool. The familiar statue of the goddess, which he now knew to be Astiana, stood overseeing everything.

"We are here," he said.

"Cidus, you need to find the key," Ciara prodded him.

He nodded and waded through the water, then swam to approach the statue. He climbed onto her feet. Clinging with his legs to a leg of the statue, he reached up to the hand that was held out. He felt the jewel within the palm. When he touched and turned it, a small compartment opened beneath the statue's armpit. He stuck his hand inside it and a key appeared beneath his fingers. Grasping it, he let go of the statue's leg and plunged back down into the pool.

Spluttering, he surfaced and held up the key. "I have it!"

Cidus swam to the shore clutching the key in his hand.

After he clambered onto the silky sand, he handed the key to Ciara.

"Now we need to go behind the falls. That means swimming." Ciara dropped her backpack on one of the supply carts.

Cidus looked at the carts bearing the supplies. "How will we transport the supplies to the portal? The carts will sink to the bottom of the pool."

Icaras had removed his pack and placed it with Ciara's. "Do not to worry about the simple things. Once we reach the cavern that houses the new portal, I will transport the equipment to us. Make sure everything is in one pile close together."

One by one the team entered the water and swam to the waterfall. Cidus entered the water last, and when he reached the edge of the rocks near the base of the falls, the water was still very deep. He grabbed the rock and pulled himself onto the ledge with the others.

The pool and waterfall were much larger than they had appeared to be upon entering the sanctuary. It reminded Cidus of the Clyss in a way, but the water did not seem to have the same magickal properties.

He followed the others behind the curtain of water cascading into the pool. Before them, carved into the stone wall was the doorway. Strange symbols and hieroglyphics had been etched into the rock much like the doors in the temple in Henderson. The door itself appeared to be cast from gold. In its center, forming a circle around the hexagonal keyhole, were the sculpted images of a dragon and a lion, their eyes made from sparkling crystals. Cidus watched as Ciara inserted the key into the keyhole. The eyes of the lion and dragon as well as the symbols surrounding the door began to glow brightly. When Ciara removed the key, the door shifted, then slid completely open.

Cidus peered inside the entryway, but the tunnel was so dark it was hard to see a foot in front of him. He wondered if the door had always been there. He and Tabeka swam in the pool so many years ago, and before he had met her, this place had been his private sanctuary. He had often taken a cooling dip but had never thought to explore behind the waterfall, assuming there was just sheer rock behind it.

"I'll take the lead." Brenn pulled a glimmer stick from his belt and handed it to Cidus, then stepped into the passage. One by one they followed Brenn into the dark passageway. The tunnel was large enough for them to walk in pairs. Jonathan walked beside him, and Taylith and Liana had taken the rear. The glimmer stick he held dispelled enough of the darkness that he could see the rock walls of the tunnel. Like the doorway, they too were etched with symbols. Cidus wondered what they could possibly mean. He had never seen this type of writing before entering the Temple of Fertility for Julia and Bernie's joining ceremony.

"What do the symbols mean?" he wondered aloud.

"Your guess is as good as mine. Astiana told us when we found the temple that it was the language of the gods," Jonathan answered.

"The language is older than Ierilia itself. Even the dragons do not know what the symbols mean," Liana said from behind him.

"I am not so sure that our parents, or Ciara's, do not understand their meaning," Taylith commented.

"Fork up ahead!" Brenn called out.

They stopped when they reached the fork in the tunnel. Cidus took a deep breath. How were they to know which tunnel led to the hidden cavern?

"You have got to be bloody kidding me!" Jonathan leaned against the passage wall.

Cidus brushed his hand through his hair. "Any ideas

which passage we need to take?"

"The hieroglyphics probably gives us the directions," Icaras suggested.

"What good does that do? None of us can read them." Cidus touched one of the symbols. It began to emit a soft glow.

Jonathan pushed himself away from the wall and touched several of the symbols. They illuminated as well.

"You are both demi-gods. The symbols are reacting to you like the ones in the temple did to Astiana. Quick, try the symbols above the passageways," Ciara said.

Cidus and Jonathan began touching the inscriptions, one after the other. Their hands moved swiftly. Only some of the symbols surrounding the one passageway illuminated. They moved to the second one. Each glyph lit up brightly, surrounding the entry in an eerie glow. "This has to be it," Cidus said. "I wonder to where the other tunnel leads."

"I suspect that will be made clear in the future. For now, you have shown us the correct tunnel that leads to the hidden cavern where we will find the portal," Ciara said.

Brenn took the lead again. Holding their glimmer sticks up high, they followed him. The tunnel was not that long. When they faced a door with the crossed swords in the center, Ciara pressed where the swords met, and the door opened, revealing a large cavern.

Cidus gasped at its beauty. Stalagmites stood scattered on the cavern floor, and stalactites resembling huge icicles hung from the ceiling. They emitted a colorful rainbow gleam, lighting the cavern enough that they did not need their glimmer sticks.

"And there it is." Cidus walked to the far wall of the cavern. The portal's plasma and its swirling mauve and white and red colors matched the beauty of the cavern.

Icaras stepped to the side. "I will transport the supplies

now."

Within seconds, the huge pile of containers, equipment, and their backpacks appeared near the portal's entrance.

"Jonathan, Taylith, come with me. We will need to be on the other side to make sure the supplies are safe," Brenn said while slinging his backpack over his shoulder. He stepped into the portal, and it swallowed him instantly. At least, Cidus decided, that is what it looked like when watching—getting swallowed by a gigantic mouth.

Using his magick, Icaras began directing the heavily loaded carts into the portal. Cidus wondered if the carts would tumble around as he had previously. He hoped the goods packed on them were secured tight enough.

He stepped through the plasma field, not relishing the thought of getting shook again, but this time he managed to steady himself and remained upright. He landed on his feet on the other side and noticed the carts had survived intact. Icaras was the last to exit from the portal.

Cidus took a long drink from his waterskin. "Where to first?" he asked, looking at Brenn.

"We need to find the other Erica first. She probably lives in the same area as where her estate is located on Ierilia. Take a moment to refresh, have a snack, then Ciara, Taylith, and Liana will take us there."

"Yes. We will fly high above the clouds so people on the ground cannot see us," Liana said.

CHAPTER EIGHTEEN

Brenn's prediction was correct. Laro and Erica lived in the same location, except it was a much more impoverished version of their estate.

The dragons landed in a clearing in a nearby forest.

"What if the other Erica is not here? She could be out on a mission for Odoxon or in his castle," Cidus said.

"I Am said Odoxon is not on this planet, and now that I Am has control of the portal, the sorcerer can no longer get here," Ciara reminded him. "Before we landed, I saw some cottages. If one can call them that. They are hovels, not even good enough to shelter animals."

"Let us move on. We will see if we can find the other Erica." Brenn hoisted his backpack over his shoulder. "Icaras, can you hide the carts and supplies for now? Let us go find our doubles."

They entered the dark forest on the lookout for any predators. But all was quiet. After exiting the darkness of the trees, they crossed an open veld and approached the shabby shelters. Some children played near what looked to be a well. Cidus stopped and turned the handle. A bucket came up, filled with foul smelling water. "This is what they have to drink?" He held it sideways for the others to see.

"That is fucking unbelievable," Jonathan exclaimed. "I wouldn't give that to the pigs."

"Pigs?" Cidus asked.

"Oh, an Earth animal my mother taught me about. Sorry, my mother included much about Earth, its population, animals, and its language for my education."

Cidus smiled. "Yes, your speech reminds me of Laura, Julia, and Erica."

Brenn halted one of the children running by him. "Boy, can you tell me where Laro and Erica live?"

The boy looked at him curiously. "Over there. You should know. You come here all the time." The boy pointed, then ran off to follow his friends.

Brenn grimaced. "Over there. I guess Erica, Laro, and I are friends here, too."

They headed for the hovel the boy had pointed out. Brenn pounded on the door. And again. After a few minutes, it opened, and a sleepy-headed Laro peeked around the corner. "Brenn, we were not expecting you."

"I need to speak to Erica. Is she here?"

"She is sleeping."

"Go and wake her."

"Not sure if I should do—"

"Laro, what the fuck is going on?" Erica appeared, a blanket draped around her body.

"You? You came back..."

"Yes. We promised we would. Can we come in?" Brenn stepped back.

"Give us a minute, okay? Laro, put some water on for tea."

They waited impatiently, all the time garnishing attention from other people and the children. Finally, the door opened again.

"I'm so sorry. We had a hellishly long meeting last night with our co-conspirators. Laro, these are the people I told you about. Our doubles from another planet." Erica placed eroded mugs on a rickety table in front of them all.

The chairs they sat on were unstable. Cidus thought for sure his would fall apart any second.

"Erica, after seeing the water in your well, we cannot drink this tea," Ciara gently said.

Erica pulled a face. "Oh, don't worry. This is made with filtered water. We don't use the water from the well."

Cidus did not touch the tea. Even with Erica's promise that the water was filtered, he did not trust it.

"Erica, what is your role on this planet, and Laro's, besides serving Odoxon?" Brenn asked.

Erica tapped her fingers on the table. "Before I answer your questions, I have a few of my own." She glanced at the dragons. "Ciara, Liana, and Taylith are your doubles, but unlike them, you have scales on your faces and shifted into dragons. Why should we trust you?" She turned her attention to Brenn, Icaras, Jonathan, and Cidus. "Any of you... For all we know, you could be just like that old bastard."

Cidus would have wondered the same thing. They had shown up in their world, doubles in almost every way, yet the Ierilians appeared to want for nothing. At home, they had resources well beyond this world's capabilities, and they had magick.

"For you to understand, then you must know how and why this world was created." Liana shifted in her chair and placed her hands on the table. "Centuries ago, when Odoxon was a young man, he wished for the two of us to be joined. I refused his suit. I did not then, nor do I wish now, to ever be joined with that monster."

"What does that have to do with him creating this pigsty?" Erica's hand flew to her mouth. "Oh wait! That fucking twisted bastard! He went after our Liana the first time we saw him. He captured her and kept her chained in the castle. We could do nothing to help her. The whole time he had her imprisoned he tried to foster hate between Liana, Taylith, and Ciara."

Liana nodded. "He created this world and my duplicate after he cursed me to remain a miniature dragon and bound me to a forest for centuries. This world and my double were his answer to my refusal of him."

Erica raised her eyebrows. "Centuries ago? How old are you exactly? I presume when he first came after you, he was young? Looking at him now, he's just a weathered wizard."

"Odoxon got his hands on a very dangerous book and a stone. He abducted two young people from Ierilia and kept them imprisoned here, as you were told before. I will not go into detail what horrors he inflicted upon them. It is sufficient to say he needed parts of their anatomy to make a potion. Using a spell from that book together with the stone, he drank the potion, and now he is once again a young man. There is no spell to counteract it. We now deal with an even more dangerous sorcerer. His powers have increased a thousandfold with the return of his youth. And with it all, his pursuit of our Liana will not cease."

"So, what you are saying is that Odoxon is your enemy on Ierilia, but you actually have a means of defense against him. Like turning into dragons."

"We have more than just the ability to shift. We have the magick to fight Odoxon, and our gods and goddesses are on our side," Icaras stated. "There is much more, but we are here on a mission. We can tell you everything else during future visits and delivery of supplies."

Brenn crossed his arms over his chest. "Now that we have answered some of your questions and before we can assist you, we need you to answer our questions."

"That is reasonable." Erica let out a deep breath. "Before the old man appeared to us, we tried to do what we could to help the people here. But it is of little use. This place is rotten, much like Earth was when I left it. Actually worse. On Earth, we didn't have the monsters that live here."

"So, you do know about Earth. Do you know how many of your people are here?" Brenn continued questioning.

"There are over two hundred of us from Earth. The last thing I remember before waking up in this hellhole was going into stasis. Though we must have crashed, there was no ship here, no wreckage. Strangely, the other crews just seemed to appear in Zenthia out of thin air, like they were transported."

"So, Odoxon renamed Cront. Zenthia? How many are unhappy here? And I do not just mean the people from Earth, but also others, the ones that were already here before you crashed, like Biryn and the rest of your team," Brenn pressed on.

"Biryn was the most optimistic of all of us." Laro shook his head, a pained look crossing his features. "He has become nothing but a drunk since Odoxon's return. We tried to create a life for ourselves when the sorcerer disappeared for a while. We attempted to make this place more habitable, but each effort failed. It is as if we are cursed. Within days, crops wither, animals sicken and die, the water becomes foul, yet we continue living.

"It breaks my heart to even think of Biryn in such a condition. And poor Cylena. She has the twins to worry about and a husband that doesn't seem to have a care in the world except where to find his next drink." Erica brushed her fingers through her hair and sighed. "Nearly all of us from Earth are unhappy, except for a few. Barry has managed to turn a small group of my people against us. They are in league with Odoxon. The people that were already here, most of them kind of accepted their lot. It is all they have known. We've had a secret group for a while now. We want to change things, but we've got no idea how. The sorcerer is powerful. How the

181

fuck does one fight one of those beings?"

Cidus understood why a man could be driven to drink. The gods knew, living in squalor the way these people were forced to would change even the best of men. If not for Tabeka, and the help of Biryn and his team, Cidus knew he could have become the same. Even now his imprisonment haunted him. It was only in the arms of the woman who owned his soul that he had found peace.

"Biryn did not drink before?" he asked.

Laro's jaw clenched. "It was like Biryn changed overnight. At one time he cared what happened to the people of Odoxus. Now he cares only for himself. Even Cylena cannot get through to him."

Taylith glanced at Ciara and Liana. "Do you think it is possible that Odoxon has bespelled their Biryn?"

"I wouldn't put it past the kurakelda," Liana said, contempt in her voice. "He created Odoxus did he not? The people here are mere toys he uses to amuse himself. Who is to say he does not torture them because *we* have angered him. As for Biryn, maybe he placed a spell on him at Zohmes' request. We can undo such a spell."

"In other words, he is using us as scapegoats whenever he gets angry with your team or if his buddy wants him to," Erica said.

"And we tend to piss off the bloody bastards quite often," Jonathan added.

Erica shook her head and gazed at Jonathan. "Actually, all he has to do is see our Jonathan, and it sets him off into a rage. He has a vendetta against you."

"What if we were to tell you that Odoxon no longer rules this planet?" Ciara said.

"I find that hard to believe. Where is my alter-ego? I would have liked to have heard that from her."

"The gods decided that only a few of us would lead this

expedition. Jonathan is Julia's son. You know Julia, right?" Ciara prodded.

"Yes, of course I do. How the fuck is that possible? She wasn't pregnant when we left Earth. If she had a baby since we crashed, that's all it would be, an infant, and Jonathan is a young man. No one grows up *that* fast. Unless there is sorcery involved?"

"That is another whole story. Jonathan, prove to her you are Julia's son." Ciara told Jonathan.

Cidus' head was spinning. How were they going to convince duplicate Erica that this was all for real? How could Jonathan prove he was Julia's son? Jonathan with his blazing red hair and looking so much like Zohmes.

"Erica, we have brought supplies. I can have them here in seconds," Icaras interjected, and thankfully diverted Erica's attention away from Jonathan.

"For how many? Do you realize there are thousands of hungry and suffering people out there? How can we help them all? Your supplies will only help so many. You've got no idea how frustrated I am, how devastated that I can't help the poor and starving."

Cidus saw the anguish on her face and felt it in his soul. He and Jonathan were going to be able to change the planet, but how? Neither of them had conquered their powers.

"We brought all we could at this time. We can bring more. And next time, we can see if we can convince Erica to come with us if that is what will prove our true intentions." Ciara heaved a sigh.

Cidus watched Erica's face. She seemed hesitant.

"Let me see what you brought us."

Icaras stepped out of the hovel. Seconds later, he came back in. "Everything is outside your door, Erica."

Erica rushed to her door and outside. "Oh my God! Really?"

Cidus had stood and followed the others. They watched as Erica opened one container after another.

"Strawberries? Oh my God! Fuck! How the flaming hell am I going to distribute all this shit? Real potatoes? Clothes? Fresh bread? Blankets? Holy Mother of God! This is like finding a pot of gold at the end of a rainbow."

Cidus had to laugh at her Earth language though many words were still puzzling. They had brought four carts bursting with supplies — as much as they could fit within the storage bays of the flyer. But Cidus knew it would not be near enough to provide for all the inhabitants of Odoxus. I Am had said that only the people from Cront and their realm had been duplicated. The inhabitants still had to number ten-thousand at least.

Brenn pulled the lid off one of the containers. "You can start with the people living in your immediate surroundings. There are also weapons. We have dealt with several of the creatures that live on this planet. The crude swords you are forced to carry will not harm them." He handed one of the proton phasers to Erica and then one to Laro, and a new sword for each. "These will at least give you a fighting chance until we are able to assist you further. There are more here for the ones that stand with you."

Erica and Laro examined their new weapons. Cidus could see by the way Erica manipulated the phaser that she had handled something like it before.

"These are very similar to our laser rifles on Earth, but they are a lot lighter. The controls look the same though, so they should be easy for us to use. Thank you." She sat the gun back in the crate to examine the contents of another box.

Cidus watched Erica hold up a dress and feel the material. Looking at what she and Laro were wearing, he could imagine her wonder. Their clothing was made of roughly woven material. It was frayed and almost hung like sacks on their bodies.

Laro stepped up to stand beside Erica. Cidus saw that his eyes were suspiciously moist. "We can believe them, Erica," he said softly, but loud enough for the team to hear.

"I wish we could go back to your Ierilia with you," Erica said wistfully, a tremor in her voice.

Ciara walked up to her and embraced her. "We love our Erica, and you are like her twin. From now on, consider us your family." She stepped back, but still held Erica's shoulders. "We cannot transport the duplicates back to Ierilia. We promise we will visit often, especially in the beginning because we need to bring more supplies. We can also promise you will have a much better life after Cidus and Jonathan have communicated with the gods on how to make this planet habitable. This will happen before we leave. I Am, the god of all gods and goddesses throughout the universe, has renamed this planet. From now on it is called Giethoren and will belong to King Biryn. I Am will instruct us who is to be the designated ruler here in the future."

"It all sounds too fantastic to be true. I thought at first this was all a stasis induced nightmare. Now I'm really beginning to believe it's all a dream." Erica popped a strawberry into her mouth. "But this tastes very real. How is it you have Earth fruit on an alien planet?"

Cidus laughed. "That is yet another story for later. We must leave. Time is of the essence."

Erica gazed at each of the team, then looked directly at Brenn. "You seem to be in charge. Laro and I are going with you on your mission to find the book and the stone."

Brenn began to speak, but Ciara interrupted him. "Rania told me they need to go with us."

"For what reason? Why would we put them in the path of danger? Odoxon is not here, but the monsters he created are."

Cidus heard the voice in his head as clearly as if the words were spoken aloud.

Because you need Erica and Laro to believe, to trust you all completely. They are competent fighters and will assist you. It is written in the book of knowledge. Allow them to join the team on this mission.

He looked at the others and knew at least Ciara had heard it, too.

"Who is Rania?" Erica queried.

"She is a goddess and speaks to us in our minds. Many of the gods and goddesses speak to us," Icaras explained.

"Really. I suppose that's believable. It says in the Bible that people saw and spoke with angels. So…this goddess is on my side?"

Ciara nodded. "Yes. It is written in the book of knowledge that you will accompany us. That is if you are not afraid to fly on a dragon?"

Awe masked Erica's face. "Ride a dragon? Hell, I'll live the fairytale! Can we have a moment to change into these new clothes?"

CHAPTER NINETEEN

"**H**oly Fuck! Laro, pinch me? We are sitting on a dragon, right?" Erica shouted.

Cidus, sitting behind Laro, laughed heartily. "It is not a dream. The dragon is real, and so are we all."

"Which one is this?"

"We are on Liana. Ciara is the purple dragon and Taylith the blue dragon," Cidus answered.

"They are fucking unbelievingly gorgeous! I'm going to write a book about all this. Well, if only I had something to write on. My tablet, computer, everything vanished along with our ship."

"Next time we bring supplies, I will ask for a new tablet for you," Cidus said.

"Do you know where this book is?" Laro asked.

"Yes, it is hidden inside a large silver egg connected to a silver chain and is in the depths of the lake near that old castle where we first met your Erica."

The dragons soared through the air at a fast pace, and Erica's enthusiasm for the flight was infectious. Cidus found he was finally able to ignore the strange feeling in the pit of his stomach when the dragons dipped and turned.

It did not take them long to reach the black mass of clouds

that hung over the island. Though Odoxon was gone, the planet he had created was still threaded with the essence of the sorcerer's corrupt soul.

"This is Incredible!" Erica threw her hands up in the air, her long curly hair whipping in the breeze.

Cidus had a firm grip on Liana's scales. "You do realize that is a very long drop to the ground?"

Laro chuckled. "I will not let her fall."

Liana followed Ciara and Taylith beneath the dark cloud cover to fly above the trees of the forest. Even Erica's excitement did not help Cidus' disposition with the dragons flying so close to the branches. A wave of nausea hit him when Liana banked left hard then glided to the clearing and landed.

"Looking a little green in the gills there, Cidus," Erica stated after they slid from the dragon's back.

Jonathan patted him on the shoulder. "He'll get used to flying eventually."

Cidus gave Jonathan a sidelong look. "I do just fine in a flyer. At least you can strap yourself in."

"A flyer?" Laro questioned.

"It is a mode of transportation we use on Ierilia. It is enclosed and flies through the air at great speeds, though they do not travel as fast as a dragon," Brenn explained.

"You mean like a mini spaceship?" Erica scrunched up her face. "The only method we have to get anywhere is by using our own two feet. We don't even have animals, like horses, to ride."

Ciara smiled. "There is much we will be able to assist you with after we complete our mission."

"We will take the path we followed on our previous quest." Brenn pulled his fleet weapon. "Be on the lookout for any of the creatures we encountered."

Cidus slung his pack over his shoulder and turned to

follow Brenn, though he wondered why they did not just use magick to get to the lake. It would be quicker and much less of a chance of meeting one of the monsters they had fought the last time.

We do not want to frighten Erica by using our magick unless it is necessary. She barely trusts us as it is. Ciara's voice sounded in his mind.

"Brenn! No! Don't go that way!" Erica shouted and yanked Cidus back. "Odoxon's experiments run wild throughout that area." She motioned to a small path at the edge of the woods. "We use this path. It is protected from the creatures and will lead us directly to the lake and the small rowboat we use to get to the island."

"Noted. We will take your path, but I will take the lead," Brenn said.

They followed Brenn to the small opening in the treeline. The path was narrow, and Cidus could see that the bushes and branches had been roughly cut. They were probably hacked through using their crude swords. They now had the new ones strapped to their backs. Luckily the area seemed to be clear of the horrible smelling eyeball plants or the vicious fanged flower bulbs.

"How does Odoxon contact you when he wishes to send you on a mission?"

Erica gave a sarcastic laugh. "Most of the time he just pulls us through a weird vortex, and we land at his feet. Other times he sends a command in our minds, forcing us to obey. When he does that we have to walk to his godforsaken island." She shifted the straps of her pack. "After we hiked our way to the castle, it was usually vacant. We would have to wait for his return."

"That must have been the times he was on Ierilia wreaking havoc on us. How long did he hold the other Liana captive?"

"She was stuck in the castle for months at a time. She'd escape, but not this time. No matter what we did, we could not free her. I know she hated us for leaving her, but there was nothing we could do." She took a deep breath and let it out slowly. "When Odoxon discovered Jonathan, he became more depraved. You saw the condition he was in when you found them. He told me you guys had freed them."

When they had found Jonathan's double, the young man appeared to be hanging to life by a thread. His body was covered in blood, bone, and tissue exposed, skin and muscle flayed from his torso, arms, and legs. Cidus was thankful Ciara was able to heal the man.

"The sorcerer was already working on his potion. Your Liana and Jonathan did not have what he needed to complete it. That is when he abducted Evior and Iridia and subjected them both to unimaginable torture," Taylith told her.

"Are they okay now?" Erica asked.

"Yes. They are healed and recovering from their ordeal."

"He is one evil son-of-a-bitch."

"That he is," Jonathan agreed. "I told you before that Zohmes is a god. I did not mention that he is a fallen god. He and Odoxon have been in league for a long time."

"A fallen god? Like Lucifer from the Bible? Although he wasn't a god, he was called a fallen angel, but once upon a time sat on the right hand of our God." Erica raised her eyebrows and looked at Jonathan.

"Yes. Zohmes wants the throne and is obsessed with ruling Ierilia. Odoxon was imprisoned for many centuries, and Zohmes managed to release him. Together, they're formidable, and now that Odoxon's powers have multiplied, it will become worse."

"The old bastard is in cahoots with Satan? What in the hell can we expect?" Erica hacked at a branch.

"Zohmes has no interest in this planet. It is, or rather, was, Odoxon's *toy*, but he will never be able to come back here. I Am, the most powerful of gods, has locked the portal to him.

You don't need to worry." Ciara smiled reassuringly.

Cidus had listened to the conversation with interest. He knew most of the stories by now…or at least as much as the team would share. Though some tales were so horrific, they were best left to the victim to tell. How would this Erica react if she knew he and Jonathan were demi-gods, Zohmes' sons?

They had reached the end of the path and faced the row of bushes with eyes that flanked the lake. "Follow me," Erica said. "We cleared a path through those stinking things."

Erica led them to a dilapidated dock. It was small and rickety, just barely large enough for the team to gather on. The boards bowed under their weight, and it swayed back and forth in the water with each step. A boat was hitched to a rotten post by what looked to be a rope made from twisted vines. Several oars rested across the stern.

Cidus climbed into the rowboat and took an oar. The boat seemed quite sturdy and could easily hold up to twenty. He was not looking forward to rowing across the lake. Hell, it would have been simpler if the dragons could have flown them to the island, but because of the clouds, that was not possible. And if Icaras whisked them there with his magick, that could freak out Erica. He sighed and began to row.

With six of them manning the oars, it did not take them long to reach the island. The thick blanket of black fog made it hard to see, but Laro seemed to know where to steer the boat, and soon they hit land. Cidus stepped from the boat, his feet sinking ankle-deep in the slimy mud of the lake.

Taylith pulled the boat onto the bank and secured the rope to a stake Brenn had driven into the ground.

"The silver egg that contains the grimoire and black diamond are beneath the island," Ciara said as she got out of the boat.

Erica scrunched her face. "How do you expect to retrieve it? You can't swim in that crap, and you don't have oxygen tanks or diving suits. The water is filthy, and it's icy." She grabbed her proton phaser and jumped from the boat. "Well, if you are planning on getting in that nasty water, come with me."

After grabbing their supplies, they followed Erica to a small clearing with an inlet. Cidus noticed she knew her way around rather well, so she had to have made this trip often.

"You will be able to dive easier here. The water is deeper in the canal. You never did say how you plan on breathing underwater." Erica crossed her arms and gave the team an inquisitive glance.

Cidus wondered the same thing. Sure, they had made many technological advances during the time he was held captive. Much more than he had ever imagined. Though he knew flyers were not a new technology, the one he had owned before his captivity had been outdated. His father had chosen to refuse much of the latest technology the king had offered.

"We have special masks we can wear that enable us to breathe underwater. Only one of us needs to go down to retrieve the egg. Volunteers?" Brenn looked at them all.

Cidus stayed quiet. No way did he want to go down into that murky water beneath the island. There could be all manner of foul creatures hiding in its depths.

Icaras spoke up. "I will go." He gave them a lopsided grin. "Remember where I came from. I swam in underwater pools just as bad during my captivity." Icaras took his backpack off and taking out his oxygen mask, put it on. "I probably will not need this, but just in case..."

Cidus had heard the story of Icaras' rescue from the rest of the team, but Icaras did not speak much of the details of his captivity. Cidus only knew that the man had been trapped for centuries in the bowels of Ierilia as some kind of giant worm.

"Good luck." He clapped Icaras on the back. "You are brave."

They stood close to the water's edge and watched Icaras disappear into the inky water.

Erica peered into the lake. "I have a really bad feeling about this."

"Erica, no need to worry. Icaras knows what he is doing. He has quite a history and is an experienced diver." Ciara stood closer to Erica.

Cidus tapped his foot on the ground waiting impatiently. The minutes seem to drag, and he was beginning to think it was taking far too long for Icaras to resurface. "Odoxon would have protected the container. What if Icaras runs into trouble? We do not know what kind of monsters live beneath the surface."

"Then we will need to go in to rescue him. We will not let any harm befall Icaras," Liana said.

"How would you know if something attacked him down there? I can't see a damn thing through the muck." Erica stepped closer to the edge of the water.

"Trust what we say, Erica. Icaras will tell us if he needs our assistance," Ciara said.

"Tell you? How?" she queried, her eyebrows raised.

Jonathan grinned. "Telepathy, at least I think that's what it's called on Earth. We can speak in each other's minds."

After what seemed like hours, the first thing that appeared above the waterline was the silver egg. It emitted a soft glow and floated slowly to shore. As it rolled onto the bank, Icaras surfaced. Cidus watched him pull the mask off and run a hand through his long hair.

"I thought I was going to the center of this planet," Icaras muttered. "I need some water."

Taylith handed Icaras a waterskin. "Did you encounter any danger? Resistance to taking the egg?"

Icaras took a long drink from the waterskin and handed it back to Taylith. "Remember, Odoxon has lost control over this planet, so even if there was a spell on the egg, it has lost its power. No danger, no strange fish, it was smooth all the way down."

"So now we have the egg and its contents. We need to use our magick to open it," Liana told them. "Cidus, Jonathan, Ciara, Taylith, and Icaras, join hands with me and stand around the egg. Erica, Laro and Brenn, step back please."

Cidus closed his eyes and allowed the chant to infiltrate his mind. His lips automatically found the words as he chanted along with the others. The chant faded. He opened his eyes, and the egg had opened, displaying the grimoire and a black gem nestled in a small container on top of the ancient book.

Ciara lifted the grimoire carefully and held it in her hands. She handed it to Jonathan. "You and Cidus must now use the spell within to cleanse this planet."

Next, she took out the smaller container with the black diamond. Shock registered on her face. "This is a duplicate. It is not the real gem."

Jonathan looked up. "So, the old bastard has fooled us again."

Cidus stood with Jonathan who continued leafing through the thick book. "Will the missing gem stop us from cleansing the planet?"

"No. The black diamond is not needed for that. Go ahead," Ciara insisted.

Cidus waited while Jonathan searched for the spell. "I've got no fucking idea what in hell I'm looking for," he muttered and looked at Cidus. I can't even read most of this stuff. I wish the gods would give me that ability at least."

Ciara chuckled. "Jonathan, rest your mind. You can read all of it. So can Cidus. You need to cleanse your mind of other matters. Concentrate."

Cidus peered at the grimoire and blanked out his mind of all thought. Suddenly, a long soft breath came from his lips directed at the pages. It was as if the pages now turned automatically, then suddenly stopped. "I think that's the spell," he said.

They stepped away from the others and joined hands, the book resting on their joined hands between them.

Cidus gazed into Jonathan's eyes. Suddenly, he felt a strong bond with this young man, a connection so unyielding, he could hardly absorb it. They were both demi-gods, they were brothers by blood. Though they had not grown up together, Cidus felt as if he had known Jonathan his whole life, a connection that could not be broken.

In unison they began to chant the spell, their voices increasing in volume. At the end of it, Cidus raised his head and spotted the lightning in the dark sky, saw the dark clouds dissipating, a mauve sky taking their place with two suns blazing down upon the planet.

"Brother, it is done," Jonathan said and squeezed Cidus' hand.

"I see that. I cannot believe we did this."

Cidus gazed around at the now verdant landscape, the clear lake, a castle that was no longer macabre, but beautiful. It rivaled the size of the king's palace and appeared to be built of white marble. Tall golden spires gleamed brightly in the sunlight. The mud-filled moat had disappeared. In its place, a lush garden of velvety green grass and colorful flowers surrounded the serene castle. Trees that were laden with fruit, berries, and nuts, formed a large orchard where the twisted forest once stood. The cheerful sound of birds singing filled the air, and several small antaur-like creatures played within the grass.

Erica shrieked. "Holy fucking shit! I can't believe what I just saw. Did you really do this? Is this the same planet? I've thought all along I was hallucinating and was still in stasis, but now I'm sure I'm dreaming."

"Remember what we told you, Erica," Liana said.

Cidus kind of had to agree with her. At times he thought he was still in captivity and everything that was happening was just a dream. But he knew now it was not, and after this mission, he would be back with Tabeka and hold her in his arms.

He wondered how Evior and Iridia were doing and how Tabeka was dealing with them. Was Iridia going to accept that she was Zohmes' daughter? A demi-goddess? He cleared his mind and concentrated on the here and now.

"So now we have the grimoire, but we do not have the black diamond. That means Odoxon is still more than dangerous. He has memorized all the spells within the grimoire and using his magick created a duplicate of the book. With the real black diamond still in his clutches, he can still create havoc on Ierilia," Ciara told them.

Erica shook her head. "This is all beyond me. How are the people on this planet going to react to the sudden change?"

"The people here believe in magick because of Odoxon's rule and tyranny, but they have only seen the evil side of sorcery. The goddess Rania told me that the god Izarus will shortly address the people." Ciara gazed up at the sky.

"You're kidding me. A real god? And we'll be able to see and hear him?"

Cidus followed Ciara's gaze and saw snow-white clouds roll in above where Zenthia and its surroundings were approximately located. The clouds parted, and a giant-sized Izarus appeared slowly from the waist up wearing his usual white-and-gold robes. They blew gently in a breeze, his hair billowing around his head. He held his staff and directed the dragon's head toward the ground. It shone brightly, bathing the whole landscape in a brilliant radiance.

Cidus wondered how the people in Zenthia and the villages in its vicinity were reacting to this phenomenon. The god's voice boomed. Even as far as they were from the city, they could hear it where they stood.

"People of Odoxus. The sorcerer, Odoxon, has been banished from your planet forever. His evil no longer reigns. The god of all gods, I Am, has smiled upon you and with the help of two of his assistants, your planet, now named Giethoren, has been transformed into a place of beauty and tranquility.

"Its soil is cleansed, enabling you to grow crops. Odoxon's horrendous creations have been eradicated. In their stead, you will find fish in your rivers and seas, fowl on the land, birds in the sky, and horses, jagos, and korobeasts.

"Treat your renewed and replenished planet well. Respect the bounty granted to you. Until the gods have chosen a new ruler for this kingdom, Erica Martinez and her mate Laro will be in charge."

Izarus faded, the clouds rolled away and vanished, and all was quiet. Cidus glanced at Erica who had fallen to her knees, her head bowed, her hands raised to the sky, her lips moving silently. "Erica, what are you doing?"

"Praying. Giving thanks to your gods, and my God, although perhaps the one this god spoke of, I Am, *is* my God. I was raised a Christian, believing in the one and true God. But the way Earth went, I began to doubt. I think I have just become a believer again."

"Erica, you heard Izarus. For the time being, you and Laro are temporary rulers. You can assign whoever you trust from your team to assist you," Ciara told her. "I am sure the people will bombard you with questions. Tell them as much as you need to. You can inform them about Ierilia and how Odoxus, or now Giethoren, came into existence, a bit about us, and you can be honest, up to a point. They need to understand that no one can ever come to live on Ierilia and vice versa." Ciara stepped back and let Brenn take over.

"From now on, you will have our assistance. Explain that to the people. Until a ruler is set in place, you and your team will be the head of all decisions and operations. Those that defy you, you will need to punish, just like Barry and his accomplice on Ierilia were punished."

"How the fuck will I punish them? How was Barry punished on your planet?" Erica demanded.

"Barry and Liam were sent to the mines to work there for a very long time. Are there mines on this planet?" Brenn asked.

Laro shook his head. "There was nothing valuable enough to mine. It was hard enough for us to grow crops to feed our families." He gazed at the transformed island. "But now, once we cultivate the land and grow crops, there will be more than enough to keep our people from starving. And who knows, maybe there will be mines in the future. Many of the Earth people are well-educated. I believe there is a geologist, and Laura is a botanist."

"A butterfly!" Erica giggled when a brightly colored salora fluttered in front of her face. "Was the whole planet transformed? I have never seen anything so beautiful. Earth was practically destroyed when our ships departed."

"Yes, the whole planet. The gods and goddesses have blessed Giethoren. Your people will want for nothing, and we will keep you safe from corruption. You must be its protectors and nurture the goodness of the people. With the cleansing of the planet, Odoxon's evil has been eradicated," Ciara explained.

"We should return to Zenthia. I imagine the others are just as shocked as we are at the changes that have taken place," Laro suggested.

Brenn nodded. "I agree. Let us see if the spell has been reversed on Biryn's double, and after that, you can assemble your team."

Erica scrunched up her face. "We will freak Biryn the hell out if we show up riding on the backs of dragons. I don't think that would go over well."

Icaras tied his hair back and shouldered his pack. "Then you must trust me to transport all of us using magick. It would take a day for us to reach Zenthia on foot."

Erica shook her head vigorously. "Wait a minute now. That zapping around to different locations hurts like all bloody hell. Every time the old bastard played Scotty with his transporter beam, I felt as if my body was getting ripped apart. We'll chance the dragons."

Cidus laughed. "I have been transported by Icaras, and it was just fine."

Erica obviously hesitated. "I suppose. If you say so."

"We would not hurt you." Ciara smiled and held her hand out to Erica. "We need to join hands. It will be over before you know it."

Erica grabbed Laro's hand and stood beside Ciara. "I am trusting you on this."

The team stood close together, held hands, then Icaras chanted softly. Cidus barely felt any movement. When he opened his eyes again, they stood near what used to be Erica and Laro's hovel. A modest, but very nice house stood in the shack's place. Lush purple grass grew in the yard, and a garden of vegetables and fruit was nestled among several nut trees. A teenage boy swung to the ground from one of the branches and ran toward them.

"Mother, Father!" The boy came to a running stop in front of them.

"Holy shit, all bloody hell, what happened to the house? Or what we used to call our home." Erica pulled the lad into her embrace.

"I don't know. Everything happened so fast. I was afraid it was the sorcerer, so I hid in the tree," Tomas mumbled. "And then the god appeared and spoke."

"It wasn't Odoxon. Just like Izarus, the god in the sky said, it was I Am and the gods and goddesses. You are safe." Erica released Tomas.

"I still don't understand." He walked away muttering under his breath.

Ciara squeezed Erica's arm. "Everything has changed. Remember? Now you need to lead us to where Biryn and Cylena live."

"Their home isn't too far from here. Wait, can I see inside first?" she asked excitedly and began for the door.

"No time for that. We need to find out if Biryn is still bespelled. Please, show us the way," Brenn told her.

Erica scrunched her nose and nodded. "Okay, I guess. It is hard seeing him drunk all the time. Laro, stay here with Tomas? I'll be back soon."

Laro clapped Tomas on the shoulder. "Come on, son. We will explore the house while your mother is gone."

Cidus could not help the wistful feeling that filled his soul as he watched Laro and Tomas enter the house. Zohmes had taken away everything Cidus had ever cared about when he had switched him with Jatron—Wildevein, Tabeka, and their unborn child. How he wished he had the chance to bond with his own son or daughter.

"Biryn and Cylena live in this direction. Follow me." Erica interrupted Cidus from his thoughts.

As Erica led them along a well-worn path, Cidus gazed at the mauve colored sky. The suns shone brightly down on a planet full of life, where before everything was dying.

Erica was shocked to see the changes, but so was Cidus. He still found it hard to believe that he and Jonathan had the power to change this place for the better. It was frightening and exhilarating, and he really was not sure if he wanted that kind of magick. It did his heart good to see people shouting and dancing, some raising their hands to the sky and praising the god who had spoken to them.

It did not take them long to reach the home where Biryn and Cylena lived. It, too, had transformed into a nice house.

"Here we are," Erica said and pointed at the home. "Or at least this is where they should live. I am not so sure, now that the gods have transformed this place into Oz."

Ciara chuckled. "This Erica's language is as mysterious as our Erica's."

They were about to knock on the door when Biryn came staggering toward them on the pathway, again singing at the top of his lungs. He stumbled over a tree-root and landed face-first on the ground. After pulling himself back up, his body swayed back and forth. He was obviously very intoxicated.

"The spell has not cured Biryn of his addiction." Cidus hated to see Biryn's double in that condition.

Liana nodded in agreement. "We have to invoke a spell to cleanse him."

They waited for Biryn to reach the front of the house, then entrapped him within the circle they had formed.

Biryn gazed them in confusion. "Who are you? Brenn, what are you—"

"We are here to help you," Brenn interrupted him.

"I do not—"

His words were lost when they began their chant. Cidus let the others guide him through the spell, amazed that the words flowed from his lips as if he had said them many times before. After a few moments, inebriated Biryn regained his sensibility and stood steady on his feet. A look of confusion clouded his face while he took in his surroundings. Biryn stepped toward the door as if he did not even see them.

"What...what is...this?"

"It is like he is oblivious of us," Cidus said, raising his

eyebrows.

"I have made us invisible to him," Icaras answered Cidus.

"Can we see what happens next? I want to make sure they will be okay." Erica shifted closer to the front steps.

Cylena burst through the door, an infant in each arm. "What is all this racket, Biryn! You woke the twins again!"

"Here, let me take one of them." Biryn reached for one of the infants.

She stepped back in the doorway. "Oh, no you don't, you drunken kurakelda. I will not have you injuring one of them because you trip all over your feet when you are in this condition."

"Cylena, love, I am not drunk. Do I smell like wine or spirits?"

She looked up at Biryn and shook her head in disbelief.

He planted a kiss on her lips. "See? It is as I said. I am not intoxicated. Now let me hold my daughter?"

Cylena grinned and offered one of the twins to Biryn. "Oh, she is going to be your favorite, huh?" Shifting her son in her arms, she gave Biryn an inquisitive glance. "So why did you come home singing? Because of what the god in the sky said?"

"God? Oh, that. Yes, I think so."

"Please...let his foolishness be over." Cidus heard her mumble under her breath.

"Foolishness?"

"Your drinking, Biryn... I hope that god who spoke to us has ended it." She turned and walked back into the house.

Cidus watched Biryn shake his head as if trying to recall what he had seen and heard. He knew the man had to be confused, and because of the spell Odoxon had placed on him, Biryn probably could not remember exactly what had happened all these years. At least now Giethoren and its people could prosper and heal.

He sighed. Maybe the power that flowed through his veins

was not all bad. They had accomplished what they came for. Well, almost. They had the grimoire, but not the black diamond. And from what the goddess Rania had told Ciara, Odoxon knew all the spells within the book. With the black diamond in his possession, what havoc could he cause on Ierilia?

CHAPTER TWENTY

s soon as Cidus reached the steps to the palace, Tabeka flew into his arms. "I am so glad you are back. My sense of doom has not left me. I was afraid for you and the others," she murmured against his neck.

"My sweet dancing queen, forever worrying. The danger on that world is gone. The mission was quite simple, really." He hugged her tightly, savoring the feel of her in his arms. He cherished every moment he had with the woman he loved. In the blink of an eye, happiness could be ripped away. He gazed down at her and lightly brushed her hair from her cheek. "How are Evior and Iridia?"

She peered up at him, sorrow reflecting in her eyes. "They are well but still recovering from their ordeal. I will ask Ciara to help erase the memories. They are so young, it is senseless to let them suffer the horrors of their torture."

"Ciara and Icaras erased the memory of their pain, but they need to remember what Odoxon did to them, especially Iridia."

"Why especially her?"

"She is Zohmes' daughter. A demi-goddess. After Iridia goes to the Clyss, she will have great magick just like Jonathan and me. She needs to retain the knowledge of what those powers can do if used for evil."

"I had forgotten." She let out a deep breath. "No, not true. I just do not like to think of her as another spawn of that crazy god."

"You raised Iridia well. She has a good heart, and her soul is pure. Her soul is not tainted by evil like Zohmes. She will be fine, and she will be a great asset in the future in defeating Zohmes and Odoxon."

Tabeka stepped back and looked up at him. "Tell me all about the mission?"

"The king is waiting for us. You will hear everything then." He kissed her tenderly, then twined his fingers with hers. "Come, my love. Let us get dinner over and done with. I can hardly wait to be alone with you."

Hand in hand they walked to the king's quarters. "Nothing happened while we were away?" Cidus asked casually.

"Nothing. Everything has been quiet, thankfully."

Jonathan and Liana caught up to them. "Those two assholes must be running out of tricks, surely?"

"Another strange word. What does it mean?" Cidus asked.

Jonathan grinned. "You don't want to know. It's an Earth term. It's bad."

Cidus leaned closer to Tabeka. "I see them mating in the near future."

Jonathan swiveled. "Hey, I heard that."

"As did I," Liana smiled sweetly and hooked her arm through Jonathan's.

Cidus chuckled. It seemed their hearing was enhanced as well because he had spoken very softly.

Jonathan knocked lightly on the king's door. Dunmore, as usual, let them into the chambers. They had not been the last to arrive. Taylith and Laura stepped into the room behind Cidus and Tabeka.

Dunmore gestured to the dining table. "Please be seated,

His Majesty will join you shortly."

Cidus pulled a chair out for Tabeka, then took a seat beside her. As soon as they had settled in, Dunmore brought a tray of glasses and a bottle of wine and served the newcomers, except for Laura. He returned to the sideboard and poured a cup of tea and a glass of milk, then set them on the table before her.

Laura smiled and took a sip of the tea. "Thank you, Dunmore. The tea is perfect." She turned to Tabeka. "And thank you for suggesting it. It has done wonders for my nausea."

"It was passed down to me from my great-grandmother. She was well versed in herbal remedies, and she had a gift for healing as well as the sight," Tabeka commented.

Cidus took a deep drink of the wine. Even though the mission had been easy enough, he was still wound tighter than a drum. He could not help feeling that something was amiss even though Zohmes and Odoxon seemed to be on hiatus. He set his glass on the table and reached for Tabeka's hand. She twined her fingers with his and squeezed.

Biryn slipped into the room with Cylena and quietly closed his bedchamber's door. "The twins are fast asleep." He led Cylena to the table and helped her take a seat, then turned to Dunmore. "Please call down to have dinner served. Also, have two dinner trays sent to the nursery. Isabella and Tanoth are watching the twins while we conduct the meeting."

"Yes, Your Majesty." Dunmore filled the king's glass.

Biryn took a drink of his wine. "The grimoire has been locked away in a safe place, but Brenn told me you were unable to retrieve the black diamond. Brenn, please continue your tale. I am anxious to hear how the rest of the mission went."

Brenn cleared his throat, then began telling Biryn about their quest. Though there really was not much to speak of.

They had not run into any resistance from Odoxon or his creatures. By the time Brenn finished telling of their experiences on Giethoren, servants entered the chambers, their arms laden with platters of food.

"That is all? You had no trouble retrieving the book?" Biryn asked after the servants had set the food on the table and left the chambers.

"After I Am moved the portal to a new location, he told us Odoxon would be unable to enter the gateway," Ciara reminded him.

Cidus pushed the food around on his plate with his fork. "I would say the loss of the black diamond was trouble enough. We also had help from Erica and Laro's doubles. They knew a path to the island that kept us from encountering any of Odoxon's monsters."

"And you left my double in charge? That poor girl! It is hard enough to deal with the Earth crews, now she has a whole planet of people to deal with!" Erica shook her head.

"Not the whole planet is populated. Odoxon only saw fit to duplicate the people from Cront and nearby villages. She has her Laro and the team to help her until the gods decide who should rule Giethoren. She is a strong woman, just as you are, Erica. She will do well in this task," Astiana said.

"We need to find out what the twisted bastard has done with the black diamond. I have a sick feeling that the two of them have something up their sleeves, and with their power amplified by the gem, we may not be able to stop them." Laura took a bite of roasted vegetables. "Bernie and Julia are back from their honeymoon. I can't wait to tell Julia that we're expecting a little dragon!"

Taylith laughed. "News has already spread on Storming Enclave—the first baby to be born to our people in centuries. We are famous. As for the black diamond, we must wait until Ciara or Astiana speak with Rania. And there will be no more missions for you, lady. After our little dragon is born, you will have your hands full keeping him from changing and flying out of his cradle." He hugged Laura.

"You're fucking kidding me, right? They can change into a dragon when they're babies?"

Taylith winked at her. "Would I tease you about something like that?"

She scrunched her nose at him. "You better be! Besides if she does decide to fly from the cradle, *you'll* have to chase her since I am not a dragon."

"You are calling the infant a her. You think you are having a girl? Taylith may be teasing you about the little one shifting, but did he warn you that twins are very common in our family?" Liana gave the couple a sidelong glance.

"It usually skips a generation, too," Ciara added.

Laura's eyes widened, and she shook her head. "No way! Uh-uh... That isn't even funny, you two!"

Everyone laughed heartily. The mood around the table was light-hearted instead of one of doom and dread. Cidus smiled as he watched and listened to the teasing interplay. At that moment he could see just how young the dragons had been when Cewrick had cursed them.

After dessert, he was glad when it was time to leave. He was not surprised when Liana and Jonathan decided to spend the rest of the evening at Brenn and Ciara's. The news of Laura's pregnancy had come quite suddenly. The couple had not even had time for it to sink in before Taylith was required to go on the mission to Giethoren. Years ago, when Tabeka had given him the news of her pregnancy, he wanted nothing more than to be alone with her and plan their future.

Unfortunately, that future had been ripped from them, but he would not let the past interfere with the here and now. He had made up his mind that he and Tabeka needed to leave Cront and take up residence at Wildevein Manor. Deep down, he knew that was where he was meant to be. His people needed him, and even though I Am protected the portal to Giethoren, he did not want to leave the sanctuary unprotected. Once he had her alone, he would talk to her about it.

Cidus took a deep breath. Alone, finally, though he wished Tabeka were with him now. She had gone to check on Iridia before joining him in the privacy of their room.

He stepped out on the balcony and gazed at the gardens below. The sweet smell of the summer blossoms drifted through the air, and the moons shone brightly down on the couple seated on the stone bench in front of the fish pond.

He turned away from Jonathan and Liana and strode back into his room. It troubled him that Odoxon had set his sights on Liana. Cidus knew that Liana had to be Jonathan's lifemate. He would not put it past Zohmes to use Odoxon's fascination with the dragon to ensnare Jonathan.

Pushing those thoughts from his mind, he shucked his clothing and entered the heated water of the tub he had started before walking out to the veranda. He leaned back and closed his eyes, his mind wandering to Tabeka.

It still felt as if he were in a dream—that his mind had finally broken from the seclusion and torture wrought by Zohmes over the years he had held him captive. What would cause such hatred within the god, that his own offspring were expendable? Why go to all the trouble to procreate, only to then want to destroy his children? And what of Astiana? What Zohmes had done to her was reprehensible. Cidus could not fathom the idea that it was possible the god had the ability to feel and give love at one time. Who or what had corrupted him?

It was he that began all evil on Ierilia so many centuries ago. Zohmes sat at the right hand of I Am. He was the favorite son. But Zohmes turned against I Am and wreaked havoc on the planet. I

Am, with the help of Rithar and the four swords, banished him to Yanata, from which he managed to escape. His obsession to once again rule Ierilia began by possessing Cewrick. Cewrick was released from the possession, but Zohmes continues on his path of destruction and vengeance. The reason he does not care for nearly all of his offspring is that their souls are not corrupted. He knows you all have powers that may be his end. Therefore, he will stop at nothing to annihilate you.

The voice had spoken clearly in his mind, but his thoughts were broken by the sound of soft footsteps on the marble floor drawing his attention. He opened his eyes and admired the temptress the gods had seen fit with whom to bind his soul.

"Tabeka..."

"A hot bath will relax us both." She gave him a teasing smile and slowly unlaced the ties to her corselet, loosening her dress, then let it slide to the floor.

His breath caught in his throat. She was even more beautiful now than she had been at eighteen. Her red hair spilled around her shoulders in gleaming waves of fire, the tips of her breasts peeking through the silky strands.

Gods, he ached to touch every inch of her pearly skin, from the elegant line of her neck to her shapely toes. She was a goddess that should have never been cast aside as mere garbage.

She stepped into the large tub and facing him straddled his hips. "I hope that was the last mission that requires your assistance for a while. We have barely had time for one another, and I have missed you."

The heat in her gaze scalded him. The beat of his heart thundered in his ears, his blood rushing through his veins straight to his aching cock. She squeezed some of the sweet-smelling soap Ciara stocked in the bathrooms into her hand, then glided her hands across his chest to work up a lather. He groaned when those questing fingers encircled his erection, her fist sliding up and down the length of him from base to tip.

Cidus grasped the back of her head and pulling her down, he claimed her mouth. He skimmed his fingers down her neck to her breasts, his lips following the trail of his fingers. He reached down and gripped her hand, stilling her movements, then tenderly kissed her.

"Gods, woman if you keep that up, I will be spent before I can pleasure you," he whispered against her lips.

"Then take me over the edge with you." She raised her hips then guided him to her opening, teasing him with the velvety softness of her core, inflaming his desire.

He grasped her hips and plunged into her, filling her to the hilt. She thrust her hips against him, taking what she wanted, giving him what he needed.

Cidus could not keep his eyes off the beauty of this woman…his woman. Her luscious breasts swayed with each movement, her long red hair a stark contrast to her ivory skin. He ached to taste, to touch… He traced his fingers up her spine and gently nudged her forward, then took one of her nipples in his mouth and sucked hard.

She moaned and arched into him, the walls of her core tightening around him. Grasping a breast in one hand, he slid the other between their bodies, finding the tight little bud of her clit. He rolled it between his fingers, continuing the ministrations to her breasts. Cidus saw stars when her walls tightened and spasmed around him, taking them both over the edge into oblivion.

Tabeka collapsed against him breathing heavily. He held her while they both caught their breath.

She kissed his chest, then sat up to look at him. "You will always possess my heart and soul, Cidus."

He raked his fingers through her now damp hair. "And you own my soul. It was yours the moment I laid eyes on you all those years ago. Promise me you will join with me as soon as we return to Wildevein."

"You have my word. I wish to do it privately, in your sanctuary, before the gods and goddesses." She caressed his cheek, then wrinkled her nose. "We should get out of this tub. I am starting to look like a zonomi fruit."

"You are beautiful, Tabeka. I, on the other hand, am starting to look like a wrinkled old man." He lifted her from the tub and placed her to stand on the floor.

"You are far from an old man. You are a demi-god, and much younger than most of Biryn's team." She wrapped herself in a towel, then held one out to him.

He took the towel and wrapped it around his hips. "My love, about that. I know it seems as if I am to be part of the team, but I have a gut feeling that I am needed in Wildevein."

She nodded. "I told you. The feeling of doom has not left me. We should return to Wildevein soon."

CHAPTER TWENTY-ONE

Cidus told Brenn and Ciara at the breakfast table of their plan to return to Wildevein.

"Are you two coming with us?" Tabeka asked Evior and Iridia.

Iridia nodded happily. "Yes. Now that Zohmes no longer rules over it, I would like to go home. Evior? What about you?"

"I will go wherever you go, love. If your parents will accept me into the family? The manor was my home, but now it belongs to Cidus."

"Of course, you are welcome to remain in the home where you grew up. I already told you I will adopt you as my son. I hope Tabeka and I can provide better memories for you, Evior," Cidus told him. "And as the oldest son, one day you will be Lord Milhella of Wildevein and ruler of the Sirona Realm. It is your right."

"It is a long journey. We should begin to prepare," Tabeka said. "Brenn, Ciara, I am so grateful for your hospitality. I hope we can repay you in the future."

Ciara smiled. "Help Wildevein to prosper. That is all we ask."

"The journey does not have to take long. How about if I

transport you there on my dragon?" Liana suggested. "Jonathan and I can use a holiday, and it will give Taylith and Laura a few more days alone."

"Iridia, before you leave, you and Evior must go to the Clyss. I Am demands it." Ciara looked at the young woman.

"I do not want to. I feel sick when I think about Zohmes, that the god is my real father. I just want to be me."

Ciara sighed. "Sweet girl, you need to do what I Am wants, or you will anger the gods and goddesses. From what I know, the powers granted to you at the Clyss will help you and will aid Jonathan and Cidus in the future when Zohmes will finally be defeated."

"So… I have no choice?"

"You always have a choice, but it must be a wise one." Tabeka took her daughter's hand. "Liana, your offer to fly us to Wildevein is generous and will alleviate much hardship traveling with a wagon and horses. Thank you."

"So be it. I look forward to a hiatus from all of Zohmes and Odoxon's games." Jonathan held up his mug of tea. "Besides, I would like the chance to get to know my brother and sister better."

"I will do as the gods say," Iridia said softly, then gazed at Cidus and Jonathan. "My brothers…" She shook her head. "I still find it all so overwhelming. It is hard to reconcile that what I grew up to believe has all been a farce."

"Cherish those memories. They can be taken from you in an instant," Jonathan stated heatedly. "Zohmes may be your sperm donor, but it does not negate the fact that Tabeka is your mother and loves you dearly. From what I have heard, you had a good life with her."

Iridia clasped Tabeka's hand. "You are right, Jonathan. It does not matter who my biological parents were. I know who my mother truly is."

Cidus had to agree, though the man who had raised him

had not been his biological father, he knew the man had loved him and his mother. In all ways, that man, Lord Seron Milhella, was his father.

"We will go to the Clyss this afternoon," Ciara answered. "When do you wish to leave?" She looked at Tabeka and Cidus.

"I think we should go as soon as possible. I have a feeling all is not right in Wildevein," Tabeka answered.

"Then we will leave right after Iridia and Evior have met with the god at the Clyss. Can you have your belongings ready?" Jonathan asked.

"Will it all fit on the dragon?" Tabeka wondered.

Liana laughed. "Easily. You came here with a wagon loaded with your belongings. Look at what we transported to the other planet. Yes, it will fit. Do not trouble your mind with such."

That afternoon, Ciara and Liana flew them to the Clyss. Only Evior, Iridia, Brenn, Jonathan, Liana, Astiana, Tabeka, and Cidus were with them. Iridia had requested that no one be present, but that was just not possible.

Cidus loved the Clyss. Oh, what a utopia if one could live here. He gazed around at the abundant life that surrounded him. It was a paradise, not unlike his secret place in the Astanica Mountains, but even nicer and more tranquil with the flow of magick he could now sense.

"Please join hands. Iridia and Evior stand in the center of the circle," Ciara requested.

Jonathan, Ciara, Cidus, Astiana, and Liana began chanting. White clouds rolled in and hid the sun. It did not take long before I Am appeared. Cidus noticed Iridia crouch to the ground, her eyes lifted to the god in fear, Evior's hand on her shoulder.

"Iridia, my child. Do not be afraid. You are my direct

descendant, a daughter of the gods. I will protect you, always. Like your brothers, you are gifted with power and magick. You will learn, with the help of Liana, Ciara, and Astiana, to wield your powers. Always remember, you are our child.

"Evior must enter the pool with you to activate his symbols though he does not have the powers of a god, he has been granted the guardian gift through the sorcerer's blood flowing through his veins. Now both of you, go to the bottomless pool and immerse yourself in its waters."

Lightning rained down upon the couple. Cidus did not see them flinch. Iridia stood up resolutely and began to walk to the pool, followed by Evior. They broke the circle to let them through and watched as she took off her dress and sandals and waded into the water. Evior took off his clothing and joined her.

Minutes passed, making Cidus wonder if they may have drowned. They had been beneath the surface for quite some time, even longer than he had been and the water had a strange effect on the mind and body. Though he knew his fear was misguided. The gods protected those they required to enter the Clyss. Evior surfaced first. He came out of the water coughing and spluttering. The symbols on his body glowed softly.

Moments later Cidus could see a soft red glow under the water slowly moving to the edge of the basin. When the light reached the shallows, Iridia emerged, the symbols I Am had placed onto her body during her healing were illuminated a bright crimson and fire danced in the bright blue depths of her eyes.

Evior rushed to Iridia, enveloping her in the large towel he had held. The light extinguished, and her eyes returned to normal.

Tabeka squeezed his fingers hard. "What has been done to my daughter and to Evior?"

"I do not know." Cidus felt guilty for not telling Tabeka how the hieroglyphics had appeared, but he had not lied. He had no idea what the symbols meant. He first thought had been that Odoxon had etched them into their skin. After Laura healed them, the glyphs became visible. But I Am told them they were placed there for a purpose. They would find out in due course when the gods or goddesses were ready to reveal the meaning of them.

"Do not worry, Tabeka. As I Am told us, the gods protect Iridia. Your daughter will come to no harm," Astiana told Tabeka.

Cidus hoped that was the case. The young woman had been through enough at Odoxon's hands, and he would do everything in his power to protect his sister from a fate he had been relegated to when he was young.

After Iridia and Evior had dressed, they gathered in the clearing, leaving room for Ciara and Liana to shift into their dragons. The flight to Brenn's estate did not take them long, and Cidus was thrilled to see that Tabeka's, Evior's and Iridia's belongings had been readied by Brenn's servants for their departure to Wildevein, all bundled into a large rope net.

Cidus and Tabeka stood in the courtyard saying their goodbyes when Astiana approached the group. "I am returning to my temple in Astanica. I have already spoken to Biryn. He is against my leaving, and I shall miss my great-grandson and the twins, but I do not trust Zohmes. He suffered a great loss when we ousted him from Wildevein and the Dreaded Peaks, and I do not doubt that he still has followers hidden within the Sirona Realm."

Cidus understood her fear, the same distrust had seized his heart. He knew Zohmes and Jatron would try to steal Wildevein back, and his people deserved his protection after so many years of abuse by his brother.

Ciara gave them a troubled glance. "I do not trust Zohmes

and Odoxon's silence either." She turned her attention to Liana. "Stay in contact with Taylith and me. We have only just found you, and I do not like being separated from you, no matter how short the timespan."

Liana pulled her into a hug. "It will only be a couple of days."

"With Odoxon in possession of the black diamond and the spells of the grimoire we cannot take any risks. Especially you, Liana." Ciara stepped out of her embrace.

"You are beginning to sound like our fathers."

"I won't let that bloody bastard anywhere near her." Jonathan stepped close to Liana.

Liana laughed. "See? I will be in the company of a goddess and two demi-gods and a demi-goddess, and I am a sorceress in my own right. I will be safe, Ciara. Now step back so I can shift."

They made room for Liana to call out her dragon. Cidus noted that Ciara's brow was still creased with worry. Maybe the dragon had the same nagging feeling that something was not right. And then there was Tabeka's reminder of her sense of doom. He shrugged the troubling mood away. He had too much to be grateful for, to fill his mind with caustic thoughts.

After Liana had shifted, she kneeled and allowed Jonathan, Cidus, Tabeka, Iridia, Evior, and Astiana to climb onto her back. She straightened, and Cidus could see she had grabbed the large bundle that held Tabeka's household goods in her foreclaws. She flapped her wings and lunged into the air, the extra weight had not even bothered her. Why would he even think that? It was like him picking up a pebble from the ground.

Tabeka, who sat in front of Cidus, relaxed against his chest. He tightened his arms around her and kissed the top of her head. He thought of her promise and smiled. Soon, he would take his intended lifemate into their little oasis and join his soul to hers. Maybe he could ask Astiana to perform the ceremony. He knew the sanctuary had to have belonged to Astiana and her priestesses centuries ago. There could have been no other reason her statue would have been placed in the gardens. Or possibly it was a tribute from the other gods and goddesses, made long after Zohmes had cursed her.

"Cidus, look. It fills my heart with joy to see the beauty returned to Wildevein." Tabeka leaned forward and pointed to the rolling hills and forests surrounding the manor property.

Cidus held her tightly by the waist. "Not as beautiful as you, my dancing queen."

It took more than a few days for them to clean up the manor. Cidus had gone into the village and hired carpenters, workers to tidy up the grounds, and women to help clean the house. A bonfire burned steadily outside the manor walls, the gates now wide open instead of locked.

Cidus and Tabeka had gone through every room, removed pieces of broken furniture, torn off all the bedding and taken down the drapes. He had summoned seamstresses to the manor to make new drapes, and he and Tabeka had bought all new bedding.

He tried to erase as much of Jatron as he possibly could, but many of the ornaments were priceless, and the furniture was valuable — at least the furniture that was still in one piece. Without a complete makeover, there would always be memories remaining, many of his childhood before he knew of Jatron.

Though he would rid the manor of his twin's influence, he would always remember the parents who had lovingly raised him, his mother for only a few years, his father guiding him to adulthood.

He and Tabeka stood looking at the dining room set up for

dinner that evening. "Maybe we will build a new manor in the future," Cidus said.

"Why? I like our home just fine with all the changes we made. The new, much lighter paint on the walls and the new murals makes a huge difference." Tabeka stepped out of his arm and straightened up some utensils.

"I hope the cook I hired is good," Cidus murmured.

"Nooneen is a great cook. I have tasted her food. She has hired helpers from the village to prepare the wedding feast for the villagers we are holding on the grounds after we join."

"Tomorrow we go to the sanctuary. It will be our big day." He stepped behind her and wrapped his arms around her waist. "Evior and Iridia have settled in nicely. Maybe we should have a double ceremony."

Tabeka swiveled to face him. "No! My daughter will have the ceremony of her life, one she will remember for the rest of her days! She has expressed the wish for the ceremony to be held in the Temple of Fertility in Henderson. Then we can hold the celebrations here afterward."

He chuckled, then picked up the bell and rang it. "Right now, we concentrate on our own ceremony tomorrow. Time to sit down for dinner, milady."

The others filed in slowly and took their seats. Cidus had never felt so proud. He was where he was supposed to be, the lord of the manor, seated at the head of the table, Tabeka by his side. His years of misery almost seemed like a bad nightmare he once had. Yet he could not quell the feeling that something was still not as it should be.

He rang the bell again to let Nooneen know they were ready for dinner. "First, I want to thank all of you for staying much longer than anticipated to help Tabeka and I get the manor into shape. We will be forever grateful. Thank you all so much. Second, as planned, tomorrow we will go to the sanctuary for Tabeka and me to join. Astiana, will you do us the honor of performing the ceremony?"

Several servants came in bearing platters of food. They set them on the table and quickly left again.

"I will be more than happy to," Astiana agreed. "And then, the day after, I would be grateful if Liana will fly me to my temple. I am sure it will be as dusty, if not more so than the manor was."

Cidus chuckled. "And we will all go with you and help you to restore it to its former splendor."

CHAPTER TWENTY-TWO

The next morning, Cidus stretched, carefully got out of bed so not to wake Tabeka and walked to the windows. He gazed out at the courtyard and gasped. The servants must have worked all night because the large area was decorated with long garlands of greenery and small flags. Big pots filled with flowers flanked the walls. Long tables stood at each side of the courtyard, and he was amazed at all the chairs. Where had they found them all? Maybe in the attic? Decorative, colored bubbles floated above. A small stage was set up with musical instruments on it. The villagers had outdone themselves.

Tabeka had soundlessly joined him. "Cidus, did you order all this?"

"No, love. This is the work of the villagers and staff."

"I am stunned."

"Our joining will not be as quiet as you wanted, my dancing queen."

"It appears so. But I am glad. They suffered much under Jatron's rule. Everything will change from now on. Come, I must get ready, and so should you. Before we left, Ciara gave me a gown to wear. I am eager to see it. She had it all wrapped up."

"We need to eat something before we dress, and before we go to the sanctuary," he told her.

Tabeka laughed. "I cannot eat. My stomach is in knots. You know, one small part of me is sad."

Cidus pulled her against him. "Why? What we dreamed of so long ago is finally coming to pass. There is no room for sadness on this day."

"I know my father cast me out. My parents abandoned me so long ago and never attempted to find me. They never returned to Wildevein. Yet it would have been so wonderful if they could be present for our joining. I know my mother would not have cast me out willingly, but my father was an overpowering man, and she bowed to his will. I wish..." A tear escaped her beautiful eyes.

"You wish your mother could at least be here. Love, I would make it happen for you if I could. Had you spoken of this before, maybe I could have—"

Tabeka placed a finger on his lips. "I know you mean well. They need to want to come of their own accord. My mother will not go against my father. He is an extremely stubborn man. News of our joining will travel. They will know."

"You have never had a vision of your parents?"

"No. I have asked the goddess, but never an answer."

"Maybe one day your father will regret what he did. Remember, everything is written in the book. If it is recorded that you will be reunited with your family, it will happen. But I understand that deep down you hoped that at least your mother could have been here today. Come, put a smile on that beautiful face and let us have some breakfast."

Cidus paced a bit as he waited for his mate to arrive. Liana had flown him and their guests to the sanctuary first, then went back to fetch Tabeka and Iridia.

To his surprise, when they arrived at his little paradise, he found the team already there. Biryn and Cylena, with the twins on their laps, sat on the grass surrounded by the rest of the team. Even Bernie and Julia were there.

"This was supposed to be small and quiet," he said softly to Ciara.

Ciara giggled. "Cidus, after all you went through, do you really think we would let you have a very quiet joining? We want to celebrate this precious day with you and Tabeka. Liana approaches. Your mate will be here in a few minutes."

It was as if the birds shared in his happiness. The small, white and pink quennisses flew around their heads, twittering, singing their song. The sanctuary was brilliant with flowering trees and shrubs, its water sparkling clear, the waterfall a soothing murmur in the background.

It held so many happy memories for him. And now, after so many years, his deepest wish was about to become reality.

He watched as Tabeka, followed by Iridia and Liana, walked toward him. She looked breathtakingly beautiful.

Her dress was mostly white. Blue laces crisscrossed to below her navel to hold the white corset covering a blue embroidered bodice that wrapped around her tightly. It had white gauzy sleeves with a blue band above the elbows, then sheer white material billowing out to below her wrists. The white skirt flared out below her hips. A sheer shawl of shimmery material draped around it held by a blue flower, then bellowing out to a full circle. Small blue flowers adorned the hem. Some of her hair had been braided into a crown on top of her head with the rest flowing down her back. A coronet of blue and white flowers adorned the braids.

Iridia and Liana wore dresses of the same shade of blue as the trimmings of his mate's dress. They both looked lovely, but no one could hold a candle to his Tabeka.

For just a few moments, his mind drifted back to the first time he had seen her dance. Her colorful skirt, the coin belt around her hips, the small top covering her breasts, her flaming hair flying around her head in wild abandonment. Oh, what he would give to see her dance like that one more time. Alas, she had sworn never to dance again. Maybe she would one day — privately, just for him.

She hardly looked a day older than when he had first met her. Even the silver strands lacing her hair seemed to have disappeared. Had he ever seen her look this beautiful? Her cheeks were flushed, and her eyes sparkled as she walked toward him.

Astiana stood just behind him. He held out his hand, and Tabeka threaded her fingers with his. They turned to face the goddess.

Astiana began to speak. "A joining of two souls should not be entered into lightly, but thoughtfully. The miracle lies in the path you have chosen together. The true magick of love is not to avoid changes, but to navigate them mindfully. You wish to join, so I shall ask you both. Is it truly your desire to become one with each other? Please speak your vows."

Tabeka spoke first. "For the young man you were, for the man you are now, and for the mate you shall be to me, I choose you to be my own."

Cidus cleared his throat. "With this ring, Tabeka, I take you as my mate, my friend, my lover, and from this day forth and until eternity, I pledge you my faithfulness." He slipped a ring onto her finger.

Astiana produced a chalice. "Cidus, take this chalice and repeat your vows."

"For the girl I first saw, for the woman you are now, and for the mate that you will be to me, I toast and drink and take you to be my own." He sipped from the chalice then handed it to Tabeka.

"Cidus, I take you as my friend, my lover, my mate, and until the fullness of time and realm of dreams where we will meet and remember and love again."

She handed the chalice back to Astiana. It disappeared, and a lit candle took its place. Astiana handed the candle to the couple. They both held it. Together, they said in unison, "This flame symbolizes the joining of our partnership. It brings the warmth, strength, and wisdom from both of us as kindling. Our flame feeds the same fire. From this day forward, we will bask in the beauty and the light of our love. May this flame keep us warm throughout all the days of our lives."

Astiana raised her arms. "Izarus, I call upon you to bless this couple."

Clouds appeared above the oasis hiding the suns. Izarus emerged, his white hair billowing around his face. He held his staff up high as he spoke his blessing.

"Cidus, you are a demi-god, one of us. You have chosen your mate wisely, the mate that was written to become yours in the book of knowledge. Cidus and Tabeka, from this day forth, you will share in each other's pain, laughter, joy, burdens, and you will help lighten them and encourage one another. You are now bound, one to the other, your souls entwined for eternity. Our blessings are upon you. Go in peace."

The clouds dissipated, and the ceremony was completed. Cidus embraced Tabeka. "We are joined, my love."

"Yes, we are."

"You look like a goddess," he complimented her. "But I cannot wait to get that dress off you tonight."

She poked him. "Is that all you men think about?"

He chuckled. "Mm, maybe not so much me, but a part of my body does."

After the congratulations and hugs, Taylith, Ciara, and Liana left to the clearing to get ready to transport everyone back to the manor.

"Did you notice the whole team was here?" Tabeka asked.

Cidus nodded. "Yes. Our quiet little ceremony did not quite go as planned. Come, we need to leave. The dragons are waiting."

When they arrived at the manor, the courtyard was alive with music and people. Cidus and Tabeka walked through the gates, and loud cheers greeted them. He was sure the whole village was present for this celebration, and probably more people from outlying farms. It made him feel good. His people were happy to be freed from Jatron's rule and tyranny and deserved to celebrate, not only their lord's joining but also their relief from Jatron's rule.

When they had first returned to the manor, Cidus had gone to the village and talked to the elders to explain who he was and who Jatron was. Now, all the villagers knew about his evil twin and what had caused the change in Wildevein. Some of the elders had mentioned a concern, about the young women that had gone missing over the years. Cidus had promised them he would try and look into it, but he was no miracle worker. He had a feeling that many of those women had been used as sacrifices, as Zohmes' priests had intended to do to Zandria.

He and Tabeka took their place at the main table. The music quietened, and a group of actors took the stage.

After the play had ended, Cidus led his mate to the clearing quartered off as the dance floor. Loud clapping and hurrahs filled the courtyard when he took Tabeka in his arms for the first dance of the night.

As he twirled her in a traditional dance, Cidus gazed at the villagers celebrating his joining and smiled at their revelry. Young and old, they had put on their best finery and created a festival the likes Wildevein had not seen in over twenty-five years.

From what Tabeka had told him, the last celebration held

within his realm had been the one where they had first met. His people and the whole of Sirona, more so than himself, deserved happiness and prosperity, and he would ensure that they had exactly that.

Several dances later Tabeka leaned heavily in his arms. "I no longer have the energy to dance the night away as I did in my youth."

He leaned down, tenderly kissing her. "Perhaps you have the energy for a private dance?"

She glanced up at him, the hunger in her eyes matching the pulse of need that flared across their bond. "Then escort me to our rooms, my lord, and I will show you just how much stamina I still have."

His skin heated and desire filled his veins. The woman was a temptation he could never deny. He nipped her bottom lip, and a giggle escaped her. "Come, my love. I do not think we will be missed."

Twining his fingers with hers, he led her through the manor door and to their suite. Cidus barely noticed the candles and the soft scent of flower petals that drifted in the air, his attention solely reserved for his beautiful lifemate. "I have been aching to get you alone all night," he whispered against her lips before claiming her mouth in an endless kiss.

Cidus wished Astiana would have given them a day's rest at least after the festivities, but he understood she was anxious to move into her own home. He had felt the same need to return to Wildevein after he had defeated Jatron.

Liana, Ciara, and Taylith had flown them to the temple. They all had a late night, and the team had chosen to stay at the manor instead of returning to their homes around Cront. Cidus was relieved that they had offered to pitch in to help Astiana get settled.

Having the people closest to her would help her deal with

the memories he knew would hound her within the temple walls. From what he had been told, Zohmes and Astiana had made the temple their home before he had turned her to stone.

Cidus took in the magnificence of the temple and surrounding mountains. It was a stark difference from the Dreaded Peaks that had been the backdrop of his childhood, and he was thankful the gods had seen fit to restore the place to its former beauty.

Astiana was about to place her hand on the elegant, ornate gold doors when Iridia burst from behind, pulling Evior along.

"Wait! Stop!"

Astiana turned to the young couple, surprise written all over her face. "Iridia, child, what is wrong?"

Cidus saw the excitement on Iridia's face and wondered what had gotten her so worked up. Her personality had been so subdued after her rescue, it shocked him that she showed such enthusiasm.

"I heard a voice." She placed her hand on Astiana's arm. "Before you enter, Evior and I have to do something. I finally know what the glyphs on our bodies mean, and what they are for. Stand back, everyone!"

After they had stepped away from the entry, she grabbed Evior by the hand. "Evior, hold on tight. When I place my other hand on the marble next to the door, you must do the same."

Cidus held his breath wondering what was to come next. It all seemed mysterious, but he was grateful that his young sister seemed to be much more at ease than she had been the day they had taken her to the Clyss.

Iridia and Evior braced their hands on the marble flanking the door, then closed their eyes. Strange syllables erupted from Iridia's lips, much like what happened to Cidus when he was pulled into a chant. Suddenly, her and Evior's bodies emitted a glow as if lit from within. The symbols etched onto their skin began to dance, almost seemed to erupt from them, then shot tiny bolts of lightning, like phaser fire, at the surface of the temple walls and surrounding mountain face. The hieroglyphics landed like fiery candles all over the grounds, encircling them, hovering above the mountain and over the valley, then slowly faded.

"Nothing unclean can ever enter this valley and this temple again," Iridia said, then opened her eyes. "The voice told me that Evior and I are guardians, and with the blessings of the gods, using the glyphs imprinted on our bodies, we are able to protect the land from evil and unclean beings."

The glow from within their bodies slowly faded and they once again looked normal.

Before anyone had a chance to react to the beautiful phenomenon, a scream came from behind Cidus, chilling him to the bone. He spun around, his hand on his sword.

Liana and Jonathan stood in front of him, Liana's face ashen, her eyes tortured.

"Liana, what is it?" Jonathan tried to pull her into his arms.

She shook her head wildly and took a step back, then another, her hands clutching her chest and her features contorted in pain.

"Too late! The guardians... Odoxon already... Ciara! Taylith!" she screamed. "Jonathan, help—"

She rushed away from them as her dragon surfaced. But what had emerged was not her beautiful golden dragon. Her scales had lost their gilded luster and were now a sickly yellowish color.

She lifted her great head and with a tortured roar, she breathed fire up into the sky. When her wings flapped, Cidus stepped back and tried to stop Jonathan from rushing to the dragon, but it was of no use. His brother shoved him aside, fury blazing in his eyes, and he emitted an aura of torment so deep that it ripped at Cidus' soul.

Liana's dragon rose, and as her large body lifted, her claws grasped Jonathan. She soared up, straight into a huge chasm splitting the sky above them.

Ciara and Taylith had pushed to the front, Taylith changing to his dragon. Before Taylith could reach Liana, the chasm vanished, his sister and Jonathan disappearing along with it. The great sapphire dragon's anguished roar thundered throughout the valley. He circled the sky once more, then landed in the clearing, Laura racing to his side.

Ciara turned to face them, tears streaming down her cheeks. "Zohmes and Odoxon. They bespelled Liana just before Evior and Iridia were able to place the guarding spell. They have Liana's soul shard, and with it, they have Jonathan, too. They have full control over Liana, but she was smart enough to grasp Jonathan. He will not abandon his lifemate."

NEXT IN THIS SERIES:

INFINITE FURY

Excerpt:

Jonathan faced Zohmes and Odoxon, appearing as the young sorcerer he had become. He was quite handsome, except for his creepy eyes. Zohmes did not look wild for a change. Jonathan shivered because he could see his resemblance to the god. Zohmes' eyes were trained on him. Glowing a bright red, they seemed to pierce his soul. Both the sorcerer and Zohmes held a black staff, Odoxon's topped by a green skull, Zohmes' by a glowing crystal.

"Welcome, children. Come here and join us. We have readied sustenance for you," Odoxon spoke.

The bastards were crazy if they thought he'd go anywhere near them. He fought the rage building within, stepped closer to Liana, and brushed his fingers down her neck, hoping to calm the tempest. Her scales felt clammy, almost as if she were sick. *Liana, please… Talk to me.* Again, she didn't respond, and the whirlwind of power continued to build inside his heart and soul.

"Like fucking hell I'll join you," Jonathan shouted. He felt as if his skin were on fire and the two bastards in front of him were covered in a red haze.

"Such a fiery temper, just like his father," Odoxon said quietly and smiled. "Zohmes, control your spawn."

Zohmes held his staff out and pointed it at Jonathan. "Son, you are not a prisoner, but I urge you to obey. Liana is under our control. Odoxon has her soul shard and without it, she is helpless."

Odoxon laughed evilly and pulled a chain from beneath his tunic. He dangled Liana's shard before them. It glowed radiantly as if it sensed its home close by. "Come, my dear."

The dragon changed, and Liana stood facing the god and the sorcerer. "Liana, don't go to them!" Jonathan yelled. She didn't even look at him. As if she were walking in her sleep, she slowly stepped toward the podium and joined Odoxon, taking his extended hand.

Jonathan felt the power within him getting ready to burst free. Zohmes pinned him with his glowing eyes.

"Do not try anything, my son. If you value the dragon, you must stand down. Soon, you will join us in our quest to gain control of the throne, the crown, and we shall rule the planet together."

"Never," Jonathan hissed.

"Then Liana will reap the consequences." Zohmes laughter boomed around them.

"Odoxon won't let you hurt her. He desires her for himself."

"Odoxon will do as I command. He might be all powerful now having the grimoire spells and the black diamond in his possession, but I am still the most feared and mightiest of all."

Zohmes' eyes seemed to shoot fire at him. Jonathan cringed under the attack. What was he going to do? He could not take the chance the god would hurt Liana. He took a deep breath willing himself to calm.

BOOKS IN THE CRIMSON REALM SERIES:

Also available, **THE LION'S STOWAWAY**, a novella based on the Ierilian world and its characters, published in an anthology with Viola Grace and other authors. Buy it at extasybooks.com and please help to support the authors by purchasing directly from the publisher!

EXCERPT:

Heading back on the familiar trail, that she could almost walk blindfolded now, she hummed a tune. That was something she missed. Music.

When she was close to her tree, a sound startled her. It was too loud to be made by one of the little furry creatures she so often saw darting around among the flowers. She stopped. Her heart sped up. She'd seen no other human in the forest since she'd lived there. Not once. The sound came from the direction of the crate.

Standing very still, she held her breath and waited. A crack, then another. Suddenly a huge lion faced her. She dropped her basket, her purchases spilling to the forest floor, screamed, and ran to the nearest tree.

She peeked at the lion from behind the trunk and started hitching up her skirts to tie them in a knot above her knees. "Go away, kitty!"

She hoisted herself onto a branch and started climbing. When she was halfway up the tree, she dared to look down. She couldn't remember. Did lions climb?

"Nice kitty, kitty, kitty." She climbed a couple more limbs but dared not go any higher. The branches were starting to get thin and might break beneath her weight. She leaned forward and peered down at the lion.

"Holy shit! You are one big cat!"

He was the biggest lion she'd ever seen. Their parents had taken them to a zoo when she and Hannah were still little. The lions had awed her and had seemed gigantic. But this one was huge. Of course, he had to be. It was an alien lion.

What in the hell was she going to do? Was it hungry? Was it looking at her for its next meal? She grabbed the piece of smoked meat she had in her pocket, pulled a chunk off it with her teeth and held her hand out. "Look, kitty. Mmm, it's good, see?"

She threw the piece of meat. It landed on the ground a distance from the tree. "Go get it, boy!"

The lion just stood looking up at her. He did not attempt to climb or approach the tree...nor did he go after the food. To her consternation, he suddenly growled. Then it appeared as if his bones were popping through his skin.

"Oh, fuck, no!"

It freaked her the hell out. It was like the movie *Thing*. An alien made itself look like a dog, but when it showed its true form, it was a grotesque monster.

She couldn't take her eyes away. It was all so crazy. It wasn't a hideous creature he was mutating into. When the transformation was complete, he had become the most gorgeous hunk of male flesh she'd ever seen. She rubbed her eyes and looked again. Was she going insane? *Okay... I'm dreaming. There is no way this is real.* She pinched herself. *Wake up, Izzy.*

Antique Trove, a best-selling stand-alone story available at eXtasy Books and all online retailers.

EXCERPT:

It felt like hours had passed when the pounding of her heart finally simmered to a steady beat. She dared to open her eyes again and screamed. Directly in front of her stood an enormous reptile with wings. With a snap of its jaws, it lowered its head and glared at her. *What the hell? Is that a dragon? This is not happening.*

Dazed, she began to climb out of the chest. If she stepped clear, she would be back in her grandmother's shop, right?

"This is a dream. It is not real," Azilia muttered.

"This is no dream," the dragon said.

She must have lost her damn mind. Even though she was out of the chest, the hallucination was still there. She held her hands, palms out, in front of her body and took a careful step back. The last thing she wanted was to be this creature's lunch. "Okay. Now I know for sure I am dreaming or going crazy. Talking dragons?"

"You have finally come home," the dragon spoke again.

"Home?" *Oh, my God. I am actually answering the beast.*

She calmed down a bit. The dragon did not seem as if he wanted to gobble her up. It was actually quite beautiful with its shiny blue, purple, and red scales. But in all honesty? A talking dragon? And where in the gods' names was she? *This is just another one of my stupid nightmares.*

"No nightmare. I assure you I am very real."

Her eyes widened, and her jaw went slack. *Seriously? The damn creature is answering what I am thinking?* She felt kind of silly as she made a V with two fingers. "Peace..." Her voice came out like a squeaky little mouse.

Also by these authors:

VEILED ELIMINATORS:

EXTRICATION

Extrications are dangerous, and Two is willing to risk it all to escape the Institute.

Two is an eliminator, a trained assassin. She has one mission—enter the portal, eliminate a rogue general, then activate her microchip to wipe her memory. But she knows a secret that would rock the foundations of the Institute's training program. Armed with only a tiny dagger, and the truth of their future, she enlists the help of her partner, Four, to escape their fate.

VIRAMA

She is an emotionless killer, a virama. Her mission — eliminate the traitors.

Seventeen knew no other existence but the Institute and its training program. Trained as an assassin since she was a toddler, she must now face the ultimate test — locate the traitors, Two and Four, and exterminate them.

For years, Seventeen has longed to escape the Institute, but a one-way ticket to Brevona was not her idea of freedom. To make matters worse, her targets were two of their own — Two, a young woman she considered family, and Four, a trainee from the male division. Sometimes you had to take what you could get, and a life outside the Institute was worth it, no matter the cost.

RECREANCY

She is a cyborg, trained by the Institute for one thing — to kill.

Twenty-four is a highly trained killer, a cyborg that owes her life to the Institute. Her orders? Destroy the rebel cell on the planet Brevona. But she has a personal mission of her own and will stop at nothing to complete it.

To put a kink in her plans, she is told she will be accompanied by a squeaky old robot, and Ninety-one, a cyborg from the male division. The mismatched duo and bot set out to find the pocket of rebels, but instead find unexpected information that will change their lives forever.

Coming Soon:

Eye of the Gods 1

DARING CHAR

ABOUT THE AUTHORS

Taryn Jameson

Taryn Jameson is a mother, artist, and avid reader who lives in an enchanted forest that sparks her imagination to create. Her latest outlet is the written word. She is the alter ego of cover artist Angela Waters.

Gabriella Bradley

Gabriella Bradley has been a writer and artist all her life, though only ventured into erotic works in 2003. Her hobbies include hiking, gardening, swimming, sewing, embroidery. Favorite movies are old timers like Gone with the Wind, Spartacus, etc. Favorite music is Abba.